Sheetrock Angel

Jeanne C. Davis

ISBN: 1-4528-8764-0
ISBN-13: 9781452887647

FOR MY HUSBANDS

OBSERVATION

Dow Corning could have warded off bankruptcy had they been able to exclude from their breast implant lawsuit those pouches of silicone found on the stretch of beach between Palos Verdes and Malibu. Pilgrims to the Santa Monica bay imagine the lives of the preternaturally attractive locals and leap to the conclusion that here they might find that elusive something missing in their own lives. Here—amid the wildly divergent populous, the tenuous landscape, the pervasive sense that anything is possible—they could uncover that core belief, that internal anchor which would guarantee them happiness. Next incarnation they'll ask to be returned as one of the indigenous bronzed gods or goddesses... which practically guarantees return as a sand flea.

chapter I

BACK IN THE mid-nineties, Audrey James was struggling through her second divorce. Sure, the first divorce had been tough, but this one should have been easier since it was from the same man.

The current struggle was to find a place to live. Audrey had been all over the world, but this stretch of land was her favorite. The Santa Monica Bay. And not because she thought it held some key to life, but because it was life in all its caprice. The beach closures due to pollution after a rain, the homeless in the parks, the overcrowding on the promenade, all served as counter point to Santa Monica's climatic and geographic perfection. She wasn't about to leave just because her soon-to-be-ex-ex-husband was here first.

Slouching near a sliver of a window in the tiny condominium, Audrey stared at the pitiful wedge of sand and meager ration of ocean.

"I can tell you're a minimalist." This, from Ernest her real estate agent, who had met her for the first time an hour ago. As she looked around the sparse interior of the glass and plaster structure she realized that he had come close. Not a minimalist, just empty. She had been looking for an adjective, one that would define this new level of self-doubt. Empty worked for that nauseating feeling in her gut, but it was the yin to the yang that she couldn't put her finger on when it came to her head. There had to be a word that explained this feeling that all of her brain cells were dashing around switching positions in search of some order. Nothing in her life quite fit. It was as though someone had stolen in during the night and had switched all of her size nine shoes to size five floor samples. In truth, Ernest was probably just assessing her finances, deducing that minimal was all she could afford anywhere near the beach. How right he was. Only the late eighties real estate bubble bursting had her in the running at all.

"No garbage disposal. A sure sign they didn't redo the plumbing when they patched the tile after the earthquake." Audrey wheeled around to find her excessively pregnant friend, Katherine Dale, lying on the kitchen floor, belly and legs protruding from the under sink cabinet. Pregnancy had given Katherine permission to inhale everything in both animal and vegetable kingdoms which meant Audrey would need to help Katherine liberate herself from beneath the basin. As she put her arms around her friend's stomach to hoist her up, she felt the baby kick.

"Wow, did you feel that?" asked Audrey.

"Did I feel that? You felt it through two layers of clothes, six inches of fat and a placenta. I felt it like a Tyson punch to the kidneys. The joys of impending motherhood." A smile forced its way to Audrey's lips.

Ernest, eager to focus their attention on a more positive aspect of the dwelling, pointed out the vaulting white walls of the vertical room: "It's you."

"I'm more cluttered than this," said Audrey.

"He's not interested in your emotional state," said Katherine. Katherine had tossed it off, but when she thought about it, "cluttered" precisely described that scrambled brain feeling.

Ernest dragged them to the next prospect, a California ranch house remodeled by a demented Tolkien fan. Cute, cottagie, all manner of tschochkes lining every ornately carved shelf. Even with her own furnishings in this impossibly busy, low ceilinged house, she would find it claustrophobic.

"Is this the real you?" Ernest seemed to be gritting his teeth.

"Ernest, if I were this cluttered, I'd slit my wrists."

"If you didn't do it while you were married to Miles, you're not a candidate." Which is why Audrey loved Katherine. Straight shooter.

The trio marched on, this time to a new duplex fashioned from what looked like hand-rubbed cherry wood. Audrey gazed around in awe. Even Katherine was speechless, an uncommon condition. Not a wall out of plumb, not a corner off a degree, beautiful lines which flowed one into the next with a harmony that evoked the climax of Cosi fan Tutti or early Simon and Garfunkle. She imagined perfect happiness here, a perfect husband, two perfect children, one of each. The image made her stomach rumble the way it did when she smelled cigarette smoke before breakfast.

Ernest moved close to Audrey and whispered, almost sincerely. "It's you." If it were, she would be wearing an Armani rather then her dress-sweats from Target.

"I'm not this perfect," said Audrey.

Ernest's look said he was sure of it. "I have a couple of places closer to Venice."

The now testy real estate agent drove the massive Cadillac in resentful silence. As Katherine filed her nails in the front seat, Audrey stared numbly out the back window.

The neighborhood was in transition. Encroaching affluence. Charming beach cottages of the twenties transformed into would-be estates on postage stamp lots. Still, they were easier on the eyes than the sixties era apartments, boxy and plain, bearing names like "The Cindy Sue" and "The Janet Ann". Santa Monica maintained the charm of diversity thanks to that anomaly, rent control. A wonderful notion redolent of humanity, doing right by seniors and the disadvantaged, but all too often perverted by development executives and junior law partners whose names miraculously appeared atop the lists of would-be renters thanks to hefty graft payments. But in nineteen-ninety-five rent control was in jeopardy, soon to be a victim of a more callused public conscience.

Audrey hadn't really been looking, had been staring at some middle distance while buildings blurred past her, when Ernest suddenly stomped on the breaks, a function of her headlock around his neck.

"That's it!" said Audrey.

Katherine looked out the window and pronounced: "That's not a house, it's a hair shirt."

"It has endless possibilities," said Audrey.

"It's nothing but possibilities. It's another stray dog and your pound's full. Don't be an idiot."

Perhaps yellow at one time, the clapboard cottage appeared to be standing only by the grace of the vines which, at once, seemed to hold it together, and to devour it. Some reconnaissance tentacles tore off large chunks of wood on their march toward what was left of the roof. Huge, warped pieces of plywood covered the windows so that the cottage seemed to stare blindly at its neglected yard. A chain link fence surrounded the small lot and gave the house the look of a dejected prison lifer.

With an assurance she hadn't felt in awhile, Audrey said, "It's me."

The word "clutter" stuck like gum to the bottom of her shoe. Audrey wished she could remove it, but didn't possess the mental solvent. The District Attorney's office back then made physical her emotional clutter: a large main room with numerous cubicles and even lone desks stuck here and there as though a clear square foot were in violation of the law of universal chaos. The atmosphere itself was cluttered with too many people, with too much to do, with too little time or space in which to do it. As a paralegal, Audrey occupied one of the lower rungs on the office ladder and her desk in the middle of the chaos confirmed this. The building itself sat on Main Street in a municipal complex: courts, police station, city hall, all within minutes of each other. Very organized, very convenient, unlike her office, unlike her mind.

Earlier in the week, Audrey had tried to broach the subject of her cluttered mind with Katherine.

"Don't even go there. It's not your mind that's cluttered, it's your life," said her friend. The next day Audrey found an expensive Day Runner on her desk. Practical solutions were Katherine's forte.

Before the D.A.'s office, Audrey had time to read, to garden. A nine to five job had always been anathema to her, so when she had stumbled into the life of a courier just out of college, she felt right at home. At first she carried packages for reduced airfare because she was willing to go anywhere to sample the local cuisine, but after awhile, her reputation as a dauntless, reliable problem solver gained her a position with the exclusive firm of Hilary and Beauchamp. Now, at thirty-five, she was not only in an occupation that required many more hours than her much lamented courier job, but she was also studying to become a lawyer, a profession for which the lack of a personal life was as essential as a dark suit.

She realized that she had been reading the same sentence in the dry deposition for five minutes while her cluttered mind had its way with her.

"Hey, I know you're hiding a porn magazine under there. What is it this time, he-men and the pets who love them?" Carl Roger's voice was as soothing as his looks were disquieting.

"You know me so well," Audrey responded without missing a beat. An attractive but not classically handsome man, Carl had a penetrating stare which, though he was her closest male friend, made her feel revealed in a way which never allowed her to be absolutely comfortable. She smiled up at him. "What are you doing over on this side of the quad?"

"Trolling for patients." Carl was the resident police and D.A. shrink who maintained an office next door in the back of police headquarters. He shoved aside some files and grabbed a stack of papers on Audrey's desk then casually sat on the cleared space as though the desk were his own. He didn't bother to hide the fact that he inspected each piece of paper he touched. "So, how goes the house hunting?"

"Great. Just bought one." She grabbed the papers from him.

His eyes locked on hers. "Bought? As in escrow?" She nodded. "What, ninety days?"

"No need. I bought "As is". I close tomorrow," she said, purposely clipping her words, knowing she would get flack from him.

A look of incredulity did a touch-and-go on the psychologist's face. He spoke in the professional voice he reserved for the clinically deranged. "Do you think that's wise?" A rise of the eyebrows to convey concern. "Can you get it extended?"

"I don't want it extended. I want out of Katherine's guest room and into my own life."

"But it's a huge step when you're...in transition."

"'In transition.' Your euphemism for 'crazy as a nude skydiver'? Don't shrink me, Carl. Save it for the paying customers."

"Busted. So, lunch?"

"Can't. Opal just gave me a stack of depos that I have to get through by tonight. Rain check?" Audrey felt privileged that Opal, the deputy D.A., had thrown the depositions to her rather than one of the other six paralegals.

Carl slid gracefully from the desk. "Sure." He hesitated, then with a note of uncertainty: "So...have you heard from Miles?"

"Yet another subject I don't wish to explore with you. We're going to run out of things to talk about."

Carl laughed easily as he headed for the door. "Never happen."

There was so much to be remorseful for in the purchase of her shabby little travesty that Audrey had been actively warding off the perfunctory buyer's remorse. Now, as Ernest assembled the final papers, signed earlier at the escrow office, she looked at the bungalow and felt the queasy stomach she usually associated with life altering experiences like missing a final exam, losing a wedding ring, smashing into the back of a car. Audrey managed to do all these things in the past few weeks. She couldn't remember being as irresponsible before--well, perhaps that once, but that was a long time ago.

Ernest handed over the keys then vanished like a department store clerk spotting a return. As Audrey approached her new purchase, she felt alone, deserted, isolated just like this caged cottage that had drawn her. But before she could wallow in her rising self-pity, her concentration was shattered by loud voices from the tawdry duplex next door.

"I'm warning you!"

"Or what?"

She looked toward the porch where a scruffily handsome man in his late twenties waved his fist menacingly in the face of a reedy man, who looked even from the distance as if he could use a bath.

"Or I'll hit you where you live. You know me. You know I can do it," said the more attractive man who wore his leather vest like a second skin. As he stormed down from the porch, he caught sight of

Audrey and stared pointedly at her until she looked away. From the distance, she couldn't read his expression. Anger? Annoyance? Interest? She looked up again and found that he was gliding toward his motorcycle, which he mounted and kicked alive in one fluid motion. The thunder-rumble of the Harley fought for decibel supremacy over the screech of the tires that left an inch of rubber split between the pavement and the noxious blue cloud which lingered in the air like a specter.

Audrey dismissed the intrusion as the price one paid for a diverse neighborhood. If she wanted homogeneity, she could live in Beverly Hills—well, actually she couldn't afford to. Back to the problem at hand: the feeling that was mirrored in the depressing exterior of her house. She noticed that she couldn't muster the same well of self-pity she had fostered just moments ago. She dug deeply to find a can-do attitude and walked inside her very own house carrying the cardboard box of tools which she had begged, borrowed, or when all else failed, bought. She had enough money to fix the structural problems and to spruce up the exterior but none left for the interior save for a minimum of supplies. That she would do herself, rather like building a fort, she thought, and remembered the California scrub covered hills near her childhood home and the heady feeling of independence when Katherine and she would escape into the wilds.

The Santa Monica library had been her source of "How To" books. They were all extremely over priced in the bookstores, though books were usually her major extravagance. When she thought of how people spent their money she always remembered her father combing the supermarket ads and pointing out to her mother where she could save twenty cents here, thirty cents there. Then this same man would purchase an opulent scarf or something equally nonessential, just to see the expression of delight on her mother's face. In her biology class at Hoover High, they had studied differentially permeable membranes. It was where she got her concept of people being differentially cheap.

Looking around the large main room, she realized that she had to decide what she could live with and what she couldn't. The walls were thick with layer upon layer of paint. If sliced through, she thought, they could be read like tree rings: here a flood/birth, now a drought/divorce, there a fire/death. She imagined she could divine the house's history if she were just patient enough to peel the paint one layer at a time. But what if the paint was all that held the house together?

She glanced around the room, her eyes drawn to a ghastly white rock fireplace standing conspicuously in the corner like antlers on a Bobcat. On closer examination, she found that the rocks were only an inch or so thick, slices of a synthetic substance manufactured to resemble rock. The fireplace itself was a fake gas unit with painted metal logs. It all had to go. She couldn't live with it. Couldn't live with anything any more that covered and concealed, distorted and deceived.

Grabbing the sledgehammer from the box, she hit the bogus rocks with all her strength. A taunting chip flew toward her, missing her eye by inches. The stone's retaliation and the meager damage her swing had caused, angered her until she found herself swinging repeatedly, willy nilly, now a roundhouse blow, now straight from above, now rapid repeated strikes until at last she had bludgeoned a sizeable hole. She collapsed in a sweat on the floor and her mind sailed off...rudderless.

Clutter. Audrey now realized why the word had struck her as so genial. Because behind the clutter, beyond the mere inconvenience of the occasional impossibility of linear thought, was something poignantly familiar: her tapes. Audrey always had been the star of her own head-movies. Early childhood tapes were on the order of sports fantasies where she would hit the game winning home run, or pass the long bomb for the tie-breaking touchdown. Her early athletic prowess was the source of her formative feelings of self-confidence. She thought that next time she felt that creeping feeling of insecurity, that nauseating feeling of shrinking inside her clothes, she would spend a few hours at the batting cage.

All these tapes had a common thread: Audrey would save the day by inventing novel ways of fixing things, fixing people. But recently, certain tapes rewound themselves and replayed with alarming frequency. The soundtrack to these head movies would inevitably be the noise of obsession. How could he? To me. Again. And the words she really wanted to bury: How could I let him? One of these Miles-tapes, which had to be on the brink of snapping from celluloid fatigue, depicted her on the witness stand pointing at Miles and explaining to the frowning judge how she had given her husband a second chance after his express promise of fidelity. Of course in real life the judge would have said, "No one's going to give you a medal for being an asshole twice." But in her tape, the judge was kindly and sentenced Miles to fifty years of reading "The Prophet".

In another tape, she made a bonfire of his many surfboards. She mapped out her own Stonehenge, positioned each board so that the sun focused on her head just at sunrise on the vernal equinox, then she torched the boards and the ritual cleansed her of him. Since the waves were his only lasting emotional commitment, she imagined Miles throwing himself on the pyre in an act of love akin to the Hindu suttee. She had no revenge fantasies about the women. They posed no threat of passionate involvement. Only the waves.

chapter 2

KATHERINE SCRIBBLED FRANTICALLY on a legal pad, shoved a bagel in her mouth and was still able to scream at her husband all because she used a hands-free headset, a necessity for Katherine since she would be mute if handcuffed. Though she moved from New York when she was five years old, Katherine's speech was tinged by the barest trace of a Queens inflection which she cultivated as part of her tough guy persona. And it was Katherine, not Kathy, Kay, Katy or even Kate, though the Hepburnesque flavor of that truncation with its after-notes of strength and patrician beauty certainly applied. Katherine was a knockout even now that her lovely oval visage had morphed to a voluptuous roundness with the pregnancy weight.

Her office was one of the coveted rooms with only one pane of glass in the door, practically private, a perk for being a fairly senior deputy D.A. Though only thirty-four, she was considered senior be-cause she had been a star in the federal prosecutors' office downtown. A Stanford Law graduate, she turned down plenty of offers from prestigious firms so she could fight for truth and justice. She wasn't looking forward to the slower pace of her pre-birth maternity leave.

Audrey dropped a file on Katherine's desk, then started to leave, but Katherine waved her back as she spoke into the headset's microphone.

"I don't care how great a deal it is, I need you there. You're not going to know what to do." She looked up at Audrey and rolled her eyes. "Fine, I'll see if Audrey'll do it.... Yeah, you'll owe her big time." Katherine hit the button on the phone to end the call.

"Lamaze?" asked Audrey.

Katherine nodded. "Tomorrow night, could you?"

"Always ready to pinch-hit."

"Well, if my husband misses any more "at bats", I'm going to have to cut him," Katherine said with feigned indifference. Audrey smiled at her friend.

"Yeah, right. And tell him he doesn't owe me. If he hadn't turned me on to Ernest, I never would've found my house."

"Oh, yeah? He owes you bigger for that one."

⌖

The man behind the counter at Fisher Lumber wore the name-tag, "Mel". He had been very helpful in his suggestions about what supplies she would need to hang her own sheetrock or drywall.

"You take these screws and screw the wall into the studs, but that's not the hard part." Mel looked closely at her to make sure he had Audrey's undivided attention. "Then you take and put some of this wall board joint compound on the corner where the walls meet or on the seam where two boards'll meet. And that's still not the hard part."

"I give up, Mel, what's the hard part?"

"The hard part's putting this tape over the joint, then laying a thin coat of the compound over it so you can't see the tape or the joint. They got guys who do nothing but tape. It's really an art."

"Well, thanks Mel, but I think you've given me excellent instructions and besides, I have a book." Mel didn't bother to wait for her to turn around before he rolled his eyes.

Since Audrey was five-foot-seven, the four-foot width of the sheetrock didn't challenge her as much as did the eight foot height. Although she carried it on its side, Audrey struggled mightily with the huge drywall panel. She found she could carry it only a few feet at a time, then she had to put down the unwieldy piece of gypsum until she could get a new grip on it. Tilting the board to its length up position, Audrey tried to grasp both sides of the four-foot width. She was in the middle of the street, making another brief dash, when a bearded face presented itself from around the other side of the board. Startled, she nearly dropped the sheetrock.

"Hey!"

"Sorry, didn't mean to scare ya," said the scruffy looking young man. Audrey scanned her memory for that vaguely familiar face and voice. It had been over a month, but she finally affixed both to the man who had ridden off on the motorcycle after the argument next door. He wore dirty jeans and the same black leather vest over a yellowing white T-shirt. His hairline receded at both temples but hair trailed over the collar of the vest in a sandy thatch and the stubble on his chin had a red cast to it. He would have been considered handsome but for his teeth which showed areas of decay near the gums.

"What're ya doin'?" He sipped his coffee from a thoroughly stained, chipped Peet's Coffee mug and inquired casually, as if they were old friends.

"A lot of glib answers come to mind, but since it's so early, you get the straight line. I'm carrying a piece of sheetrock."

The man assessed her with a nod. "Wanna hand?"

Audrey's mother had been the queen of adages and all the old ones about gift horses and spiting one's face raced through her mind before she could muster a civil, "Thank you. I'd appreciate that." A man of his word, he used one hand to help carry while the other still gripped his coffee. He seemed to swagger even when carrying the awkward board.

"You ever hung sheetrock?"

"No, but I have a book..."

"Yeah, well, I seen a law book before but that don't make me a lawyer. That's what you are, right?" Another adage, this one about good fences making good neighbors sprang to mind. Irritability colored her words as she spoke quickly, uncomfortably.

"Actually, I'm a paralegal...but I'm going to law school...well, not this semester because of this, and other things..." Her tone became suddenly sharp, accusing. "Why did you think I was a lawyer?"

"Terry next door." He nodded toward a dissipated young woman watching them from the front yard of the duplex, lethargically pulling at weeds on a lawn teeming with them, casually glancing in their direction now and then while puffing on her cigarette. Audrey waved and received a barely perceptible nod in return. "She's pals with your real estate guy, Ernest. Small neighborhood, everybody knows everybody's business." They maneuvered the board through the front door.

"That doesn't thrill me." The living room was still a shambles with pieces of plaster and ersatz rock strewn hazardously about. They picked their way cautiously through the debris, then rested the sheetrock against a wall near the gaping corner where the gas fireplace unit remained exposed behind the studs.

"Why? You got secrets worth keepin'?" asked the stranger. Audrey felt acutely uncomfortable with his directness but mustered bravado.

"Don't we all?" The man smiled for the first time and, for the first time, Audrey relaxed a bit.

"B'lieve you're right at that," he said. "Tell you what, I'll help you get that wall done. Luck and your good looks put you right in the way of a taper." Or an axe murderer. The thought surfaced like the yellow caution signal Audrey used to stop for but now raced through.

"Look, I don't have any money...I've over-extended myself..."

"Don't need no money."

"And I'm not interested in, well, you know, anything...reciprocal." The man smiled again, this time with a slight smirk, as he looked her up and down.

"Don't say no 'til you been asked. I'm just offerin' to help ya out here."

"Why would you do that?" asked Audrey.

"A person need a reason to do a good deed?" She had been reared to believe that good deeds were like breathing, something done naturally, without thought. But life had made her a bit more realistic. Also this man was too sure of himself on the one hand, while on the other, he exhibited the festering quality of an open wound. The combination didn't inspire trust. He moved toward the coffee maker on the floor nearby, and helped himself, filling the mug that seemed to be permanently affixed to his left hand. He took her confused silence as an affirmative. "Maybe you're right--this day 'n age. Okay, I'm atonin'."

"Would this be atoning for a felony or anything I should worry about?" He took a long sip from his cup, eyeing her from above the rim.

"What are you scared of?"

"I don't know. You forcing my neck into my borrowed chop saw...?" He laughed with a child-like spontaneity that surprised her.

"Yeah, well, you'll get to know me. Find out I ain't such a bad guy. You get that sheetrock hung and I'll tape it for you. You're the lucky person that gets my atonin'." He held his mug aloft in a toast to her, then abruptly left. Audrey stood there a moment, wondering if she could have imagined the entire encounter. The whole experience seemed highly improbable. The door had just closed when Katherine threw it open again.

"Who is that hunk?"

Audrey had to think a moment. "I don't know."

"You don't know?"

"A friend of Terry's."

Katherine stared at her. "Terry who?"

Audrey thought again, then shook her head absently. "I don't know."

⌖

The security lights in the employees' parking lot blazed with wattage that out shone the sun on a hazy day. In the early nineties amnesia about the oil crisis of the seventies reigned. Energy was cheap and plentiful. Unlocking the driver side door of her battered Jeep Wrangler, Audrey looked up to see Carl jogging toward her from police headquarters next door to the D.A.'s office.

"Hey, hey! What is this, banker's hours? It's not even nine p.m. yet," said the police psychologist. Audrey threw her things into the car and smiled back at him.

"I'm reclaiming my life. After twelve hours, I'm leaving whether I'm finished or not."

"And you'll use the spare time to teach seminars on how to enjoy all that spare time."

"Gimme a break, I'm not as bad as Roland H☞☞s. He's the first in, last out. I think he actually lives in the air conditioning ducts."

- 15 -

"Yeah, well, it wouldn't hurt to cut yourself a little slack while you're going through all this emotional shit."

"I love it when you use psychiatric terms." Audrey hoped she had cut off further comment on her mental health. Carl always wanted to talk everything to death, a hazard of the profession. Why do you feel that way? What do you think caused that? Is that your head or your heart talking? Apropos this last, he was a romantic first and a shrink second. Love as panacea. An uncomfortable moment passed; Carl had something to say, but couldn't quite get it out. Finally, Audrey broke the silence.

"What?"

"I got a call from Miles...He wants to talk."

"Really? I thought he'd be too busy screwing his co-producer up in Calgary."

"Hey, I wouldn't know about..."

"Then you'd be the only one who didn't." Carl had the misfortune to be one of Miles's few close friends which meant he probably did know. Carl took a deep breath, then finally looked at her again.

"He does love you."

"I don't doubt it. He just is who he is. Why did I have to marry him twice to realize that? What happened to my judgment?"

Carl smiled at her and broke the tension. "Well, if that house is any indication, I'd say it's gone the way of my low forehead." She smiled back, grateful for the reprieve from the toxic subject of Miles. As long as she could keep the images of their life together in a mental lock-box, she was able to function.

"When did you see my house?"

"I drove by right after you closed escrow. It needs a lot of work."

"I wanted something I could make my own."

"Something that would allow you to fix it?"

"Do you want to be my friend or my shrink? Because both doesn't work for me." It shocked her even as it flew out of her mouth. There were few people in the world with whom she could be direct. Saying this forced her to realize that Carl was on the short list.

"Sorry. Friend. I'll try to leave my couch at the office. So, when am I going to get to see it?"

"It's not ready for entertaining."

"Oh, yeah? Since when do I have to be entertained?"

She looked at Carl and thought of the times he had been there for Miles. For her. "You don't, you're family...Practically lived with us," said Audrey in a vaguely accusatory tone.

"Do I detect some veiled blame?" She put a hand on his cheek in a gesture that found the middle ground between a caress and a slap.

"Nope. If anything you kept us together too long." She got into the car and closed the door, but rolled down the window. He reached in and tousled her hair in a brotherly fashion.

"See ya," he added as he headed off into the artificially bright night. Audrey gritted her teeth. She had survived the ordeal. She had talked about Miles and hadn't broken down. She was over him.

<hr />

Audrey put the key into the door of her bungalow, now painted white and looking presentable in the blaze of the motion tripped security lights. But once inside she felt threatened by the exposed beams, the dark corners, the walls which looked as if they could betray her by sealing their windows and trapping her inside forever. She turned on a work light that dangled from a beam spanning the open ceiling. A small animal scurried to escape the sudden glare. Her breath caught. Standing in the middle of the room, she could only see the destruction, none of the potential that had kept her absorbed in her task these past weeks. A futon with a ragged quilt served as her bed in one corner of the havoc. A glance toward the bedroom revealed a room filled with boxes and furniture huddled in its center as if even the inanimate couldn't stand to face, alone, the menacing walls around them.

Audrey swallowed in an attempt to relieve the dull throb at the back of her throat. She swallowed and held her breath hoping that not breathing could hold back the convulsive sob she felt pushing up like a lava dome. Miles was up in Calgary shooting the made for cable movie, "Stampede". Audrey had been up to visit him once, but didn't stay long. Pots and pans hadn't flown. In fact, the actual "D" word was pronounced over long distance lines. How long the process would have taken a hundred years ago. Now their marriage was over at the speed of sound. The locked box of Miles burst opened. Pain and disappointment spilled out. She began to sob. And sobbing helped, the physical release coupled with the vaguely ludicrous picture sobbing presents to the mind's eye. The foreign tones, wracked from the soul, split the conscious so that while pain vents through primordial grunts, the mind views the body with humorous disbelief.

So while sobbing and watching herself sob, Audrey at first didn't pay attention to the loud voices issuing from the duplex next door. When she did, they were at such a pitch that curiosity eclipsed her self-pity. Her sobs shortened to sniffles, then lessened to simple tears as she walked to the window. A half moon illuminated the three shouting figures: a woman tugged frantically at a man who punched and kicked another figure on the ground. Audrey raced to the phone and called nine-one-one.

"Emergency operator," a calm voice responded.

"Three people are fighting, kicking, hitting."

"Address of the altercation?"

"Around 413 Idaho. You can't miss them they're in the front yard."

"We've notified police. Your name?"

"James. Audrey James. I live next door.

"Stay where you are. Help's on the way."

"Thank you." Audrey hung up and went back to the window. The woman was yelling at the man who continued his assault of the body now lying in a heap on the ground.

"That's enough. You're going to kill him!" said the woman.

"That fuck sends you to strong arm me?" said the aggressor between kicks.

When the woman jumped on the attacker's back, he threw her off violently and she lay momentarily motionless on the grass. Audrey bolted through the front door and stood on the porch at the point closest to the adjacent yard.

"I've called the police. They'll be here any second." The attacker wheeled around and looked up at Audrey; the man on the ground crawled to a beat up Corolla and sped off. As the attacker moved toward her, Audrey recognized the reedy man. The stranger with the coffee mug had been shouting at him when she had taken possession of her home. As he strode up toward the porch, she could see that his thin frame was wrapped in long rangy muscles. A week's growth of beard, coupled with hair that looked like it couldn't have been washed since that last shave, was incongruous to the expensively cut blazer he wore over his Levies. He shook his fist at her.

"You stay the fuck out of my business, bitch. And when the cops come, you didn't see shit. You got that?" Audrey was too stunned to respond. The man ran toward an expensive looking motorcycle parked at the curb, jumped on and hauled off down the street.

Now the woman approached, and Audrey recognized Terry, the young woman the stranger had pointed out in the yard next door. She didn't appear to be injured but she walked with the fatigued gate of the infirmed. Her hand dug furiously into the pocket of her baggy jeans from which she pulled a flattened box of cigarettes. She lit one before she looked up at Audrey.

"I'll take care of the cops. Just stay out of it. You don't know what's going on. Leave it that way," said Terry. She cut off a response by turning and sauntering back over to the duplex.

Audrey retreated into her house, which now felt more alien than ever. An unfaithful husband had made her previous home impossible to live in, but at least she had felt physically safe. She had never considered that she needed the protection of a man, had always thought she could take care of herself, but then she had never felt as alone as she did now. As the red and blue lights strobed through her blinds, she lay down on her futon and thought she wouldn't tell Katherine about the fight. Katherine wouldn't have said "I told you so", but she would have quietly called a high priced security firm and paid for an alarm, bars on all the windows and a phalanx of patrolling guards. Audrey wasn't ready yet to surrender to paranoia. So far that province belonged exclusively to Mom.

chapter 3

AUDREY AWOKE WEARING her clothes of the night before as sunlight streamed through the dust-streaked windows. The light bulb still dangled, its illumination now consumed by the dawn. She turned it off and changed into a pair of sweats.

A search of her makeshift toolbox produced a cat's paw, a sturdy metal lever with a slightly curled end, ideal for her purpose. Mel, at the hardware store, had advised her to buy a Johnson bar—which, he added, was called a Johnson bar long before everything else in the world was called a Johnson. But the large hickory stick with the short flat metal scoop at the end was unwieldy even if it did allow a better leverage ratio, so she used the cat's paw to rip the base boards from the wall in the living room. One section required her full body weight to attain enough leverage, but instead of coming free in one long piece, the base board broke, catapulting her backward onto her rear end where she landed right at the feet of the man with the Peet's coffee mug. The flush in her cheeks surged with a force that made her think she might burst a blood vessel. She looked up at the unkempt figure that towered over her.

"I didn't hear you come in," she managed.

"Didn't think you could, over all that gruntin' 'n groanin'. This here's my sister, Judy—I mean, Frances."

As Audrey rose, she saw that a girl had been easily concealed behind the man's bulk. Frances, slouching within a black leather jacket, scowled at her brother. She appeared to be in her mid-teens, but the vacant, waif-like look could have belonged to someone much younger. Audrey extended her hand.

"Pleased to meet you. I'm Audrey."

Frances looked disdainfully at the hand then turned away. "Yeah." The sulky girl threw herself onto the futon.

Audrey looked down at her rejected hand then offered it to the man. "And your name is...?"

He grasped it warmly. "Fred Engel." He nodded toward Frances and said in almost a whisper. "She's part of my atonin'."

"Listen, that guy you were shouting at on the porch next door? He was beating up somebody last night. I called the police."

"Did he know it was you that called?" asked Fred.

"Yeah, I went out and told him they were coming."

"Bad move. Just steer clear of him." He looked over at his sister and said pointedly: "Everybody needs to steer clear of Street." Frances leapt up and strode over to her brother until she was inches from his face. She spat her words.

"Fuck you, Fred. Street's my friend, too, and I can see who I want, when I want."

"This ain't open to discussion," her brother responded laconically.

"Nobody asked you to screw up my life! You're so full of shit. Think you know everything. Does Miss Lawyer here know she's got a junky working for her?"

"Ex-junky and it ain't nobody's business—" The young girl obviously had no fear of her brother, in fact, the siblings seemed familiar with the choreography of this particular dance.

"Once a junky, always—"

"And you oughta know. Look, just sit your ass down over there and after I finish here, I'll buy you ice cream or somethin'."

Frances, deflated by her brother's inane remark, shook her head and retreated to the futon where she pulled out a Walkman and stuck on the headphones. "I can't believe how lame you are. Ice cream. Like I'm twelve, or slow."

Audrey scraped her wits together and moved toward the coffee maker. "I'm sorry I don't have anything but coffee—"

"I don't want anything, except him out of my life. I wish you'd die like he did!" Frances snapped before turning away from them.

"Would that be St. Kurt? Or our old man?"

"Don't like even put them in the same sentence," Frances shouted from the futon.

"St. Kurt's been dead over a year. Time you got over it."

"I will like never get over it. If you died, I'd be like over that before it happened!"

Fred shook his head, dismissing his sister. He pulled a cassette tape out of his pocket. "You got a tape player? Can't work without Eric." Audrey nodded and unearthed a small boom box from a carton near the kitchen.

"That music is like so Jurassic!" said the teenager. Fred popped the tape in and began humming to Clapton's "Before You Accuse Me".

"A lot of Clapton's good stuff's before my time, too, but the man's a god, like Mozart or Buddy Holly." He tossed over his shoulder to Frances: "Sorry, no 'Teen Spirit' today." He added to Audrey in a near whisper: "Her real name's Judy. Renamed herself 'Frances' after Cobain's kid." Then, turning his attention to the joints Audrey had fashioned between the existing walls and the new piece of sheetrock: "Not bad. Even mitered the corners into the walls. You figure that out yourself or did ya read it in a book?"

Audrey wondered why this both pleased and embarrassed her. "Sewing 101. I figure construction's just like sewing, only the materials are heavier and less flexible."

He threw a gob of wallboard joint compound into his rectangular pan. "Sewin', huh? Well, however ya get to it, I guess." He caught her eye and cocked his head, beckoning her closer. "I ain't lettin' her outta my sight 'til she's in rehab."

Audrey was surprised by this almost paternal interest in his sister. She couldn't solidify a take on this man. When Frances revealed he'd been a junky, her imagination had conjured pictures of his waltzing in and stealing everything she owned, but now she felt something resembling admiration. He wasn't just paying lip service to the concept of atoning; he was acting on it.

"Have you found a place for her?" Audrey asked as Fred carefully laid a coat of "mud" on the crack where the existing wall met the new sheetrock.

"Naw. They all cost a fuckin' fortune. She's on a waiting list at this joint run by the county."

Warmed by her perception of his nobility, she wanted to reward him, wanted to water this seed of kindness, which she had been so suspicious of initially. "Listen, you're helping me. The least I can do is call around and see if I can find anything."

He looked directly at her for the first time that day. The scrutiny caused her to squirm, which she masked by picking a nonexistent speck off her sleeve. "Thanks," he said, then turned back to the wall. "Now I'll show you about tapin'. And you ain't learned it in any sewin' class."

Audrey glanced at the troubled girl, then back at Fred who unrolled a length of drywall tape. Here was an average Joe who had seen the error of his ways and was now making the world a better place, one deed at a time. She was glad he had stumbled across her.

Audrey tried to concentrate on the deposition in front of her, but the room hummed with the general bustle of a busy afternoon, Xeroxing, reading, word processing. People with sheaves of paper crisscrossed the central bullpen inches from her desk. Concentration was essential because it was her job to redact the document, to cull through the mounds of blather and highlight the salient testimony. She fought to focus her mind on the page, but the battle was decidedly lost when she looked up and found Fred standing in front of her desk as though he had materialized. He held a small bubble-wrap envelope and shifted his weight nervously from one foot to the other.

"What are you doing here?" It was out of her mouth before she realized how it sounded.

"Hey, if it's a problem..." He looked out of place in his work clothes; the same dirty jeans this time with a paint stained and ripped T-shirt.

"I didn't mean it like that," she fumbled.

"So this is where the D.A. is, huh? You know him?" He continued to survey the room warily.

"I've been in a couple of general meetings with him, but I don't have much contact...Is there anything I can help you with?" She felt vaguely uncomfortable with him here in her workplace, though she couldn't say why, wouldn't own the thought that she was embarrassed by his appearance.

"So you couldn't just, like, walk into his office, ya know, if the notion took you."

"Well, no, not really. I'd have to go through channels." His expression momentarily clouded, then was instantly brightened by a too quick smile.

"Just seein' how important ya are. Listen, I came by to tell you I'll need to sand and put another coat of mud on that tape tomorrow. I'm leaving town Saturday." She liked him with the detachment of admiration, so the momentary disappointment she experienced took her by surprise.

"Oh. Oh, well, I'll leave the key under the mat. And maybe I can get off early."

Fred seemed distracted by something down the hall. "Yeah. Maybe I'll see ya." He waved his packet at her and headed toward the door. A glance down the hall revealed Carl and Opal heading in her direction. Katherine also poked her earphone-clad head out of her office. All seemed to take particular interest in the unconventional visitor as he slipped through the door.

"Who's that?" Carl asked. Audrey resented his proprietary tone. She presumed Carl was looking out for Miles's interest even in light of the divorce and so begrudged him his concern because it smacked of monitoring.

"Just a guy helping me at the house."

Katherine tore off her headphones and joined the group angling for a glimpse of Fred as he slipped out the door. "Missed him again, didn't I."

"Looks like it," Audrey responded.

"A friend of yours, too?" Opal asked Katherine.

"I just know he's some guardian angel who's helping with her wall."

"Thought you were doing it yourself?" Carl's voice had a note of suspicion, which irked her further.

"I am. He just volunteered to help out."

"Volunteered?" Opal looked at her skeptically.

"He's atoning."

"Well, watch yourself," said Carl. Audrey shot him a look of displeasure. She was close to calling him on overstepping the bounds of friendship.

"I'll be careful, Dad. So, did you move your office over to this building?"

"I'd like to. The coffee here's better."

"He was helping me with a case." Opal nodded toward the deposition in front of Audrey. "Are you almost finished with that?" Audrey cringed because, though Opal had explained it casually, it really wasn't her business what Carl was doing in the building and her boss had just said as much. She leafed through the final pages.

"Five more pages."

"So about an hour?" asked Opal. It took Audrey a beat to realize her boss was teasing her. Relief followed by pride at being singled out by this familiarity imbued Audrey with confidence.

"You need it that fast?"

"Hey, cut her some slack. She's in divorce hell," said Katherine. Carl looked at Audrey and smiled.

"Yeah, but she paved the road with good intentions."

⌇

Audrey's parents had argued both sides of the "road to hell" question. Her mom came down firmly on the side that good intentions were good no matter what; while her dad pointed out that the missionaries had decimated the native Hawaiian population with their good intentions.

Her mom had a mantra about treating everyone with kindness, holding doors open, always smiling, being indiscriminately solicitous. When Audrey was a teenager, she rebelled against smiling at everyone. She figured a downward glance or a far off gaze would be interpreted as mysterious. Greta Garbo wanting to be alone. It didn't take her long to realize that she missed being filled up by the response a smile evokes. It opened the sluice for that natural flow of energy from one being to another. As she matured, she found that the flow was all too easily blocked by chemicals, hormones, or just a bad day. She understood that when she smiled at someone, she was saying: "I trust you with my smile and hope you will trust me with yours." The few times her smile had been interpreted as a come-on, she had easily parried the response with humor. Katherine had said she was asking for it. Smiling at strangers meant you were a hooker.

As Audrey approached, her house seemed to glow from within, the warmth radiating from the interior lights at the windows and streaming from the slightly open front door. She pushed the door fully open and saw Fred bent over in front of the fireplace, as though he were trying to look up inside. When he realized she was there, he stood abruptly, moved to the corner he had taped, and ran his hand over the invisible seam.

"If you didn't know where the tape was, couldn't hardly find it."

"It's a beautiful job, Fred. Thank you."

"Yeah, well, glad I could help out. Don't fire up the gas jet 'til I get back and check it out. They can be dangerous if they haven't been used in awhile." Audrey nodded. He'd be back. He just said so. The idea pleased her.

"I've been thinking about trying some molding around the windows, maybe the doors…You think I can handle it?"

He smiled at her. "I think you can handle anything you set your mind to." She smiled back at him, thankful for this boost to her self-confidence. She started to say something, but hesitated. Fred picked up his tools and moved toward the kitchen on the opposite side of the large room. "I'd best get these cleaned up and get outta here." The physical distance he had put between them gave her courage.

"Are you in some kind of trouble?" He paused briefly before putting his tools into the kitchen sink.

"Nothin' I can't handle, but I need to put some distance between me and Street, the guy you saw next door, before one of us does somethin' we'll regret." As he meticulously cleaned each tool, he demonstrated that he had respect for his craft, a respect he didn't extend to his appearance, and perhaps didn't extend to himself.

"What about Frances?" Audrey inquired.

Fred scrubbed harder at the bits of caked compound on his blade. His face hardened with determination or was it pain? "She got busted last night. I thought she was in her bedroom talkin' on the phone. She snuck out." His tone rang with self-recrimination. "I got me a job with a buddy buildin' this house up in Mitchell…a little town up North. I'd wanted to take her up to our cousins' place in San Jose 'til I got her into rehab. That way I could, you know, see her on weekends and shit." Audrey moved to the kitchen area, but still kept her distance.

"Don't you worry about her being in jail?"

Fred looked up at her, the water still flowing over his hands. "At least she won't be usin' and it's CYA, not real jail. My mom won't make bail for her that's for sure. She's at the end of her rope with Judy—I mean, Frances. When I get me some cash, I'll come down and get her." Audrey suddenly had the urge to hold him, to take him in her arms and pat him on the back. To tell him things would work out. She'd see to it. She'd fix it for him. Instead, they locked eyes.

"You're a good brother," she said. Fred pointedly resumed his clean up. Guilt suffused his voice.

"Naw. It's my friends what got her into this. But I'm gettin' her out. And I got insurance on her. They'll leave her alone."

"Insurance?"

He looked up and eyed her almost suspiciously, then packed his tools in his bag. "Nothin'. Look, you'll keep workin' on that rehab place, huh? Gettin' her straight's the only thing that matters in my life right now. She's the only thing in the world I give a shit about." Audrey's nod was lost on him because he looked everywhere but at her to conceal the water barely visible on his lower lids. His mirthless laugh seemed forced. "Well, her 'n my hog. I love my hog." His discomfort seemed to dissipate. He handed her a scrap of paper. "Here's my number up there. You get into any construction problems, you call me, okay?"

"Thanks, I'll do that."

He grabbed his coffee cup, wrapped it in a stained cloth and stuffed it in his bag. As he started to leave, Audrey picked up one of the shopping bags she had brought with her. "Wait." She opened the bag and pulled out two pounds of premium coffee and an oversized mug with "Fred" painted on the side in bold letters. "I figured you could use it. It's your only vice."

Fred accepted it gratefully. "Only monkey I got left. Thanks." He pulled his stained Peet's Coffee mug out of his bag and handed it to her. "It ain't much, but ya might use it for paint and such."

"Thank you." She watched him leave, watched through the window as he secured his bag to the back of his Harley, watched as he drove off without a backward glance.

chapter 4

EVEN IN THE mid-nineties the Venice boardwalk was a cliché: outrageousness piled on the already camp. For every talented street performer, there was a guy with a guitar wailing like an alley cat, jingling the collection box that doubled as percussion. The bike path teemed with bikers, skaters, and joggers dressed in a minimum of spandex all oblivious to one another as they cruised in their own Walkman worlds.

Jody Maroni's was the dietarily correct place to eat the most incorrect of all junk foods: sausage. Theirs was made from chicken and duck with exotic herbs and spices so that one could speak to his sausage in Chinese, Hindi, or Spanish.

On a bench with a good view of the people parade, Katherine, belly bulging onto her thighs, shoved a huge sausage sandwich into her mouth. Audrey looked on in awe, doing her utmost to keep a straight face, but the sight of her very pregnant friend attacking the impossibly large sandwich forced the corners of her mouth up. Katherine's sausage-lust seemed to have her undivided attention and she didn't look up when she said:

"How's your mom?"

Jolted, Audrey flashed on how she could be somewhere enjoying the sunshine of life-appreciated only to have a thick nimbus draw over her at that word, "mom". Her response had become the stuff of ritual, a tea ceremony where the formal movements were more important than the beverage.

"They're always trying some new drug."

"One'll work someday," Katherine said.

"Yeah," Audrey said with the conviction of a jaded politician. She noticed how malleable her spirits had become, able to be bounced like a sphere of silly putty to oxygen deprived heights then squashed flat as a crepe from one second to the next. Looking back at her friend, she made a conscious effort to recapture the feeling of delight experienced moments earlier. Katherine assisted her by taking another absurdly large bite.

"That kid's going to be well insulated," Audrey said.

Katherine peered back at her friend in mock derision, offering glimpses of partially masticated pieces of sausage as she spoke. "Oh please, like your idea of a healthy breakfast isn't an oatmeal cookie instead of a chocolate chip. Besides, I'm good most of the time. Every once in awhile you gotta be bad. Speaking of which, how's that hunk?"

It took a moment for Audrey to realize whom Katherine had meant. "His name's Fred and he's up North."

"Fred? Who's named Fred these days? And what do you mean, up North?"

"Up helping a friend build a house in northern California."

"Wait a minute. You let him go? You got too many hot looking men in your life? What's wrong with you? Go get him!"

Audrey took a too large bite of her own sandwich so she wouldn't have to respond immediately. Of the two, Katherine always had been more comfortable with her sexuality. To Katherine, sex was as natural as eating. To Audrey it was more like a religion, which demanded contemplation and discussion, preferably with a like-minded individual. The attendant rituals of stated attraction, total acceptance, and mutual commitment were often too tedious for the casual suitor and Audrey speculated that many a good man had given up simply because he was disinclined to run her gauntlet. She envied Katherine her ease.

"First of all, I don't think..."

"Good, you're not equipped to right now," Katherine interjected.

The glare Audrey tried to formulate vanished when Katherine popped the last of her sausage into her mouth causing her cheeks to bulge. How did she finish that so quickly? And how could someone she had known over twenty years still make her smile just by being herself? "First of all, I don't think he's interested in me—he's got to be at least five years younger—but beyond that, I'm not interested in him. We have nothing in common. He's an uncomplicated guy... not drawn to, you know, reading, discussions, stringing a couple of sentences together with a conjunction."

"So he's a conjunction short of a compound sentence. That's not what we're looking for here."

"I'm not saying he's dumb."

"Sure you are, but you like him, right?"

"I'm not sure," said Audrey. "I mean, I admire him sort of, but there's no meeting of the minds, no spark."

"You don't have to like him to...enjoy him." Katherine's knowing look hammered her point home.

"You know I'm not into that."

"You should be. You could use a good roll in the hay."

Katherine's response shocked her. "What a 'guy' thing to say."

Katherine grabbed Audrey's arm in both her hands and earnestly looked into her eyes. "Not a 'guy' thing. A human thing...Don't shut down."

Audrey held this notion in the front of her mind, careful not to let it filter any deeper. It would only add to the clutter, only cause her to devise a new tape that would fix the problem in her mind but not in her life.

Katherine understood that she had hit a nerve. She loosened her grip and patted Audrey's hand. "There's gotta be something you like about him. He helped you with your damn drywall."

"Yes, he did. And he loves his sister...I like that a lot."

❦

"I've got bagels." Carl felt this was adequate warning, supplanting knocks, doorbells and traditional salutations. He walked through the front door, ajar as it was to catch the breeze, and past Audrey, who was in the middle of slicing a piece of door molding, straight to the little end table supporting the coffee maker. He picked up the stained Peet's mug and poured a steaming cup. "Don't mind if I do."

"Use the other one, that's mine." He eyed the clean Monet Water Lilies mug, then handed her the Peet's along with the bag of bagels. Filling the pastel cup, he studied her with suspicion.

"I get the company china? Since when am I so privileged?"

"I've already used this one."

"Not something that would've bothered you before. Am I sensing some alienation here."

"I've warned you about the couch persona."

"Oh, you're just grouchy because you've lost some sleep. Am I right?"

"I've been sleeping like a baby."

"Waking up every two hours, crying for milk?"

"Get some new material." She threw the bag of bagels at him. He caught it deftly and tried to convey a studied indifference.

"I heard you called 911 the other night. Why didn't you tell me about it?"

"Because it was just a couple of guys fighting. No big deal."

"Well, you should've called me so I could check it out."

"And you'd have done what? Put them on Prozac?

"Hey, I'm a man of action. I'd have bludgeoned them with my list of anger-management programs."

"My hero." Audrey held up a length of window molding. "Are you going to help me with these or are you just here to baby-sit for Miles?"

"I am here to execute your slightest whim...as usual."

"Yeah? Well, execute this over that door." She tossed him a length of molding, mitered on both ends, and nodded toward the doorway leading to the bedroom.

⚞⚟

She had been coping with life toward the end of her marriage, managing to handle both law school and work, although it left little time for Miles. Still, she had been coping. It only began to unravel when she learned of his latest infidelity. Initially, she had been as skeptical as the rest about this second time around, more skeptical than Carl, less so than Katherine. She knew all the adages about leopards not changing spots, apples not falling far from the tree––Miles's father had been a profligate womanizer––and people only changing if they wanted to. It was this last which she fastened onto. This time, he had said. This time he was ready.

"We'll have some kids. That'll keep me home. I've sewn my wild oats. This time it'll work."

It was too easy to blame Annabel. Annabel had been one of the reasons she had stayed so long in the first incarnation of their marriage. Miles had bought the yellow lab as a puppy when they were first dating. She felt privileged when he asked her to name it. Annabel was perfectly accepting of anything and anyone; this made her a lethal watchdog with the potential to suffocate a burglar in a deluge of slobbering kisses. Miles and she lived in constant fear of that lawsuit.

They had been divorced about a year when Audrey received the call from a sobbing Miles.

"It's Annabel."

"What? What happened?"

"You know how she always sneaks across the street to swim in the Scarnecchia's pool?"

"Yeah?"

"She was hit by a van," said Miles. "One of those `Homes of the Stars' tour things."

"Oh, Miles, where are you?"

"At the Santa Monica Animal Hospital"

"I'll be there in ten minutes." It was after midnight, but Audrey raced to the animal hospital, ostensibly to be there for Annabel, but to be there, primarily, for Miles.

She had done everything she could think of to make it work: quit her courier job so she wouldn't be gone, taken a paralegal certificate, stayed near him as much as his work allowed. The second time around would be better. She wouldn't make the same mistakes this time. He wouldn't have any reason to be unfaithful.

Granted, their sex life had never been the stuff of fantasy. It was always colored by his feeling that her demand for fidelity somehow controlled him at his core. He had said as much in one of their rare stabs at couple counseling. He also said that he felt he would come around to being faithful if not pressured by her. For her part, she couldn't understand how she could not pressure him, if pressure meant expecting fidelity. She promised him a clean slate, but the slate had been written on often and erased carelessly. She read all the books about not being a victim and tried not to see herself as one, but the nagging thought remained: it was somebody's fault.

⌦⌫

Audrey used her chop saw with concentrated precision to cut a carefully marked piece of crown molding, a much trickier operation than the flush-with-the-wall window and door moldings. The large circular blade sliced a cut so clean it didn't require the slightest sanding. As she negotiated the steps of the ladder, the long board bowed and wobbled but what satisfaction it was to see the precise corner fit against the piece already in place. She sank a temporary nail to hold it, then looked down the twelve-foot length to the far corner. The length was right, but the cut was at an inverse angle.

"Shit!" The temporary nail lived up to its name as Audrey ripped the molding from the wall, leaving a small crater in the nail's wake. Throwing the board across the room where it splintered against one of her new window casings, she wanted to scream her frustration, but knew she wouldn't get satisfaction from a scream unheard. Whom could she scream at? Spying the phone, she thought of calling Katherine. But how do you explain the intricacies of crown molding angles to the uninitiated? Besides, Katherine would just offer to pay someone to do it for her. A comfort, and not. Suddenly, she raced around the disorganized room until she found the scrap of paper reading "Cabin Motel". She punched in the numbers on the keypad. After a couple of rings, he answered.

"Yeah?"

"I just ruined a twenty-dollar piece of crown molding." On the other end of the phone line, Audrey imagined Fred lounging on an overstuffed love seat in his cozy cabin-like room.

"And who's this? Whoever it is, bet you can find the answer in your sewing book." Although Fred was obviously teasing her, Audrey still felt a bubble of insecurity rising in her throat. God, she missed her old confidence.

"It is in my sewing book...sort of. I did it right the first few times, but then I screwed up."

"You didn't make yourself a pattern," he said. In the background, she heard the television channels change one after another.

"Out of what, paper?"

"Some of that old base board you tore off. Mark the pieces up, down, inside corner, and outside corner. Once you can see 'em in front of you, you always put it in the saw right. And remember the construction words to live by: `Measure twice, cut once.'"

Audrey thought about how comfortable it had been to work with him and how surprisingly easy it was becoming to talk to him. "How'd you get so smart?"

"Don't tell nobody. Got it cleverly disguised, but my brain's my secret weapon. Anything else?" The abruptness of his question brought her up short. Obviously the conversational ease had been all on her side.

"No...No, that's all. Guess I'll see ya."

"You don't even want to know how I'm doin'?" Relief made her almost giddy. He wanted to talk. She wasn't presuming too much of their brief association.

"Of course I do. How are things going?"

"Fine." Audrey waited for him to continue. When he didn't, she again felt a palpable discomfort. The roller-coaster ride was more than she could stand from one innocuous phone call.

"Good, good, I'm glad. Listen, thanks for the tip. I'll call you next crisis."

"Yeah, you do that. See ya." A full-throated laugh escaped Audrey as she looked at the dial-tone-blaring receiver. She hadn't entirely lost her sense of humor. She could still get a kick out of making a fool of herself.

The next day in the office she realized that she was once again looking at the telephone as if it were somehow responsible for what transpired on the other end. This time she wanted to throw it across the room. Amid the din of the bullpen, she placed it back over her ear and strained to hear for a moment, then shouted back:

"I wonder how many suicides occur while people are waiting for rehab slots." She listened to the woman on the other end explain how busy her department was and how there wasn't a snowball's chance in hell that she would help her through the complex network one had to negotiate in order to enter any public assistance system. "I know it's not your problem, but it should be!" Audrey slammed down the receiver, then looked up to see her boss shaking her head. Opal wasn't the type to lose control. Audrey doubted she would appreciate that quality in a subordinate.

"Remind me to stay on your good side," said Opal. Audrey cringed.

"Sorry, a little of my natural charisma leaking out. Honestly, I can usually hold my tongue better than that. I'm just frustrated with the impossible maze that's our mental health system."

Her boss placed a file on her desk. "You need some professional help?" she asked.

Audrey shook her head emphatically. "The sister of that guy who was helping me can't afford anything but a public program."

"That man who was here the other day?" Audrey nodded, surprised Opal remembered.   "Well, `Deputy D.A.' should hold more weight, but 'widow of Judge Nichols' is what usually gets me through to the right people. I'll call around for you."

"You're kidding. Really? Thanks. Thanks a lot."

"It's in my best interest. You wouldn't be distracted and I could count on you to continue giving me a hand on the Sitwell case."

"Absolutely...I mean, I know how important it is, and I promise whatever you need I'll be there for you." Audrey had been waiting for an opportunity like this. If she could just impress Opal with her work, she might be considered for the much sought after, soon-to-be-open job of Opal's legal assistant. No longer a desk among many, but an office with a door. Maybe a less cluttered office would mean a less clutterd brain.

"Just keep up the good work on the depositions." Opal nodded toward the file she had placed on the desk. Audrey watched as her boss walked confidently down the hall toward her office. The thought crossed her mind: "That's who I want to be when I grow up."

In her early fifties, Opal looked some years younger, but strain lined the face that Audrey imagined had turned heads not long ago. Her husband's death had taken its toll. Still, her air was of competence, of authority wielded often sternly but always fairly. She was attractive, bright and exuded strength, all things Audrey admired, but the quality she truly envied was her belief in herself, in the absolute rightness of her decisions. It was a quality Audrey had possessed but had somehow mortgaged, then lost almost without noticing it, until she found that she now questioned every decision she made. If she worked closely with this woman, maybe some of that confidence would rub off.

With the crown molding, the new doors, and a fresh coat of paint after hours of stripping off the ancient layers, the living area looked almost finished. Audrey's dinner had been a bowl of home-made clam chowder that Katherine dropped by on her way to a restaurant with some of her husband Coburn's potential buyers of ornate post-modern pre-Columbian artifacts. Where did Katherine find time to make homemade soup? Supernatural powers? It was as logical as anything that had occurred to her lately.

Audrey looked down at the rough plywood beneath her feet and envisioned gleaming hardwood floors. How hard could it be? The scrap of paper was still by the phone. Was it just waiting there for her to invent this excuse to call? When motivation is questionable, better not to question. She punched in the number.

"Yeah?" Fred's voice was flat, bored.

"So, do you think I could do my own hardwood floors?"

"Ain't you ever heard of "Hi, how are ya?" Now his voice was warmer.

"Hi, how are you?"

"Fine. No."

"No?" She couldn't hide her indignation.

"You doin' real hardwood floors'd be like me makin' myself a pair of pants. I could do it, but I wouldn't wanna wear 'em."

Not the answer she wanted. Her budding confidence in her home renovation capabilities had been mitigating her loss of confidence elsewhere. Her voice reflected her disappointment. "It was just an idea."

"You might be able to handle this new prefab stuff...looks just like plank but it's in three foot boards and it comes pre-finished. Ask around about it."

"Okay, thanks. So...everything going all right up there?"

"Yeah, great. I'm watching Bonanza, smoking a cigar."

"That sounds exciting," her intonation was dryer, more sarcastic than she had meant it to be. The long pause made her sure the conversation was, again, going nowhere. "Well, I guess I'll call you next crisis."

He let another uncomfortable interval pass before he spoke. "Actually, I was gonna call you tonight. I kinda need a favor. You know, if you can't, it's okay...I really was atonin' and not expectin' anything back 'n all that."

Having been discouraged due to her lack of success with a rehab slot, Audrey was genuinely pleased at the prospect of being able to help him. "Name it."

"Looks like they're gonna drop the possession charges against Frances. They'll know Friday. I was wonderin' if you could bring her up here, you know, to my cousins?" The request surprised her. Was it purely for his sister? Was he expecting to see her? Be with her? She decided it didn't matter either way. She would like to see him again because he brought her out of herself. He was...interesting.

"Of course, I'd be happy to."

"If it's, you know, too much trouble..."

"I could use the break myself." She could hear him expel his held breath.

"I'd be real grateful. Talk to you later."

Again, she realized she was staring at the receiver. Most people Audrey knew were starting to add phone lines: fax, beeper, modem. Opal and Katherine even had phones that they could fit in their purses. People were never out of touch, connected by electronic tentacles to others they no longer had time to see and to places they no longer had time to go. They were too busy being connected. Now Fred's phone call had nudged her life in yet another direction as phone calls had in the past: the one from Miles about their dog, Annabel; Katherine at three in the morning announcing her engagement; the hospital confirming her father's death.

chapter 5

KATHERINE, ON HER mountain bike, was not as sleek a sight as she had been forty pounds ago, but what she lacked in grace she made up for in enthusiasm. Audrey jogged along beside her on the beach bike path below the soaring Santa Monica bluffs. She looked up at the towering Washington Palms, almost willowy above their neighbors, the more stalwart date palms. Both varieties queued North to South at the cliff's edge and today leaned slightly eastward because of the strong prevailing ocean breeze. Normally, due to the sun, but particularly during the Santa Anna conditions when the winds bellow out of the desert, the lanky Washingtons bend westward and peer over the cliff at their lost comrades below. The bluffs had terraced themselves over the years, had sloughed off and formed irregular little tables of earth. Occasionally a huge palm rose parallel to the cliff on one of these outcroppings. Had it skied down with the moving avalanche of earth or had it grown from seed on that mobile patch of ground. Whatever their origins, the huge trees' roots extruded at ninety degree angles into the earth, a visual reminder of the tenacity required for life in coastal California.

The Pacific Coast Highway between the bluffs and the exercisers was jammed with a mixture of luxury cars from Malibu and economy cars from the valley. Audrey gave a quick thanks to the powers that be that she could walk or bike to work. The thought of being trapped in that herd smacked of prison and recalled her mother's expensive incarceration. Audrey shook her head to rid herself of that fleeting notion.

The sun rose over the city behind the two women, elongating their shadows before them, which played constant hare to their hounds. Katherine pedaled her bike comfortably while Audrey pounded the pavement, straining to keep up.

"So, you think I should go?" asked Audrey.

"Of course you should."

"Maybe Opal will give me a half day off tomorrow."

"Want me to ask her for you?" said Katherine.

"I think I'd rather do it myself. I'm, uh, angling for her assistant's job."

"I know. It's the worst kept secret in the office. I also know I'm not her favorite person but sometimes a little extra support helps."

"Thanks, but I'll give it a try myself." Audrey felt the uneasy silence. "Will she think I'm a slacker?"

"Hardly. She piles more work on you than on anybody except maybe Roland H☞☞s."

"Yeah, I figure he has the inside track."

"A half a day isn't going to make any difference one way or the other." Katherine's voice rang with forced casualness as she unconsciously picked up the pace. "So why would you want to work for some shrew rather than your best friend?" There. It was said. Now it wouldn't hang between them any more.

"I wouldn't care if I disappointed her," said Audrey.

"I wouldn't care if you disappointed me."

"I would."

"But you wouldn't disappoint."

"I would at some point, just being human," said Audrey.

"Yeah, yeah," Katherine responded dismissively, then let a long interval pass. "So call the guy. Tell him you're coming up."

"I already did."

"Without my okay?" Katherine's indignation was feigned.

"I knew you'd support me."

"Support and encourage," said Katherine. "What's it been, three months since you dumped Miles? Time to get your butt out there."

"I'm not necessarily getting my butt out there. I'm just doing a favor for someone who did one for me."

"I don't care why you're doing it. I don't care what you do. I just know that you're going to be kissing a lot of iguanas before you find another toad that you like."

"Iguanas and toads? Beginning of an animal obsession?"

"I'm listening to my mother and treating Coburn like a dog; we've never been happier. I scratch his butt, he thumps his leg and follows me anywhere."

Audrey laughed but figured there was a kernel of truth in there somewhere. Katherine and Coburn had been through the ringer, but they seemed to have emerged stronger than ever. Only his frequent absences still caused a problem.

There was the coveted door to the coveted office. Audrey knocked lightly and thought how wonderful it must be to have that little slice of privacy. Annie would be leaving in a week and the position of Opal's assistant finally would be vacant, as would this little enclosed antechamber to Opal's office.

"Come in," responded Annie an attractive second year law student. Audrey hoped her envious glances around Annie's office didn't offend her.

"Does Opal have a couple of minutes for me? It's sort of personal."

"I'll check." Annie picked up the phone. "Can you see Audrey for a few minutes or should I schedule her?" Annie nodded into the phone before she put it down. Audrey wondered how many times she herself had used body language as futilely.

"Go on in," said Annie.

Her boss's office was opulent by public service standards, because of her personal furnishings: a pleasing love seat, a Chinese silk carpet and a couple of expensive Chagall lithographs. Opal always wore beautifully cut but conservative suits, timeless suits, ones she had been forced to wear for the past couple years with no additions to her wardrobe because, rumor had it, her late husband badly mismanaged their finances. Opal's hands constantly searched for something to occupy them, removing and replacing the cap of a pen, incessant doodling, twirling a strand of hair just behind her right ear, all telltale signs of an ex-two-pack-a-dayer. Cigarettes had also left a vocal legacy, a slight rasp that punctuated the ends of her words begun in an otherwise bell-clear alto. Opal utilized the hair fidget as she motioned Audrey to the seat in front of her, which caused Audrey to grab a lock of her own hair, then to drop it when she realized she was mimicking her boss.

"What can I help you with?"

"I was wondering if I could take half a day off tomorrow. I'm way ahead today and I'll take work home with me." Her boss smiled at her and seemed genuinely interested.

"Still fixing up the house?"

"Actually, I'm giving a friend a ride up North...the sister of the guy who came to the office the other day."

"The rehab candidate. I'm still working on that," said Opal smiling at her. "I know you'll make up the time. In fact, you can take the whole day if you can redact that widow's depo...what's her name?"

"Herring," Audrey put in quickly.

"Herring, right. If that's on my desk before you leave tonight, I'll see you Monday. Just let me know where you'll be, you know, in case anything comes up."

"Sure, great," said Audrey. "Thanks a lot."

She almost danced down the hall. Audrey had worried about requesting a half-day and now she had a full day off, quite a rarity in the D.A.'s office. The spring in her step must have been evident because as she turned the corner toward the bullpen, Carl approached from the other direction, looped his arm through hers and swung her around three hundred and sixty degrees.

"What was that?" Audrey laughed.

"You looked like you were ready to swing."

"You know me so well."

"And I'm ready for a long bike ride. How about tomorrow after work?"

"Sorry, I'm going to be taking a friend up North."

"Oh, yeah, where?" Carl's voice had a forced casualness which conveyed that he knew it was none of his business.

"A place west of San Jose called Mitchell."

"Who's the friend?"

"Frances, the sister of the guy who helped me out." Audrey spoke deliberately and realized that she wanted Carl to report back to Miles. Realized that on some level she hoped it would get to him, would evoke a stab of pain below Miles' lower left rib. That's where hers had been.

Carl seemed to swallow his immediate response. "Cool. I'll take a rain check," said Carl.

It was the first day she could remember that she hadn't awakened to one of the revenge fantasy head-tapes in which Miles fared so badly. Instead, she felt a physical sense of well being. Of excitement. Optimism. As she pulled up in front of the county detention center, she happily pushed aside even the thought of not thinking about Miles. She hoped she could make a habit of it.

For the novice, the county justice system constituted a form of punishment in itself, from the overcrowding, to the indifference of the overworked officers, to the depressing physical characteristics of the jail where juveniles of all ages and offenses were temporarily housed. Audrey thought that perhaps Frances was experiencing some of this negative conditioning as she sulked toward the Jeep. Still, Audrey felt it her duty to make this trip a vacation of sorts, a reward for choosing to stay with her cousins rather than falling back in with her old, questionable friends.

Audrey opened the door for her but got only a peeved expression from Frances for her trouble. "How are you doing?" No response. "We'll take the coast." Still none. "It'll be a gorgeous drive." The girl crossed her arms in front of her and looked straight ahead. Audrey's mood plummeted. The door crushed her newfound sense of wellbeing as it fled the car.

At Pismo Beach, Audrey spotted an ice cream shop and turned to Frances. "How 'bout a malt, soda, sundae...something fun?"

Frances continued to look straight ahead. "I don't, like, pollute my body with sugar."

"I guess artificial sweeteners are out of the question?" This at least provoked a glance from the teenager, though it floated somewhere between disdain and pity. Audrey yearned to bring up the drugs she polluted her body with, but figured the irony had to have been pointed out to her before. She ducked into the ice cream shop for a mint-chip cone and thought about what people missed when they denied themselves simple pleasures such as this. As she savored the cone, she mentally ran through a list of expensive things she would forego in exchange for this current taste bud bliss. She stopped when she came to an office of her own and considered that she would trade eight or ten such experiences for a quiet office.

Half the fun of a car trip was traveling the road to gastronomic ruin, so farther up the coast at San Simeon, Audrey finished a burger with the works, then wiped her hands on the chili saturated napkin and climbed back into the car. "What d'you say we take a look at Hearst Castle?"

Frances maintained her thousand yard stare out the front window. "So we can, like, see where a millionaire old guy kept his actress mistress?"

"You've been here before." Audrey's flat statement was met with a sigh and a roll of the eyes. She put the car in gear and wished she were piloting a Gulf Stream.

The oppressive atmosphere in the car remained whether she flapped her gums in small talk or left the air vibrationless. Besides she had long since tired of the sound of her own voice and the radio was useless near the cliffs. The clock told her she had at least three more hours to endure. When she was a child, the summer days crept by endlessly until she actually anticipated a return to school. Just last year, she had raced from job to school, to home, hoping for an extra minute, an extra second from the racing clock. Now her internal clock's mechanism seemed to be bathed in molasses. Probably not what Einstein meant when he posited that time was relative.

Near Big Sur, she realized she had closed Frances out as effectively as the young girl had shut her out. Audrey pulled into the parking lot of the restaurant, I AM THE EGGPLANT, and opened her door without asking if Frances wanted to join her. The girl's voice startled her as it cracked the silence. "Finally, like, something I can eat," said Frances as she slammed the car door.

The predominant color of the diner-style restaurant was that particular purple that the French call aubergine, the Italians call melanzana and Americans call eggplant. No wonder their food tastes better.

In a booth by the window, Audrey smiled up at the older woman who handed them menus. The woman smiled back warmly and Audrey noticed a fragment of her well-being returning.

"Thanks," Audrey said. Frances said nothing, of course, but studied the menu. When the woman returned Audrey ordered the lasagna while Frances grilled the waitress.

"Can I, like, get the mixed vegetables with a little life left in them or does the cook think the only good vegetable is a dead one?"

"We can make them a little crunchy if that's what you like," said the waitress sweetly.

"Do they have, like, any animal products in them?"

"You can get them with cheese or tofu."

"The tofu and be sure they don't mix it up," said Frances. "I'm a vegan." The woman nodded and moved off.

Audrey smiled at Frances. "You didn't mention you were a vegetarian."

"It's cruel to dominate and devour other life forms," said Frances as though quoting some text.

Though Audrey was a confirmed omnivore, she liked the girl's reasoning for not eating animals and wasn't about to point out that plants were life forms, too. "That's a very compassionate view. When did you decide to become a vegan?"

Frances looked at her with undisguised contempt. "It's not, like, something you decide. It's, like, something you are." The finality in her tone brought the conversation to a screeching halt. Frances looked out the window. Audrey gazed around the room until her eyes lit on the sign: I AM THE EGGPLANT. She smiled to herself at a memory, then decided to give camaraderie one last shot as she told her story with enthusiasm.

"The name of the restaurant reminds me of a flight attendant friend of mine who tried to tell an Indian passenger that the airline forgot to load his special vegetarian meal. The irate man screamed at her: `Madam, you do not understand. Don't you see? I am a vegetable!'" Audrey smiled at Frances looking for any kind of response, but the girl's face remained a taciturn mask, while her voice dripped sarcasm.

"Any other cute little stories?"

As her smile faded, Audrey's voice hardened. "You know, I'm getting real tired of your attitude. Particularly of the hypocrisy of someone who eats health foods, but takes drugs. You can make a choice about how you view the world every day. Even though this isn't exactly a peachy time in my life, I expend a lot of energy looking for the good, the kind, the happy."

The suggestion of a cynical smile formed on Frances's lips. "And do you find it, Ms. Saccharin?"

Audrey's jaw clenched in time with her fists. "Sometimes...when I'm not wallowing in self-pity." She threw some bills down on the table. "Take your time. I've lost my appetite." She strode out slamming the slam-proof door hard enough to make the eggplant cutout quiver.

Maybe it was a good thing she didn't have kids. She wanted to slap Frances. Snap out of it, she'd say like some thirties gumshoe. Can't you see that it's morally wrong to be the instrument of your own destruction? Don't you realize that life provides enough instruments of devastation, enough mine fields fraught with real danger? Audrey didn't like to dwell on them, those twin pitfalls of happenstance and fortune. Didn't like to examine the relationship between caprice and culpability.

When Aristotle claimed that a life unreflected upon wasn't worth living, his student countered that a life unlived wasn't worth reflecting upon. Audrey leaned toward the student; she believed that a person's first duty was to live, to embrace what was out there, and then to consider it, if you had the time. Her mother's vulnerability made her a champion of those in life's margins and this engendered in Audrey the perceived responsibility for other people's happiness. Her mom's influence made Audrey a guilt-toting idealist who truly wanted to believe the best about everyone. The line she fed Frances about seeking the good, kind and happy was, for her, a life style, consciously chosen to avoid her mother's abyss.

Now, sitting under a tree near the restaurant, Audrey took a deep breath and tried to regain the feelings she had enjoyed at the outset of the day. Optimism. Excitement. She watched a pelican dive crazily and crash into the water before regaining altitude with a beak full of fish. A smile forced its way to her lips, then was cemented there by the roar of a sixty-five Mustang which raced by, engine thudding like a Chris Craft. A red sixty-five had been her dad's pride and joy. It now rested on blocks in Katherine's spare garage. Audrey remembered her early childhood as being happy, never lonely like the accepted portrait of the only child. She envied Katherine her brothers and sisters for their sheer number, but when she thought about it, she wouldn't trade places with her. Audrey's parents had been her playmates, her mother in particular, and that had provided an exclusivity that she reveled in. When she was older, she looked at her emotionally disturbed mother and thought of her as starring in her own Tennessee Williams play. But while she was young, her mother belonged to her.

Her mind was beginning to relax in this warm memory haze under the beautiful tree overlooking one of the most magnificent landscapes in the world: Big Sur. She savored the moment, registering the deep blue of the water, the azure hue of the sky. This was how you survived. By appreciating.

Frances approached her gingerly, doggie bag in hand. "So, what have you found that's good, kind or happy in the past twenty minutes?" Audrey looked up at her. How much courage had it taken to speak those few conciliatory words? She patted the ground next to her and Frances fluidly folded herself into the lotus position.

"Let's see. I saw a pelican crash on the water, then come up with a beak full of fish...I saw a '65 Mustang like my dad's...that definitely made me smile."

"My dad liked cars."

"See there? We're practically twins."

"Did yours drive 'em, like, drunk?" Audrey thought of her father's nightly cocktail but knew that he never would have taken such a risk. She viewed him as genetically incapable of breaking the law. She shook her head.

"Mine married his to a light pole." Frances said this matter-of-factly, without a trace of irony. Audrey put a tentative hand on her shoulder.

"Did he...?"

"Oh, they, like, divorced him from it before they buried him."

Audrey had to suppress a smile at Frances's choice of phrasing. After a moment: "My dad died when I was about your age."

"Yeah? How'd he die?"

Audrey shrugged. "He just dropped dead."

"Did you like him?"

"I adored him."

"Well I hated my dad. I wished he would die and he did."

Audrey rose and offered a hand to the complex young woman. "You're a very special young lady, but you're not that powerful. Nobody is."

"Still, he's dead, isn't he?" Audrey decided not to press the issue. As they walked toward the car, Frances offered the doggie bag.

"Here. I told them to add fat and preservatives so you could eat it." Audrey laughed. Frances was one interesting young lady.

After their initial breakthrough, the drive had been like a slumber party with often frivolous but sometimes telling exchanges between friends. Frances delighted Audrey with imitations of her friends and family.

"My mom would say things like `Now Fredrick, don't you think you should apologize to your father for sayin' such a thing?'

"Frederick? His name's really Frederick?"

"I know! Fredrick! He'd die if he knew I told you. Anyway, Fred would go, like, `I didn't mean he was a monkey. Just a Neanderthal,' and my dad would get, like, all purple in the face 'cause he didn't know what a Neanderthal was and, like, he was afraid to ask 'cause sometimes Fred'd call him something good just so it'd embarrass him when he'd say `Don't you call me that'."

"Sounds like you had some fun in your house, even if your dad wasn't in on it."

"Not much. You and your dad must've gotten along."

Audrey nodded. "Do you miss yours at all?"

Frances became quiet, but not in the sullen manner she had affected before. Now she seemed to be in search of something, like an archaeologist plumbing a tomb, hoping to find an artifact.

"I don't know, like, it's hard to explain." She sat silently a long moment, then: "I miss the dad I wanted to have. But the person I don't think I'll ever get over is Kurt."

"Kurt?"

"Kurt Cobain," said an incredulous Frances.

"Right. Nirvana, sorry."

"That's why I took the name Frances, after his baby. I always hated Judy anyway."

"Grief takes time and sometimes grief for different people gets sort of mushed together."

"Whatever." She looks at Audrey for a long moment. "Kurt's been dead almost a year and if anything I feel worse now than ever. It's like this black hole in your life. Makes you want to do things—anything—that'll get you a little light."

<hr />

Pulling up outside a modest house in San Jose, Audrey felt a pang of regret when she finally came to a stop. Frances looked out the window toward her cousin's home.

"You're really gonna to make me do this? I mean, it's like getting dropped in one of those fifties sitcoms," the teenager whined.

"You're the one who chose to come up here."

"Chose? It was, like, come here or be in Purgatory." Audrey had presumed that it had been Frances's choice since her mother was legally responsible for her.

"Couldn't you have stayed with your mother?"

"That's what I mean. I'd have to hang out with her all the time."

"Doesn't sound like a bad alternative to jail."

"Same thing." When Audrey shot her a skeptical look, the girl added, "Almost."

Audrey decided she wouldn't return to her teenage years for all the chocolate in Switzerland. "Well, it's the right decision," said Audrey. Then in a self-mocking tone: "And you can work on finding something good, kind or happy up here."

"Yeah, right," but the sarcasm in her voice was mitigated by a slight smile.

"Come on, you'll be happy just knowing how much cooler you are than your cousins."

Now the teenager's smile broadened. She hoisted her knapsack on to her back. "Yeah. That'll be sweet." As Audrey walked her up the driveway, Frances actually grabbed her hand for a brief touch. Audrey squeezed it back and the two held a momentary, awkward gaze before Frances nodded a goodbye.

"See ya," Audrey said with an extra note of cheerfulness which covered the surprising sadness she felt. Frances took a few more steps before turning back toward Audrey.

"I never did anything really bad. Just some drugs and things... Well, there was this old guy, but I didn't really do anything...I didn't know it might, like, hurt anybody."

Audrey approached her. "Did you? Hurt someone?"

"I didn't, I mean, he liked me, but, you know, somebody..." She sighed. "It doesn't matter. It wasn't like some life or death thing. I'm clean now and that's all, like, history."

Fred appeared from inside the house and waved to them with his beer can as he started down the stairs. "Hey, gals!"

Frances grabbed Audrey's hand and squeezed it again. Audrey held on for a moment. "Wait, let's talk about this. We've got time," said Audrey. But Frances just shook her head, turned, and walked past Fred, nudging him with her backpack and nodding toward the beer can.

"That wagon ride didn't last long."

He took a playful swat at her retreating figure. "It's just a beer."

Audrey shifted her weight from one foot to the other, feeling awkward, uncertain of her place in the mix now that she had delivered her charge. Fred took her hand and pulled her gently toward him then planted a kiss on her cheek. "The friend I'm workin' for's having a barbecue tonight. Thought we'd drop your stuff off at my place then go over there."

Audrey shrugged. "Sure."

chapter 6

ONCE THEY GOT to the Cabin Motel in Mitchell, Fred asked her to sit with him on its little porch before they went inside. They both sipped at beers. He was personable, chatty in a familiar way that Audrey chalked up to the beer. He rambled on about the house he was working on for his friend, Nate, and how he liked doing a variety of jobs besides just his taping specialty. He suddenly focused on her.

"So was she a royal pain in the ass?"

Audrey smiled. "No. It took awhile for her to warm up, but when she did, she was delightful." She smiled back at his wry grin.

"First time I ever heard that word in the same sentence with my sister." Audrey looked at him askance. "Don't get me wrong," he continued. "I know she's a good kid. It's just that most everybody else won't take the time to get past her..." He groped for a word but finally gave up. "You know what I mean?"

Audrey nodded. She knew exactly what he meant.

Inside the Cabin Motel was a letdown for Audrey, but then most expectations were. And if this seemed to conflict with her ability to look on the bright side, it was in fact an adjunct. Look on the bright side. When you're disappointed, look for the brightest spot in the dump.

She surveyed this dump and realized that she had envisioned a perfect little haven for her unlikely saint, but Fred's room at the Cabin Motel defined tacky. It did have beautiful pine walls. That was the bright side, but his clothes were thrown all around the room. Airing out? And there seemed to be a layer of grime on everything, lovely walls included.

When she was a courier, she spent half her life in hotel rooms, some nice, some barely adequate. In each one she managed to fashion a tiny corner of familiarity: a small pillow, a coffee or tea making kit, a chair she could pull up by a window and a book, always a book. That sense of a place being her own, in turn, made her feel like she belonged. She identified with the room, regardless of decor, country or length of stay. And though each of the surroundings might have been different, she felt protected by her personal items, like a turtle, his shell.

If this space reflected Fred, she wasn't sure she wanted to get to know him any better. Then it struck her that it wasn't the space. It was the beer. He had slipped off his anti-hero-as-savior pedestal and more closely resembled the itinerate addict that he was.

He emerged from the shower with the small towel stretched around him, the two corners barely knotted at his waist. An exposed white thigh contrasted with his tan athletic torso. Audrey felt a flash of appreciation...or was it lust? He tossed the empty beer bottle, presumably drunk in the shower, toward the wastebasket where it banked off the wall before falling inside. He then pulled two more beers from the cooler.

"Want one?"

"Sure." She took the beer. Audrey couldn't remember when she had felt as out of place as she did at that moment, four hundred miles from home with a man she barely knew. If she had possessed any judgment at all she would have been sky diving, hang gliding, shark bating or any number of more appropriate activities than being here...with him.

As casually as if he were in a locker room, he dropped his towel and began to dress in front of her. Audrey developed an insatiable interest in fireplace ashes. His movements were spare, no wasted energy, just a comb through his wet hair, two strides to the pair of jeans which hung by a belt loop hooked around the partially recessed rabbit ears on the TV, then a smooth dip to the floor to retrieve a T-shirt which he sniffed before putting on. He seized his leather vest from a hook by the door, the only article of clothing treated with any respect.

"Grab that." He indicated a ski jacket thrown on a ratty looking chair by the fire. "It gets cold on the bike." She stood for a moment, nervously looking at the half-finished beer in her hand, while he opened the door. "Ya comin'?"

Audrey fumbled into the jacket, amazed by her own complicity. "Sure." She chugged the remainder of the beer and followed him out the door.

A couple of dozen people, all with beers and smiles, milled around the spacious back yard which sported a half-court basketball area at one end where five boys and three girls ranging in age from seven to sixteen played an aggressive game. A large attractive woman in her early thirties radiating the efficiency and accessibility of a supermom came toward Audrey carrying a tray of deviled eggs.

"Hi, I'm Skitch. Have a deviled egg?"

"Thanks. I'm Audrey." She took one and bit a chunk out of it, trailing a gob of yellow stuffing which landed on her sweater.

"I'll get you a napkin."

"That's okay, I'm used to wearing my food." Audrey managed to pluck the lump of yoke with two fingers and replace it on the remaining egg white before sliding it into her mouth.

"So, you gals get your names straight?" Fred approached, popping another beer and guzzling half of it before he looked at Audrey.

"No thanks to you," said Skitch with a wry inflection.

"You want another?" he asked Audrey.

"No thanks." Her look didn't disguise her displeasure. Why couldn't he cooperate and be the person she wanted him to be? She needed to believe he was on the straight and narrow, that he had turned his life around, that it was possible to fix one's own life.

Skitch offered the tray to Fred. "How 'bout a little egg to soak up some of those suds."

Fred waved her off. "And ruin my high? No way." Skitch flashed Audrey the female "men will be men" look that transcends time and culture, then moved off to foist cholesterol on other incautious guests.

Audrey studied Fred. "When you reclaim a vice, you don't do it in half-measures."

"Yeah, well, I ain't done any drugs so it's not like the old days... It's just a beer."

"Or eight...but who's counting."

"Seems you are. Listen, it's a party. Chill." He held the beer up and looked at it with reverence. "This just helps me outrun some devils...stop too long 'n they catch up to ya."

"Well, you'll have a good vantage point to watch out for them, because I'm driving home."

"You can't drive my hog. I love my hog!"

"There're a lot of things I can't do, but driving your hog isn't one of them." Fred's beer soaked brain wrestled with this concept momentarily then allowed it to pin him. He polished off the bottle.

✦

Nate Bower, Skitch's husband, was a stocky, affable man who wielded his long handled spatula like a baton, as though he were conducting a symphony from behind his mega-grill which smoked a huge fish along with the requisite hot dogs and hamburgers. His guileless appraisal of her was not offensive, though she imagined it would have been from someone else, since he seemed to take in every inch of her body as if studying her for some future exam.

"You're a couple of cuts above Fred's usual girl friends."

She realized he was attempting a compliment. "Thanks. What's usual? Besides younger."

"I don't know...quiet but loud."

"As in, sedate in dress but with a booming voice or not much for words but her attire speaks volumes."

"Number two," Nate said through a laugh. "Yeah, you're okay."

"You're pretty nice yourself for giving him a job."

"Yeah, well, he didn't say, but I figured he had to get out of town for awhile. And I can always use a hand. Him and me go back to junior high. So, you guys seein' each other long?"

"I wouldn't call us seeing each other. He helped me out with some work on my house and I helped him out by bringing his sister up here to his cousins'."

"Yeah? He seemed real excited you were coming up."

"Really?" This frankly surprised her.

Nate nodded. "Well, you're all right by me."

Audrey smiled at Nate's disarming friendliness. She felt guilty about the comparison the moment it popped into her mind, but he reminded her of Annabel, the Golden Lab Miles and she had owned. She wanted to scratch Nate behind his ears.

Half-carrying, half-dragging Fred to his Harley-Davidson 1340 Dyna Wide Glide two hours later was more difficult than Audrey anticipated. He draped himself over her shoulder then moved his feet only enough to keep her from scuffing the toes of his cowboy boots. Audrey felt like she was carrying the weight of all her shortcomings. All the times she had taken the extra soap in hotel rooms, all the times she should have let another motorist go first at a four way stop, all the times she should have visited her mother and hadn't.

The porch light glinted off the immaculate exhaust pipe of the huge motorcycle. Audrey paused at the thought of powering it, because with that projection came a surge of excitement that was quickly engulfed by a wave of fear. But as she put one foot in front of the other, the fear and excitement neutralized each other, because along with her new found distrust of herself, came an emancipation, a release from the ingrained taboo, the cultivated phobia of riding a motorcycle again. It was as though the same storm that left her rudderless also released her from the fear of being out of control.

Fred offered neither help nor resistance when she lowered him onto the back of the machine. She pulled the helmet over his lolled head then put on her own. When she hopped on the front and kicked the monster alive, the report from the engine reminded her of the sound of the hooves of thousands of migrating wildebeest which had left her awe struck one Kenyan night. Audrey spoke to Fred sternly.

"Okay, Fredrick, I want you to sing something in my ear the whole way back. If you stop singing, I'll think you're going to pass out and I'll pull over."

"What'll I sing?"

"I don't care. How 'bout nice Puccini aria."

"I don't know that group. How 'bout some Clapton?"

"Fine." He rested his head on her back and sang toward her ear: "Tears In Heaven". She gunned the engine and let the sound vibrate in her lungs. When she let the clutch out, she couldn't keep the smile from her lips. They sped off into the darkness. Yes, she could drive a hog.

⚚

It was the only thing that her trusting parents had strictly forbidden. No curfew, few restrictions, near total freedom, all because Audrey had always toed some imaginary line in her pursuit of perfection for her parents. Both, though, had placed an absolute ban on motorcycles. Of course it made them irresistible even to someone who wasn't otherwise given to anarchy. Sarto Charles, Katherine's boyfriend, had taught Audrey to ride his Harley, and Audrey had become very proficient by the time she took off into the mountains on her rented Suzuki GT250, admittedly a disappointment after Sarto's Harley. Katherine had no interest in riding one herself and was quite content on the back of Sarto's, but riding alone had been a mandatory element for total rebellion.

As the teenagers sped up the Angeles Crest Highway, Audrey felt the delicious freedom of the forbidden wind in her hair and knew why her parents had been so adamant. It was the highly addictive, luscious sensation of inexorable forward movement, a more immediate feeling than Audrey had ever experienced: hurtling though the atmosphere, dancing with the explicit taboo at tantalizing speeds.

As the trees whizzed past and the asphalt blurred to an oily black ribbon, young Audrey felt like she had pressed the fast forward button on her life. But the heady adrenaline of power decayed into the hot adrenaline of fear when, at a point up ahead, the ribbon vanished into a hairpin turn. She saw the sand as she approached. She slowed for the turn, slowed for the sand, leaned into the curve. What she hadn't seen was the Ford Pinto parked on the other side, poised like a dog marking its territory, rear tireless wheel in the air on a jack. She leaned farther, trying to make the now tightened turn, but her tires hit the sand and she slid sideways under the car, dislodging the jack, collapsing the handlebars, wedging her fragile body beneath the vehicle, gas pouring over her, engine still running. It was the first time in her young life that death had occurred to her. She tried to work herself free, visualizing the sparks igniting the gasoline, replaying every car explosion she had ever seen on screen. Katherine and Sarto had been far behind her, dawdling to be alone. Would they arrive in time? Would she die in an inferno? Would her parents ever forgive her? She saw feet. None that she recognized. Then heard someone yell from farther away.

"Idiot, get away from there! It'll blow up." The shiny, laced shoes protruding from white bell-bottoms didn't heed the warning. They found the jack, raised the car and pulled her out.

The acne scarred face of the young sailor was the most beautiful she had ever seen.

"You okay?" he asked. Audrey nodded dumbly.

Sarto and Katherine arrived and fussed over her bleeding limbs, the scrape on her chin. The sailor melded into the amorphous mass of spectators, as Audrey stood rooted in shock. It was her first brush with death and her first realization of the life-altering impact of anonymous goodness.

Of course, no rebellion is complete without its discovery. She lied to her parents. Told them the injuries were caused by a fall from a skateboard while careening down a treacherous hill—never mind that she hadn't stepped on a skateboard in years. Her parents believed her simply because she hadn't lied to them before. Hadn't had a reason. They believed her until the rental company contacted them about payment for their mangled Suzuki. Her father had always done the right thing. Obeyed the law. Didn't challenge authority. But he screamed into the phone that he knew they had insurance and that he would sue them until he owned their homes, cars, and pots to piss in, if he ever heard from them again. How dare they endanger his daughter's life? Audrey's heart swelled. She had always loved her father but now she realized how very much she admired him. She got to admire him every night for the next month of her grounding.

⌖

The crunch of the gravel roadway served as a percussive under layer to Fred's singing into the back of her hair. His voice recalled the mating screech of a peacock as he wailed through Clapton's "Layla", singing both lyrics and guitar licks. Audrey pulled the motorcycle as close to the front door of the cabin as possible, then peeled him off her back. She struggled to support him to the door, and made it just past the threshold where earth's gravitational pull won out. She congratulated herself on the foresight not to have removed her helmet as her head crashed against the gritty pine floor. Fred's helmet had popped off, but as a result, he just shook his head once, smiled at her through slit eyes––that drunk's smile that appears blurry even to the sober observer––then curled into the fetal position and passed out. She rose and switched on the overhead light. Audrey considered leaving him there in a heap and making good an escape. Instead she dragged Fred toward the single bed where a nudge in that direction sent him sprawling across it, face down, half on, half off. She pulled at his boots until they finally came free, then tried to drag him fully onto the bed by getting on the bed herself and tugging.

In a swift move, he was on top of her, holding her face in his hands, kissing her. "You'll help me keep 'em away, won't you?" Echoes of alcohol in his speech, but also a painful sincerity. He kissed her neck awkwardly. She wriggled under him, trying to extricate herself.

"Fred...Fred, I don't think this is the best time—"

"And you'll help Frances. You'll take care of her for me. You're my angel." He kissed her hard on the mouth. She pulled away.

"Wait. Listen, listen I don't have...protection," she stammered. Wobbling to his feet, Fred removed his wallet and scattered the contents on the floor. He sifted through the cards, receipts and paltry cash until he came up with a dog-eared packet that he waved like a winning lottery ticket.

"Yo!"

"Yo?" Audrey felt like she was viewing someone else's life through the wrong end of a spotting scope. Surely she wasn't in a sleazy motel room with someone she hardly knew, contemplating sex with a man whose idea of foreplay was monosyllabic dialog from a Sylvester Stalone movie. Where was her judgment?

Fred's jeans dropped toward the floor, but he was too eager to stop and pull them off altogether, so he waddled toward the bed flinging his vest to one corner and pulling off his T-shirt along the way. Audrey watched half in amusement, half in amazement as he pulled the condom on. She couldn't keep a smile from her face. Slipping under the covers, she removed her sweater. He dove onto the bed, fumbled with the covers then tore at her jeans clumsily, but effectively. In an instant, he was on top of her, moving with urgency, his beard-stubble scratching her face. At first, Audrey balked at the lack of preliminaries.

"Hey, slow down." He did and after a moment, she started to respond, began to remember what she had been missing. Began to let go of thought and allow her body to transport her to...He had stopped.

"Not that slow." Audrey stared over his shoulder, moved her hips a little--no response. "Fred?" After a moment, she heard a low, labored breath. After another, a full on snore. Perfect. She had gone against the patterns of a lifetime and it had produced precisely the effect she had imagined, this, perhaps not conscious, but less than subtle, rejection. It was easy to admire Katherine's less complex, more straight forward—yes, she thought—more healthy attitude toward sex, it was another to try to adopt an effortlessness that didn't come naturally to her.

She sighed, hauled herself out from under Fred, struggled into her sweater, yanked up her jeans and walked out the door. Could she stay awake long enough to drive back to L.A.? She looked up at the night sky where a breeze persuaded the tall pines to sway in front of the full moon. Backlit clouds framed the image. Driving on such a night wouldn't be too bad, though the clouds looked dense, as if they might harbor rain. The thought of dealing with Fred in the morning made her cringe, but she was too tired to drive very far. She would grab a few hours of sleep here, then sneak out before he was up in the morning. Closing the door against a chill, she moved to the fireplace where she built a small fire then grabbed one of the blankets from the bed and curled up in the ancient chair. She watched the fire until her eyes closed under the weight of her disappointment in herself.

⋈

The phone rang insistently. She was in trouble because Opal wanted her to answer it and she couldn't find the phone. She burrowed through mounds of paper that seemed to multiply even as she struggled inside them; mountains of paper that engulfed her like quicksand. Finally she swam to the surface of consciousness and by the faintly glowing embers in the fireplace, saw Fred pick up the phone by the bed. She was awake in the town of Mitchell in the Cabin Motel with a marginally-conscious drunk.

"Yeah? Who's this?" He sat bolt upright. "If you fuck with her in any way, I'll fuckin' kill you. You understand me? I'll be there. But you better fuckin' understand me." He slammed the phone down.

"What is it?"

Fred jumped out of bed, pulled up his pants, crammed on his boots and vest and flew out the door, trailing the word: "Nothing."

"Fred!" She tore after him, but he was already on the Harley, kicking up dirt and pebbles as he raced off. Through the veil of light rain, she watched as the taillight disappeared around the corner.

⊱⊰

How long had she been pacing? She imagined she could see a depressed pathway in the pine floor between the fireplace and the door that she kept opening at the slightest sound. She threw another log on the now sizable fire hoping the blaze would stop her involuntary shudders. She was dressed and ready for action, though she didn't really know what that meant. What could she do? What needed to be done?

Her frayed nerves spiked at the jangle of the old, black, rotary phone. She raced to the nightstand and grabbed it.

"Fred?"

"It's Nate, honey."

"Nate?"

"Fred's had an accident...a bad one." It's another dream, she thought. This feeling that the room was closing in on her was just a prelude to that moment when she would wake up and see Fred lying in the bed across from her chair. Better yet, she would wake up in her futon at home and all of Mitchell would be dispelled by consciousness.

"Did you hear me Audrey? Fred had an accident. He's dead." She didn't need to answer Nate. She knew when she was dreaming.

chapter 7

FOCUS. AUDREY TRIED to keep her mind focused on the slippery road. The mist falling through the redwoods made the windshield too damp for the wiper's intermittent mode and yet too light for a constant wipe. The stuttering screech of the wiper blades added a discordant sound track to the disjointed images flashing on her head-screen. These tapes weren't her carefully orchestrated rescue fantasies. They were fractured images. Images of her own motorcycle accident intercut with images of Miles making love to Opal. Her husband and her boss? Where was that coming from? Now one with Katherine on the back of Sarto's motorcycle. No. Coburn, Katherine's husband, is driving. She's pregnant. He's going too fast right toward the hairpin turn. The one Nate described moments ago. Was this how people developed phobias? A couple of coincidental traumas? What would they name hers? Anglephobia: fear of turns with angles less than ninety degrees? Would it be confused with the fear of British people?

Up ahead, red lights sliced through the spongy darkness. As Audrey pulled her Jeep up to a group of police and firefighters, Nate ran toward her in an attempt to cut her off.

"He's gone, honey. Nothin' you can do here." But she absently shook off his steadying hand and walked down the two-lane highway that hugged the side of the mountain. There was the familiar angle. The road abruptly jutted out toward the sea, then wrapped back around the cliff. She gazed down at the skid marks which she walked deliberately, like a sobriety test. The black rubber tracks split and converged, visually communicating his loss of control, etching a final message into the highway, an arrow vanishing into a gash in the twisted guard rail. Close by, a truck with a winch hoisted something from below. A rescue worker signaled to the man in the cab.

"Easy, easy...that's it. We got it." He swung a blanket-shrouded, cage-like stretcher back over the highway where two other men helped steady it to the ground.

Nate tried to dissuade her, but Audrey needed to see the body. Needed to prove to everyone that there had been some gigantic mistake.

A large man in plain clothes with a badge hanging on a leather flap from his pocket pulled the blanket back to reveal Fred's distorted, bloody face. Audrey looked at the misshapen remains of the man she had known. Or not known. As the policeman pulled the blanket back up, she fought the urge to gag.

"I'm Detective Penn. You the girlfriend?" Audrey nodded like an automaton; her tongue had grown thick and unmanageable in her mouth. "So, you guys had a little fight and he takes off...that it?"

Something in his dismissive manner sharpened her senses. Anger sliced through the clutter in her brain. "No. No...he got a phone call in our hotel room."

"Yeah? Who from?"

"I don't know." Without an attempt to hide it, the detective rolled his eyes at Nate. Her anger boiled over. "He did! And he said: `If you fuck with her, I'll kill you."

Penn looked her up and down like he would a hooker. "So maybe he had another girl stashed up here and somebody else was doin' her?"

It took her a second to realize the implication. When she did, she answered him coldly. "I don't know. I do know that he was mad at a guy named Street back in L.A. He said he had to put some distance between them before one of them did something stupid or foolish or something like that. And before that they were yelling at each other right next door to me."

"Next door to your hotel room?"

"No. Next door at home."

"Which is L.A.?"

"Santa Monica."

Penn sighed as if the ordeal of speaking to her was exhausting him. "How long ago'd this happen?"

Now Audrey released a long breath, this one in frustration, knowing how her answer would be received. "I don't know, a few weeks? Listen, I have no idea who called, but that person was responsible for his death."

Penn stared at her a moment, then looked around casually. "Hasn't rained in awhile, we get this light mist and it's like riding on a river of grease. He loses it around the corner. The only guy that had something to do with his dyin' was him."

"But the call…"

"Honey, if it makes you feel better, the angel Gabriel called him."

Audrey looked at Nate with an expression that pleaded for support. He seemed reluctant at first, but finally he stepped close to the policeman. "Listen, Leo, he was at my house tonight and he said, 'They're catchin' up with me', but he didn't say who. Don't you think you should at least look into it?"

Now Penn dismissed both of them with a look. "Sure, Nate, I'll put some men on it." He walked away. Audrey felt the rage of the discounted, the misunderstood, the impotent. Nate put a comforting arm around her and, like a toggle, her feelings switched from anger to sorrow. She buried her head in his shoulder and finally let herself cry.

"Listen," said Nate. "I gotta go tell Frances. I hate to ask, but could you…"

"Of course I'll come with you."

⌖

The living room was decorated with an eye toward function, a heavily woven fabric on the densely stuffed couch and an industrial grade, variegated carpet that wouldn't show dirt. Audrey and Nate had tried to call ahead so that they wouldn't just show up on the doorstep, but the phone wasn't working. Fred's Aunt Janet was crying so hard that her husband had to pull her from the room just as the sleepy Frances entered. Audrey rose from the couch and crossed to the teenager. Nate stood with his hands in his pocket studying the carpet fiber as if he would be tested on it later.

"What's wrong?" asked Frances immediately. Audrey looked at Nate who still didn't look up.

"Fred's had an accident, Honey," she said.

"Where is he? I want to see him. What hospital—"

"He's dead, Sweetheart," said Nate glancing up briefly before resuming his contemplation of the carpet's fascinating nap.

The stunned teenager showed no emotion at first. "I said I wanted him to die. Guess he took me seriously."

Audrey grabbed her and hugged her. "Oh, Frances, don't think that for a moment. I'm just so sorry." The young girl's initial resistance melted away when Audrey wrapped her arms around her. Frances broke into loud gasping sobs.

Nate followed Audrey back to the Cabin Motel. He started to get out of his truck but she approached the cab.

"You go on home. Skitch'll be worried sick."

"You sure you won't come back to the house?"

"I'm sure. And thank you, Nate." He patted her hand, then drove off. She waved to him as she walked up the path toward cabin number nine. When she reached the door, she saw that it wasn't completely closed. She thought back. Hadn't she slammed it? Hadn't she flown out, reached back, and slammed it? Audrey took a couple of wary steps backward, but then, appalled by her timidity, she kicked open the door. Pressing herself to the side of the jamb like she had seen in so many cop movies, she listened with increased alertness. But her breath resonating within her ears was all that she heard; even the clutter noises in her brain had subsided. Every sense was poised at maximum alert.

"Who's there?" she demanded of the darkness. Cursing under her breath, she darted inside and fumbled for the light switch. The sudden glare exposed a room in shambles. The mattress was slashed down the middle, the over-stuffed chair was now under-stuffed, its gray cottony matter lay in discrete yet contiguous clumps like ground fog. Both of their possessions were strewn around in what only could have been a methodical search. After each piece had been examined, it had been discarded in an orderly march from one end of the room to the other. The contents of Fred's wallet, which he had scattered earlier, now lay in a heap, his one gas card on top, the license beneath. Had there been any cash? She thought so, but couldn't be sure. Dazedly looking around, she saw that even the lining of her blazer had been slit, as had the bottom of her overnight case. Possibly out of frustration, the ransacker had smashed Fred's coffee mug. Shards of it lay at her feet. The sound of it shattering echoed in her head.

⌐≈⌐

Audrey felt as though she had drunk a cask of wine. The injustice of an undeserved hangover rankled. Her head ached, her body rebelled at movement and her overriding impulse was to pull the covers over her head and to sleep past the approaching millennium. But she had to get off her futon and function. She had to go to work. And she had to convince someone that Fred's death was not an accident.

Katherine had been worried about her but seemed to dismiss Fred as irrelevant when Audrey tried to make her case for murder over the phone from Mitchell.

"I feel so responsible. I told you to go up there. I should've had him checked out," said Katherine.

"I'd already decided, remember?"

"Still, I shouldn't have encouraged you. He could've been Ted Bundy for godsakes."

"He was an ex-junky," Audrey admitted.

"If you'd shared that little tidbit, I definitely would've had him checked out."

"Didn't want you to worry," said Audrey.

"It's not like I'm your mother..."

"Lucky you." Audrey immediately regretted the disparaging remark, but Katherine let it pass without comment. She had listened to the account from picking up Frances at the jail to the ransacked room, probing Audrey for the details like the prosecutor she was. Katherine had wanted to jump on a plane and drive back with her, but Audrey wouldn't hear of it.

"You're sure you're okay to drive?"

"I'm fine," said Audrey. "But the police up here are treating me like some ditz. It wasn't an accident, Katherine."

"Accident, murder, who cares at this point. The guy's dead. If it were an accident, then you'd be wasting your time looking into it. But what if it was murder? You ask the wrong questions of the wrong people and they come after you."

"You're a prosecutor. How can you even suggest that?

"Because I'm your friend first."

Audrey sighed. "So I'm just supposed to let it go?"

"Right. He's gone. Just let it go."

He's gone. Let it go. Not likely.

Two strong cups of coffee got Audrey out her own front door, but she halted abruptly when she reached the porch.

"Hi. I hear you had some excitement this weekend." Carl held his tall café American in one hand and the newspaper in the other. He lounged on the porch steps with the ease of ownership. Audrey looked down at him.

"Katherine called you."

"Actually, I called her to see if she knew when you'd be back…in case we could've taken an early run or something."

"I was otherwise engaged."

"So I've gathered. Wanna talk about it?" Audrey sat down next to him and released yet another sigh. She wondered if she'd ever breathe effortlessly again.

"Did Katherine tell you that I think Fred was murdered?"

"Yes…" Carl drew out the word like the shrink he was.

"And you don't believe it either."

"It's not a matter of believing. It's just something better left to the authorities up there."

"I could tell by their attitude they weren't going to do anything."

"Give them a few days. See what they come up with." Audrey shook her head, disheartened. He put an arm around her. "Come on, I'll buy you a greasy breakfast."

Audrey smiled. He knew her so well.

Opal's assistant's desk sat empty. Audrey cast a long yearning look at it as she approached the inner office door.

"Come in," came Opal's muffled voice in answer to her knock. Audrey poked her head in first, then gingerly made her way inside.

"Hope I'm not disturbing you."

"I thought I looked bad this morning," said Opal, shooting Audrey a concerned look. "No offense, but you look dreadful." Opal's harsh assessment made Audrey smile.

"I know. I'm staying clear of the coroner for fear he'll want to autopsy me."

"Not that bad. Sit down. What's up?"

"Well, um," Audrey lowered herself into the seat in front of Opal's desk. "You see, I, uh, ran into some trouble..." Audrey mentally groped, then blurted out: "The friend I went up to visit was murdered...or died."

"Whoa!" Opal rose and crossed to the other side of the desk. She leaned against the arm of the loveseat and placed a hand on Audrey's shoulder. "Just relax and tell me about it from the beginning."

"There isn't a lot to tell. He got a phone call in the middle of the night then flew out of there on his motorcycle. A few hours later they dragged him up from the cliffs."

"And you think somebody, what, ran him off the road?"

"Maybe. During the call, he screamed: `You fuck with her and I'll kill you.' That and the fact that our room was ransacked while I was gone."

"A bit too coincidental," said Opal.

"Not to Detective Penn. He just figured we'd had a fight. When I told him about the room, he said, `Sleep somewhere else, I'll try to get somebody out in the morning.' He didn't. Oh, I also told him about trouble that Fred had with a guy named Street a few weeks back. He dismissed that, too."

"You've been through the wringer. How was it left?" Opal sat back down behind her desk and twirled a strand of her hair.

"`Go home, little girl. The big boys'll take care of it.'" Opal looked at her skeptically. Audrey caught it and backpedaled. "All right, maybe not in so many words."

"So, you got pretty close to this guy." Nodding weakly, Audrey stood, then paced in front of Opal's desk.

"I did and I didn't. It's odd, because I feel like I owe him, not just for helping me with my fireplace wall, but because he challenged me to do things I never would have attempted if he hadn't given me the confidence. And I liked the way he wanted to help his sister. Guess I feel I owe him now because, I...I don't know...I discounted him while he was alive." Audrey realized that she had been rambling without considering that she was talking to her superior. "Sorry, I'm running off at the mouth."

"Don't worry. Listen, I'll put in a call to our friends up in...where was that?"

"Mitchell."

"Just to let them know someone's interested. I can't do much more; in our line of work we have to play by the rules. Meanwhile, some good news. I found a rehab place willing to talk to the sister."

Audrey couldn't believe something was going right in her life. Like Fred, someone had reached out, had wanted to help because that's just what he or she did. Katherine had teased Audrey about having to help everyone in the world, but there were lots of people like her. Like Opal. Trying to help. Trying to fix things.

"Thank you. That would be so great for her. I offered to bring Frances back with me, but her aunt thought she'd be better off staying up there. You know...family, a stable environment, at least until the funeral. Who knows? Maybe she won't need the rehab."

"And maybe you'll win a gold medal in gymnastics," said Opal not unkindly. "Once someone's heavy into drugs, rehab's a long shot."

"Well, I have to try," said Audrey. Opal nodded thoughtfully, then stood to indicate the meeting was over.

Audrey rose and looked at her boss almost sheepishly. "If there's anything I can ever do for you—"

"—Just keep up the good work."

"I will. Don't worry," Audrey said too eagerly. As she left, she reflected that Opal had looked more drawn today, more over worked. Her boss needed a new assistant and Audrey wondered why she hadn't appointed Roland yet. She figured she no longer had a shot at the position after sharing all her extracurricular problems. However nice Opal had been, she couldn't have someone as distracted as Audrey on point during the Sitwell case. Sitwell was a big one and Opal had been preparing for it for months. A serious prosecutor couldn't afford to have an assistant whose brain could be hijacked by head tapes. Audrey conceded that she had just blown any possibility of getting that coveted little office.

Back at her desk, Audrey attempted to tame its anarchy, as if cleaning her desk would somehow clean her mind. There, in the back of the drawer, lay the Day Runner she hadn't had time to fill out yet. She flipped to the address section and entered the only name and address she knew by heart: Katherine's.

chapter 8

THE MARBLE MARKERS, flush with the ground, glinted here and there in the bright sun. Bouquets dotted the undulant hills. The surroundings celebrated while the bereaved mourned. The cemetery was one of the numerous Southern California park-like areas which sanitized death for the current crop of residents who had all been reared with the knowledge that someone else would take care of a family's detritus. No longer did Aunt Millie lie in state in the living room so that relatives could see and feel the reality of her death, believe in it as a further step in life. Bodies were whisked away before any unpleasant odor could befoul the memory of the loved one. Even open caskets didn't have the immediacy of living with the dead. Once a kindly mortician had done his work, the deceased never resembled the real person whose spiritual energy had fled back to the universe. The final insult was to be homogenized in one's grave, made to wear a universally accepted countenance of repose. Fred wouldn't be made to suffer this petty indignity. No mortician, no matter how practiced, could bring repose to his face.

The couple of dozen people around Fred's grave were mostly older, few young adults and fewer children. Fred's mother sat next to Frances who wore her leather jacket thrown over her short black dress. Audrey had invited Katherine along for moral support. Carl had invited himself.

The trio stood near the back of the group listening to the pastor talk about a generic young man, not the complex individual Audrey had glimpsed. Or had she conjured this complexity to justify her interest in him?

On the opposite side of the grave Audrey noticed her neighbor, Terry, talking to Nate. She looked around for Street, the reedy man, but he wasn't among the mourners. Audrey had tried to contact Terry a couple of times since her return from Mitchell, but she was never at home and hadn't returned any of her messages.

The preacher droned on. "And finally, we ask that You please take our son Frederick's soul up to Heaven to dwell by Your side."

Fred's mother blinked back tears as she fingered the cross around her neck. The dated hat and thrift store veil spoke of a person more than a step or two behind the times. She could've been an extra in a fifties movie. Audrey wondered if this had something to do with Frances' dismissal of her. As she studied the woman, she realized that Fred's mother looked to be in her sixties, which would mean Frances, at fourteen or fifteen, had been a late in life baby. At that moment, Frances looked over at her. Audrey smiled and waved, but the girl just gazed with vacant eyes.

The preacher's voice rose in color and volume. "Let him be enfolded in the love of Christ. Amen." The crowd responded "Amen".

The preacher nodded to Fred's mother, who stood and picked up a handful of dirt. She threw it into the grave, then looked toward Frances who stared at some middle distance. Finally, clearing his throat loud enough to get her attention, the minister signaled for the girl to rise. After a moment, she walked like a somnambulist to the grave and tossed in a white rose. She didn't linger, didn't look at the casket, just tossed the rose with a casual wrist flick and moved on. Soon, other guests began to file by and drop their own flowers.

When it was Audrey's turn, she looked down into the neatly carved earth where the coffin lay in splendid symmetry, dead center. She tossed her bunch of daisies and watched as they bounced barely perceptibly before they rested where she imagined his hands would be folded. Daisies always represented a Spring-tinged life force which tasted of a cleanliness she imagined was present only in nature.

She realized that she was holding up the line and turned to apologize to the person behind her.

"Take your time, honey," Nate said as he threw his rose into the grave. Audrey smiled as he took her arm and steered her a few feet away from the grave before wrapping her in a big bear hug.

"Real sweet of you to be here for him," said Nate. "He'd have appreciated it."

"Well, I wanted to give my condolences to his mom and to be here for Frances."

"You go on ahead." He nodded toward Mrs. Engel who greeted the line of mourners a few feet away. As she left Nate, Audrey noticed that Frances had wandered off down a grassy hill. Momentarily torn by the impulse to comfort her young friend, Audrey opted to express her sympathy to Mrs. Engel first. That's when she saw him. Fred, not ten yards away. So certain was she, that she nearly shouted his name. Luckily, the name caught in her throat as the man turned around. He didn't even superficially resemble Fred from the front. Why had she felt so certain?

She joined the condolence line. When it was finally her turn, she offered her hand to Fred's mother, which the older woman clasped warmly.

"Hi, we've never met, but my name is Audrey James and I've just, rather I was just recently acquainted with Fred..."

"A pleasure meeting you dear. Call me Margaret. Are you a friend from Florida, then?"

"No. I met him here...I just wanted to let you know that he helped me do some work on my house and he wouldn't take anything for it. He was just doing a good deed." Audrey felt self-conscious about the tears that sprang to her eyes.

Margaret put a comforting hand on hers. "He was like that. Oh, he had his share of trouble, but you got to see the real Frederick." Audrey took Margaret's hand in both of hers. They stood joined like that for a long moment.

"Thank you for raising such a fine person."

"And thank you, dear, for bein' so kind as to tell me," said the amiable woman. Audrey's preconception of Margaret had been colored by negatives: that her children were into drugs, that her husband seemed to have had a drinking problem, that she wouldn't post bail for her daughter. But this kindly, sad and serene individual was not at all what she had expected.

Audrey wandered through the small groups, which had formed like water drops on a freshly waxed car. Scanning the grounds, she finally spotted Frances under an oak tree, intent on pulling at something in her hands. When she drew nearer, Audrey could see that Frances' intensity was focused on ripping apart leaf after leaf from the tree above.

"Hello, Frances."

Frances's startled response was nearer to a convulsion, but she was able to compose herself and even to sound detached. "Hey...wha's up?" said the glassy eyed girl.

Audrey tried for a lightness she didn't feel. "Not a whole lot. How are you doing?"

"I got my wish. He's, like, out of my life."

"Don't do this, Honey." Audrey held up her palms in a gesture of helplessness. "Your wish had nothing to do with it."

"Sure it did. You know how some people have a guardian angel? Well I, like, got a guardian devil. I want somebody out of my life, and he takes care of it. First my dad, now Fred."

"That's not the way it works." Audrey tried to put a hand on the girl's shoulder, but Frances shook it off. Audrey stepped back, hesitated a moment. "Listen, I have a little good news...I got a line on a really great rehab place."

Frances sniffed and resumed her leaf slaughter. "I don't, like, need it. That was Fred's thing. Okay, I've, like, done some drugs. But I don't, like, have to. I do 'em when I feel like it."

Reproval colored Audrey's voice. "Like, before your brother's funeral?"

Anger ignited Frances' previously dull eyes. "I took a page from your book. I found something good, kind, and happy—and I popped it. And it's none of your fucking business. You're not my mother!" Frances stalked off toward a line of cars.

The depth of the girl's rage stunned Audrey. They had become friends, or so she had thought. Beyond that, Frances represented a debt that Audrey felt she owed Fred. His sister's sobriety had been the focus of the final portion of his life, and Audrey wanted to pick up the torch. Fred couldn't rest in peace until his sister was taken care of, couldn't rest until someone knew the truth about his death. The reluctance of the police only strengthened her resolve to do whatever she could to help Frances and to find who was responsible for Fred's murder.

Walking back toward the crowd, she saw in the distance her elusive neighbor, Terry.

"Terry," she shouted. The slender woman turned and made eye contact with Audrey, but then glanced quickly away. Audrey walked briskly in her direction, but Terry casually disengaged from the clutch of people she'd been standing with and moved toward the line of parked cars. Audrey picked up the pace and hailed again. But instead of stopping, Terry quickly ducked into her car and sped off. Audrey shook her head, still seeing the image of Terry, gaunt and haunted making momentary eye contact, then looking—what? Scared? Angry? Perhaps just annoyed? Audrey felt rooted to the ground as she stared at the car as it disappeared around a curve.

"What're you doing? Taking a little mental time out?" It was Katherine.

"I'd like to," said Audrey. "Hey, why don't they have brain dialysis?"

"That's one of those ideas that will happen in a couple of decades and you'll say 'Hey, I thought of that' and nobody'll care."

Audrey patted Katherine's stomach. "You will."

Katherine took Audrey's hand and walked toward the queue of cars that lined the curb at the edge of the impossibly perfect grass. Live grass for the dead.

Audrey squeezed Katherine's hand. "Listen, thanks for the support. Not that I need it...floundering in divorce hell...killing the first guy I sleep with..."

"Ah, you killed him. Mystery solved. Call me a romantic, but I wouldn't mind going out that way." Carl seemed to materialize beside them. Though the cadence had been jocular, there was a dark undertone to this speech.

"You know what I mean." Audrey tried to sound casual but she wouldn't have volunteered the information to Carl and it disturbed her that he overheard. She no longer wished that he would tell his friend. She didn't want to use the dead man to hurt Miles. Not that Miles didn't deserve to be hurt; Fred didn't deserve to be used.

"Yeah, yeah." He bent and brushed kisses across both women's cheeks. "I've got a patient. Can we grab a bite after work tomorrow?"

Although he had spoken to Audrey, Katherine responded. "Sure, as long as you're out by nine when my husband gets home."

"I happen to know how volatile your husband is, so if you don't mind, I'll take a rain check for one of the times he's in Timbuktu."

"Fine, as long as you show up for my bon voyage into motherhood tomorrow," said Katherine.

"Wouldn't miss it, though it scares the shit out of me to think what a bitch you'll be without your work."

"Hey, I'm going to be working at relaxing."

"Don't sharks die if they stop moving?" Carl asked.

"My point exactly," said Katherine. "The two weeks leave was Coburn's idea, but I'm determined to live through it."

Carl's eyes held Audrey's briefly. "So, dinner? We should talk." He turned and strode toward his car, confident of her acceptance.

"Talk or listen?" she shouted after him. He turned and walked backward for a moment.

"Both."

"As long as you remember couch rule."

"Done."

Katherine watched with particular interest as he loped off. "That's the one you should've stuck with."

"Yeah, except that he was my husband's best friend."

"You were divorced."

"Didn't matter."

"Too bad. He's an even-keel, steady as a rock kind of guy. I know neurotic actors are so much more attractive."

"Before you damn him to normality, I think you forget he was a cop first--not your sanest profession--then he becomes a shrink-- truly your most loony profession."

Katherine looked at her friend and shook her head. "This, from the mental health poster girl."

"A cop/shrink. Be wary of people who want to save the world," said Audrey.

"Yes, and of pots denigrating kettles."

She was right, thought Audrey. But what was wrong with wanting to save the world? Why should people be wary? It had popped out of her mouth like one of her mother's aphorisms. Does a stitch in time save nine? And who sews these days, anyway? Ask the environmentalists as they point to the rip in the ozone. Ask yourself why you've swept something under the rug that you should have dealt with. No one cares about a stitch in time any more.

Audrey loved the food here, loved the casual atmosphere, and loved the fact that, when she first heard the name of the restaurant, she thought it denoted the spectrum of music from rock to Wagner rather than the chef's name: Rockenwagner.

Katherine and she always planned to be moms together, but Audrey hadn't chosen father material. Katherine's husband, Coburn, wasn't exactly Bill Cosby but he was supportive of her pregnancy. When he was around. When he wasn't in South America. Which was why he didn't take Katherine to get her amniocentesis and Audrey did. Coburn missed a flight from Ecuador.

Katherine, never a fan of needles, nearly chose the fourteenth floor window over the prospect of having a huge one stuck into her abdomen. Audrey held her hand and reminded her of as many laughable incidents from their childhood as she could recollect. Somehow most of them didn't pack the same hilarity as they did when the two of them would rewrite history over a couple of glasses of wine. Puking stories from high school lose something in a sober translation. Still, she managed to take Katherine's mind off the dreaded needle by bringing up a particular story, which had remained a bone of contention for years.

On a camping trip with the drill team, the two girls had shared a minuscule tent. While the others were sound asleep, Audrey and Katherine finished a quart of malt liquor between them. Sometime in the middle of the night, one of them threw up all over the tent and its occupants. Since the evidence was so widely scattered and the quarters so close, it wasn't immediately conclusive who was puker and who was pukee. As the dreaded needle entered Katherine's stomach, she again argued her case.

"I was used to drinking so I had more of a tolerance, therefore you must have been the one who hurled."

"I don't want to have to get into this while you're in such a vulnerable position, but the trajectory path clearly showed it came from your side," said Audrey.

"It was a three foot wide tent. There was no clear trajectory, just an incriminating blanket of—"

"If you ladies don't mind, I need all my concentration for this." The doctor looked as though he'd been riding a storm-tossed sea in a dingy. He steadied his needle hand and withdrew three separate vials of fluid from Katherine's uterus.

Katherine looked up at Audrey. "Just thank your lucky stars you aren't going through this pregnancy hell."

"Oh, don't get all mushy about it."

Now, after too much of the bratwurst special, Katherine was being sent down the road toward maternity by her office mates, who held her in varying degrees of esteem. Katherine was always in a hurry. Things had to be done immediately—more quickly if possible. She was exacting with her subordinates but the most severe taskmaster with herself. Never one to suffer fools, neither was she unkind nor unreasonable in her expectations. Most people performed top quality work for Katherine because she lived up to her own high standards.

Carl was included in the group by dint of friendship and because he offered to pop for the champagne. Opal attended because she was technically everyone's boss, just beneath the D.A. himself. Opal was painfully aware that the support staff would rather work with Katherine who had swept into the D.A.'s office as the golden girl from the feds.

The festivities had gone on for over an hour when Opal turned toward Audrey and spoke in a soft voice. "You really did a great job on that Herring depo. You have a gift for redacting. Gave them only what discovery required, and you were right on point with your suggestions at the end. I know there's a lot going on in your life right now, but you know Sitwell better than anyone else in the office. If you think you can handle it, I'd like to give you a tryout as my assistant."

Incredulous, Audrey momentarily wondered if the champagne had gone to her head. "Me? You'd still consider me?"

"Unless you don't think you—"

"I can handle it. Absolutely! No question. Just let me know what you need." The word s shot out rapid-fire.

"Right now I need us to get back to the office before we're all thrown in the drunk tank." Opal nodded toward the empty champagne bottles. Audrey smiled at Opal, then stood and raised her glass toward Katherine.

"To the mom-to-be. We would have gotten you cute baby gifts, but we decided to take ourselves to lunch instead."

Katherine raised her champagne glass filled with sparkling grape juice and clinked Audrey's. "And a good choice it was. If I see one more cute sleeper, I'll puke."

Audrey joined in the polite laughter, but knew that her friend's feigned indifference to her pending motherhood was for her benefit. She sat down and leaned her head close to Katherine's. The women put both arms around each other and spoke in low tones with foreheads touching.

"Sure you'll puke. You get weepy in the supermarket looking at disposable diapers," Audrey said.

"Well it's not like it's the `be all, end all'."

"Don't try to make me feel better."

"I'm not, it's really—"

"—really great. And I'm thrilled for you. Just know that you might have to let me have half of this one."

"Fine. I get the top half."

⌇

Carl made a U-turn in front of Audrey's house. He hopped out of his convertible Miata, then stopped a moment, inspecting the recent work Audrey had done. The walkway was fashioned from used bricks nestled one against the next. Some extra bricks lay scattered nearby on the dirt where the first shoots of grass muscled their way to the surface. Carl picked up the bricks and stacked them neatly beside the walkway. Audrey watched from behind her screen door, then stepped out onto the porch. She smiled at him, but shook her head.

"I dunno Carl. There're three in that stack and two in all the others. I don't think I can live with that." He picked up the offending brick and hid it behind his back.

"It's gone." He then replaced the brick, perfectly aligned with the one beneath it before she even reached him. They hugged a greeting, then Audrey, remembering a note in her pocket, dashed toward the duplex next door.

"Just a sec. I'm going to leave another note for Terry, Fred's friend." Carl watched with interest as she knocked on the door. When no one answered, Audrey held her hands up as if to say, "I tried", then joined him at his car, the Miata, the little sports car that never seemed to fit Carl.

<hr>

A few years back, Santa Monica's Third Street Promenade sprang as if full grown from the head of Zeus. When Third Street was just a street like any other, it was a text book example of local small business decay after the arrival of a shopping center. Now it was the shopping center's turn to cry. The spruced up walking street boasted hip shops, theaters and restaurants, which siphoned all the foot traffic west of the four-oh-five freeway. It also became a popular international tourist attraction. Street performers proliferated, as they did in Venice, but with half the chance of random gunfire. Performers needed permits and police patrolled the promenade on bicycles from their kiosk smack in the center of the action. Regulated pandemonium.

Emerging from a sedately trendy restaurant, Audrey and Carl walked up the promenade in the direction of Wilshire Boulevard at the opposite end of the three-block development. Her head swam in a bubbly mist. She liked the feeling. It muted the clutter, silenced the head-tapes that haunted her. Carl watched, amused by Audrey's unsteadiness on her feet.

"Okay, you've been avoiding talking about him all evening," Carl prompted.

"Miles?"

"Fred...or Miles. You choose." This time when she stumbled, she looked back at the smooth pavement, certain that she would find an ankle-high wire.

"Pandora's box...I don't want to think about it."

"Pandora already unleashed the crap. You'd just be recycling."

She loved that about him. Loved his wry eye on the world that still left room for optimism. "What a take you have on things." He shrugged but was obviously pleased. "All right," she said, "I'll talk about Miles for one block, then we have to change the subject. Agreed?"

"You got it."

She took a deep breath and it felt like a stage three smog alert, her lungs ached, constricted. "I always had unswerving faith in my judgment. Even during the first divorce I was able to say: `I was right to marry him at the time, now it's right to divorce him.' But then I went back...why?" She had never asked anyone else that question, even Katherine. It was too embarrassing.

Carl studied her. "Because you love him?"

"Yeah...but that's not good enough." She tried to clear the champagne bubbles from her head because she knew that this was important. Emotionally, she equated self-examination with what she imagined a colonoscopy would feel like physically and therefore generally avoided it. But she wanted to be as clear as possible with Carl so that he wouldn't be compelled to probe her further. She continued in what she hoped was a thoughtful, deliberate manner. "I always felt off balance with Miles, partly, I think, because I had this idea of how life should be with him. It never was the way I pictured it, but I'd try to make things fit. Then I'd feel more off balance when they didn't. I just knew Miles would never be there if I needed him. Still, I went back. Where was my judgment?"

"I don't know...Duluth?" he asked as he looped his arm through hers.

"Never been there."

"Obviously," he said.

Audrey laughed and teased him back. "Like, who's talking? A guy who gives up being top cop to be bottom shrink..." She heard the implied put-down only after it was out of her mouth and did her best to backpedal. "I didn't mean bottom like bottom, I meant like in new..."

Carl felt the barb but covered. "Hey, I never claimed to have good judgment."

Pressure was building in her chest. Somehow Fred had become jumbled up with Miles in her mind-clutter. She didn't want to talk about this but she felt she would burst if she didn't.

"I don't know why this is hitting me so hard. I didn't love Fred, didn't know him really...but he was there when I needed him. He just appeared and helped without asking for anything. He was just there for me." Carl put his arm around her, as the alcohol seemed to take more of a toll on both her balance and her slurred speech. "And Miles was never there, not really...he always held back. And Fred was...he just was there. He was like, I don't know, an angel...my own sheet-rock angel." The confession suddenly sobered her. She pulled away from Carl and walked quickly as if to outrun her embarrassment. Carl followed at a discrete distance, allowing her the physical span she seemed to need.

"You said he was atoning. The good deeds he did for you probably got him into heaven or helped his karma so that he won't come back as a warthog."

She turned to face him, waited for him to catch up, and smiled slightly. "Think so?"

"I know so." Carl glanced up and saw that the end of the block was near. Though she had said she exempted him, Audrey had never hidden her disdain for mental health professionals whom she thought were, on the whole, ineffectual. Perhaps that was why Carl took a long breath before he spoke. "Listen, you can always talk to me as a friend, but if you ever want to talk to someone professionally, I've got some great—" Audrey lurched away from him as if he had dangled a straight-jacket in front of her.

"That's the trouble with shrinks. A person can't have a minor nervous breakdown without them thinking you're ready for the loony bin."

"I'm not saying that. We all need help sometimes—"

"—Well, I'm not off the deep end yet. Okay?" Audrey whirled away from him.

"Audrey! Audrey, come on." But she was half-way down the street, leaving Carl to consider yet another change of profession.

⌖

They pulled up in front of the bungalow, both staring straight ahead. Audrey opened her car door and started walking up the brick path.

Carl followed her to the sidewalk. "Listen, I'm chewing on my foot here, afraid to take it out for fear the other one'll leap in. Please don't be mad at me."

"I'm not mad, I'm...I'm just tired." She continued up the walkway, then turned back before entering the house. "Thanks for dinner. I'll, uh, my treat next time." She slipped inside but didn't turn on the light. Instead she leaned against her new window molding and peered out through the shutters.

Carl stood by his car for a moment, then moved to the walkway. He looked down at the brick path, everything perfectly in line except for that one brick. He picked up the brick and hurled it half-way down the block.

Audrey turned away from the window. Still just inside the door, she crumpled to the floor then sat there Indian style, staring off into the darkness fractured only by shafts of the security lights streaking through the shuttered windows. She knew of the respect Carl had earned as a policeman, and she knew of his many awards and community service medals. Audrey wished he were one still, that he wasn't a shrink. As close as she felt to him, there would always be that reticence born of her distrust of the profession. Counselors in general could help the marginally impaired, could help those who had simply lost their way, show them the marker buoys delineating the shipping lanes, help with slight course corrections, bounce signals off of them and soon see them back enroute to whatever level of contentment they had drifted from. But she had been around a lot of psychiatrists, and they hadn't helped her mother. This rationale rang hollow, even as it tolled through her muddled brain, while the fearful truth chimed clearly: they would see that she was her mother's daughter. Had Carl come to that conclusion? He told her that she needed help, as much as told her that she was nuts.

She put her hands to her head, vice-like, as though the pressure she exerted might squeeze out the truth and leave her at peace again. She looked up to see the wall above the fireplace. Fred had taped it. He had been there for her when she needed him. Moving to the wall, she ran her hands lovingly over the undetectable seams. She leaned her head against his wall and willed herself to melt into it.

⚞⚟

Audrey tossed and turned in her bed, eyes moving rapidly behind her lids. The quilt was bunched over to one side. She grabbed for it, then drew it back over her. Feeling a slight resistance, she twisted back around, opening her eyes slightly. There he was, clean-shaven with a shorter haircut. Fred was naked with his arms open to her.

"I knew you'd be here for me," she muttered.

He kissed her, warmly, tenderly.

chapter 9

AUDREY, ALONE IN her bed, awoke to a shaft of sunlight whose little particles--or waves--seemed bent on prying her eyes open. They succeeded with one eye, which quickly snapped shut at the assault. Suddenly, she jerked up to a sitting position and looked around suspiciously, recalling the dream of the night before. She laughed out loud at herself, then pulled a pillow over her head to block out the offending photons. What had she been thinking? Drinking on a work night. But despite the incipient hangover, she felt much better this morning. The dream had left a contentment that muffled the clutter in her brain.

And then she felt the sensation of the mattress next to her sinking, as though a body had insinuated itself. Her eyes widened beneath the pillow when she heard the unmistakable rustle of a newspaper. Her brain searched frantically for a clue. She had been out with Carl and would have remembered if she had asked him to stay. She wouldn't have. She had learned that lesson and would never cross that friendship barrier again. And she wouldn't have picked up a stranger, not unless she truly was off her rocker. She screwed up her courage, sat up, and came face to face with Fred. He had a partially healed cut above his right eye, but was otherwise extremely clean cut looking. Gone were the beard stubble, the lanky thatch of hair, the slightly gross teeth and in their place were beautifully smooth skin, razor cut, clean hair and teeth ready for a toothpaste ad.

He nonchalantly read the paper in the bed next to her, naked. "Hope you don't mind, I took a shower," he said. "I know you like your men clean."

She screamed. But even as she did, she tried to remember if she had ever mentioned her preference for fastidious and clean-shaven men. He clamped a hand over her mouth, then pulled his hand away and kissed her, long and hard. She jerked away and bolted from the bed, clutching the sheet to her.

"You're alive!"

He smiled at her and resumed reading the paper. Gone was his lazy drawl and in its place, a crisp, articulate style of speech. "Not exactly. Remember anything from that physics class? Energy is constant. I'm energy. You're sensing it, then you're draping me with flesh."

"Really?"

"Or not." He went back to reading.

"Oh, God! I have lost it, haven't I?"

"It's not the end of the world." He said this offhandedly not bothering to look up.

"Well, excuse me for being upset just because I have visual proof that I'm out of my mind."

He put the paper down and gave her his undivided attention. "So you might have a touch of schizophrenia. You hear voices, well, a voice, and see things...me, that aren't necessarily in everyone else's everyday reality. On second thought, don't even consider schizophrenia, such negative connotations what with your mother and all... Think of me as a figment...with pigment."

She stared wide-eyed at him, then hurled the accusation: "You don't talk like that," and added to herself: no one does, thank God. But maybe he was real. Faked his death. He said his brain was his secret weapon, perhaps the whole lazy sounding drug-like speech was his cover. He took a step toward her, now modestly wearing her favorite bath sheet. She darted between two wardrobe boxes as if not seeing him would somehow eliminate him.

"I talk like this now. Guess you wanted someone more erudite. You certainly wanted someone with more...physical empathy." He reached in and stroked her cheek with the back of his hand.

She batted it away. "Don't even bring that up! I don't have to be Masters or Johnson to figure out that this probably has something to do with my lousy sex life." That confirmed it. She knew that she had never discussed her sex life with Fred. She was nuts.

"Relax. Just go with it." He flopped back down on the bed.

Audrey stepped out from between the boxes, clutching the sheet to her, then looked up as if diagramming sentences on the ceiling. "Well, if you're a figment of my imagination, and I know it, then I know I'm nuts. But if I know I'm nuts, I must have some vestige of sanity, otherwise I would think this was perfectly normal." She looked to him for confirmation.

"I'll buy that," said the clean man.

"And if I thought you up...I can un-think you." Her powers of concentration were thrown into overdrive; eyes squeezed closed, face contorted.

"Well, you didn't exactly think me up, not consciously anyway."

"What, are you one of my multiple personalities? Am I going to find out hundreds of people have been time-sharing my body?" She looked down at her body as though it had already betrayed her.

"Mmmm unlikely...But you might think of me as a manifestation of your good judgment. What did you call me? Your sheetrock angel."

She had only said that to Carl, so this—whatever he was—must be a product of her mind like one of her old head tapes that kept replaying. Now she was in familiar territory. She would banish it. She had banished tapes before. A smile supplanted the anxiety on her face.

"You don't exist." She put her hands over her ears and moved into the bathroom, while speaking in rapid monotone. "Once upon a midnight dreary/while I pondered, weak and weary,/Over a many quaint and curious volume of forgotten lore,/While I nodded, nearly napping,/Suddenly there came a tapping,/As if..."

Fred shrugged and resumed reading the newspaper.

⊱✦⊰

She moved the shower head selector to the equivalent of "flagellate". The water hit her back with the feel of snapped leather, just what she needed to shock herself back from her visit to Mom's world. There was a familiarity in what had just transpired, a déjà vu quality that connected to the tapes in her head, and now, she had to admit, to their counter part where she would physically act out the scenes she was viewing in Panavision on her mind-screen. She would be walking down the street or driving along and suddenly realize that she had been mouthing the dialog from one of these tapes. A surreptitious glance around for witnesses usually assured her that no one had seen, but occasionally, she would meet the eyes of a wary stranger, who, as embarrassed as she, would quickly avert his eyes, feeling like a voyeur to some salacious proclivity of hers.

Audrey passed off these episodes as bits and pieces of day dreams, looked upon them as part of her creativity seeping out, mostly in the shower, in the kitchen while chopping onions, or, as poet Stevie Smith told the Queen when asked whence came her ideas, "While Hoovering, Mum." She figured everyone had them to some extent, otherwise what did one's brain do while it was on hold?

This Fred episode, however, was different. He was tangible. Since Audrey hadn't been able to see them, she imagined her mother's apparitions were made of more gossamer stuff. Cotton candy-like, she thought when she was six and first tried to see that unseen person.

It was nineteen-seventy and clothes designers were flirting with the outrageous, but Audrey's mother clung to the Jackie Kennedy look for dressy daytime wear. She often wore a navy Courreges dress that had broad white boarders around the neck and sleeves and the same fabric in a strip down the front. Her mom's taste around the house ran to costumes with a gypsy flavor, but when she would "go to town" she would don her Jackie tribute dress and wear the small, gold cylinder earrings which concealed cotton soaked in perfume. That perfume wafting through the house meant "town" to Audrey. It meant dress up, clean behind your ears and act like a lady. It meant a trip to the dentist and then lunch with her father afterward. Audrey searched her closet for the new skirt and blouse because she felt she was getting too old for kid's clothes. Missing school was exciting, but tinged with a vague guilt. She had learned by example from her father to follow the rules.

Audrey ate the bowl of cereal with bananas that her mom left on the breakfast room table. Glancing out the front window she saw her mother talking to someone, though she couldn't see whom. She picked up the pocketbook she had been delighted to find in her stocking last Christmas and positioned it carefully on her arm, as she had seen her mother do with hers. She walked painstakingly so that the purse wouldn't move from its perfect position on her arm between wrist and elbow, and she was careful to pull the front door shut until she heard the click that she had been taught to listen for.

When she approached her mother, Audrey looked around but saw no one else.

"And furthermore, I see no point in arguing with you about this. You know I will prevail, I always do." Her mother took a long drag on her ever-present cigarette. "I will do as I like whatever your feelings are on the matter." Her mother was speaking in the dramatic tone she usually reserved for their play-acting. Audrey narrowed her eyes, trying to discern the person her mom clearly saw. Gingerly she circled her mother and the other entity, attempting to determine just where her mother's eyes were focused. She speculated that this experience was like her current study of words in Miss Carol's first grade class, where letters which she could identify singularly, suddenly took on a meaning when strung together, like: C-A-N-D-Y. Her mother obviously saw one of those grown-up secrets like the letters turning into words. Audrey accepted that she simply didn't have the tools yet to decipher the experience.

Well, she had them now.

Audrey dressed and left the house without a further encounter with her apparition. She worked all morning on Sitwell depositions champing at the bit to call Mitchell for any new developments, but Opal had instructed her to wait to give her Bay Area contacts a chance to report back. At least Opal took her seriously. Both Katherine and Carl remained cool at best to her speculations about Fred's death.

Audrey considered staying by the phone during lunch, but it was the last day Robinson's would have her eye cream with the useless, yet essential, free gift. Useless in that she rarely used any of the articles included in the little plastic zip bags. Essential in that she felt cheated if she didn't get one.

Now she walked back toward the office, taking the Main Street freeway overpass, trying to concentrate on the Sitwell strategy, but being hijacked by tapes of Fred, Frances and the murder scene, which all vied for time on her head-screen. Yet no matter what the visual, beneath the audio track lay the thrum of doubt. There had been other times when she had questioned her judgment, and by extension, her soundness of mind, but they had been more in the realm of wondering if she were the only one who had trouble navigating within relationships. Whom to trust and when. She always managed to sort out whatever the issue was and to go on her merry way. She would this time, as well...after she got some answers.

The hair on the back of her neck seemed to rise, an experience she read about but never before felt. She didn't need to turn to know that he was there. Sauntering casually beside her in his clean cut chinos and polo shirt, he could have been mistaken for her boyfriend or husband, well, if anyone could have seen him. And what was with the clothes? He looked like the after photo in a makeover from grunge musician to GQ model. She resorted to the Poe defense, the rapid monotone thought-block.

"And the silken, sad, uncertain/rustling of each purple curtain/ Thrilled me--filled me with fantastic terrors never felt before;"

Fred smiled at her. "I love this part. I almost have it memorized, too." She just glared at him, resumed. He chimed in. "So that now, to still the beating/of my heart, I stood repeating,/'Tis some visitor entreating...'" He stopped and pinned her against the railing of the freeway overpass, speaking with his mouth close to her ear, his breath warm and humid. "What are you doing? You think you're going to 'Poe' me into oblivion? You're only going to drive yourself more nuts than you already are."

This was too much. She hadn't read about multiple personalities physically threatening one another. Fighting for time in the one body, yes, but physically accosting each other? What if someone from work saw her doing a back bend over a freeway overpass? "Why am I imagining you so much more obnoxious than you were in real life?"

Fred took the direct response to him as a sign of a truce. He smiled at her. "Because you're imagining your soul mate."

"God! I'm so much sicker than I thought." Her soul mate did not look like Fred. True, he was cleaned up now, and well spoken--more like Carl than Fred--but she couldn't find the remotest link to the fantasy men she had conjured in her youth. They were always artists, but successful; sensitive, though strong and decisive; intelligent but not pedantic; okay, fantasies.

"I should have myself committed, shouldn't I? I mean, I could be a danger to myself. I could have you throw me off this bridge." She warily looked down at the freeway below, then suspiciously back at Fred.

He shrugged, released her. "Hey, I'm just here to help out. You need me, you call me. I'm your judgment hot line." She put her hands back over her ears.

"In stepped a stately raven from the saintly days of yore. Not the least obeisance made he..."

"I'm gone." And with a friendly wave, he vanished. She looked around, then continued, gingerly, across the overpass toward the Civic Center. She could make this go away. Her mother lived with it for long periods without...well. Failing that, she could blot him out with poetry.

<hr/>

Audrey was in fifth grade when poetry was force-fed her by Mrs. Greenland, who also had been partial to folk dancing and gardenia perfume. But it was her teacher's anachronistic belief in rote memorization that distinguished her with the students. Fourth graders shuddered when they opened their year-end reports containing the following year's teacher assignments. Audrey believed that life had come to an end when she saw that she had been assigned to Mrs. Greenland's class. She heard the moaning from the fifth graders who claimed that you had to memorize a poem a week and recite it aloud in front of the class, a small poem at first, then an added stanza each week until gangly girls and ungainly boys had to spew forth the likes of "If" and "The Jabberwocky".

Mrs. Greenland started with a choice between two Emily Dickinson poems: "Chartless" and "Parting". In the former, Dickinson states her certainty of heaven as if the way were marked upon a chart. Few chose that one. The second was by far the more popular because it contained the word "hell" and you could say it in front of the entire class without getting into trouble. "Parting is all we know of heaven, and all we need of hell." It was a line Audrey had forgotten until her father had been wheeled out with the sheet over his head.

Audrey claimed to loath poetry throughout, but managed to get through her recitations without the prompting needed by many students. They also had to memorize the states and their capitals, the Presidents of the United States and the entire Mississippi River system. She ground through them all, but found that she had a peculiar fondness for Edgar Allan Poe. First "Annabel Lee", then "The Raven". She was fond, too, of Kubla Khan. Did she have a particular penchant for drug-crazed poets, those with ravaged minds? Did she empathize with them? Identify with them?

Now even poetry seemed to bring her back to the essential question of her grip on reality. Cut yourself some slack, she thought. The split from Miles had been a trauma. Fred's death had been a trauma. Moving was always a trauma. And a larger more diffuse fear shimmering in the distance like the aurora borealis: a murderer out there...somewhere. The sum of these things seemed to overload her mind like a socket with too many electrical cords ready to short. No, that didn't work as a model because she felt—truly physically felt— an excess of electricity caroming through her body, randomly hitting distinct targets in her stomach, her head, her back, her groin. Where does love go when its specific target is no longer available? When it ceases to careen around in your body, does it spew forth onto the first appropriate or inappropriate person? But what if you don't let it; then what happens? Is this what happens?

To say that Audrey was grateful for her new office was to say that she had a passing fancy for chocolate. She adored her door, delighted in her desk, though it was still piled high with the paper deluge of law. She hung a couple of framed museum posters to brighten the otherwise drab walls, and, over Katherine's objection, also hung a faithful oil reproduction of Van Gough's "Irises" that Katherine produced in high-school before she developed her mania for financial security which precluded time for fine art.

As Audrey spoke on the phone she tried to straighten the stacks of papers. "Yes...well, I happen to think she's a great gal, but I'm afraid your daughter doesn't feel the same about me. We sort of had a misunderstanding at the funeral." As Audrey listened, Carl tapped on the glass panel of her door. She motioned him in, but continued her conversation. "I'm sure she is." Carl picked up her Day Runner and thumbed through it. "Will you ask her to call me, either number, home or office, whenever she can? Thanks so much. Bye." She smiled at Carl who appeared relieved at this reception.

"Am I forgiven?"

"Nothing to forgive."

"Yeah there is," he said without looking at her. He picked up a post-it pad and scribbled on it, then ripped off the top page and handed it to her.

"I.O.U. one favor?" Audrey looked at him skeptically. "What for?"

"For irritating you. Isn't that enough?"

Audrey laughed. "If I got one of these for every time you irritated me—"

"I know, you'd never see the top of your desk...not that you ever have."

"See? I already need another one."

"Instead I'll take you to lunch some time this week to celebrate your promotion. We'll talk about anything except getting you to talk to somebody."

"Actually, I already found someone to talk to." His face displayed a genuine delight. She had been teasing herself about her own voices, so was caught off guard when he pursued it.

"Man or woman?"

"Neither."

"I can look it up." He flipped through her Day Runner till he found the calendar.

She grabbed the book from him playfully. "He's a guy, okay? Besides, you won't find it in there. He's a secret."

"Friends don't have secrets," said Carl.

"Everyone has secrets." And they allowed their eyes to lock as they rarely did.

Opal entered from the door adjoining her office, carrying her purse and jacket. "Sorry to interrupt. Hi Carl." She looked at the papers on Audrey's desk. "Did you finish checking all those leases?"

"Yup. They're right here." Audrey pulled a large box of papers from the other side of her desk.

"Great," said Opal who then looked at Carl. "Don't you have an appointment?" Carl exchanged a knowing look with her.

"Don't you?" He opened the door--the coveted door with the coveted window--and with an exaggerated bow, ushered Opal out.

Audrey wondered whether they would talk about her, perhaps compare notes on her emotional volatility. Poor thing, they'd say, just about around the bend, isn't she? But then, maybe it wasn't that apparent to others. Maybe she could add paranoia to her list of symptoms. She recently noticed that she had been counting things in eights. During her ballet classes years ago she learned to count in various times but since she had taken aerobic classes, the whole world seemed to march to an eight count: stairs, vacuum cleaner thrusts, finger taps while waiting for an elevator. She read that artist Jonathan Barofsky numbered every single piece he had ever created no matter how obscure: a doodle, a sketch, a note. She knew her counting was a sign of obsession, knew it wasn't healthy, yet couldn't see herself as compulsive--just look at her disorganized life. Perhaps she read too much. Or not enough.

She reminded herself that this was probably a perfectly normal reaction to stress. All she needed to focus on were helping Frances and finding some justice for Fred. After they were taken care of, Audrey would allow herself a minor nervous breakdown...as long as it didn't interfere too much with her life. As her mother's had.

Glendale sits on the verge between the San Fernando and San Gabriel valleys. Does it belong to East San Fernando or West San Gabriel? This should have been a negligible identity problem, but Audrey's mom took her city's geographic ambiguity personally. It began as a dinner discussion, which seemed benign on the surface but in reality was a matter of grave importance. At first, Audrey's father didn't notice the signs: the agitation, the darting eyes, the repetitive folding and unfolding of her napkin. By the time he did notice, it was almost too late. Even at eight years old, Audrey knew that once her mother ventured beyond a certain anxious point, nothing but a sleeping pill and twelve hours in bed would calm her down. Sometimes her dad could avert the slide toward hysteria by coaxing her mother away from the subject which had aroused her anxiety.

"If you can't say for sure where you are, how do you know you're there at all?" Her mom made the question sound more like a desperate plea. With one ear cocked toward the radio which provided a recap of the world's stock markets, her father responded with obviously divided attention.

"I wouldn't worry, hon." Audrey kicked her father under the table and widened her eyes to indicate that he should pay attention. She saw him glance toward the cigarette that her mother had lit in the middle of the meal, and knew he would recognize this sure sign of agitation.

"Well," her father began, searching for the proper anxiety free direction; "Sometimes there are signs, like in Disneyland. Remember when we took Audrey on the tea cup ride when she was tiny and—"

"She ruined that beautiful smocked dress I spent hours on all because you let her have popcorn and that giant sucker." Her mother stopped folding her napkin and even smoothed it in her lap. Her father laughed and spoke of the fireworks they all loved. He had taken her back into the past where things might not have been perfect, but at least they couldn't change, couldn't frighten her with their newness, their unpredictability. Even as a child, Audrey realized that her father held some alchemists formula which could transform the base metal of her mother's neurosis into the gold of her true nature.

Once, when there was a general panic in the stock market, her father had to work late calling customers, filing paperwork, and holding the boss' hand for fear he would leap off their two story building. He called numerous times to assure Audrey's mom that he would be home soon, but as the evening wore on, her mother became more and more agitated. The nine year old Audrey felt her mother slipping from her child's grasp, felt the fear of losing the battle for her mother's mind, felt that her defeat was coming from forces within her mother and yet her mind grappled with the dichotomous notion that she was battling some entity distinct from her mother. Audrey tried to hold on to her by telling her stories, a pastime the two had shared since Audrey was old enough to speak.

"Once there was a fairy princess who ruled over the land of Seashell, and she gave everybody three wishes and the little girl got to wish for a little brother or sister, and for her dad and mom to live forever, and the fairy princess said they were such good wishes that she could have as many wishes as she wanted forever and ever. And so she wished for—"

"Her prince wasn't coming back," her mother began. "He was going to be held captive forever. And there was nothing she could do because she could no longer speak. Only the prince had the key to her voice." The frightened Audrey just stared at her mother, willing her, unsuccessfully, to acknowledge her presence.

As an adult, Audrey reflected on the paradox of having a mother who was the personification of unpredictability and yet who was unable to tolerate instability in the world at large. From a distance, Audrey could understand that her mother was sick, but that distance didn't assure forgiveness.

chapter 10

IT WAS DARK by the time she bought her groceries and picked up her dry cleaning. The porch light glowed as she walked up the brick path, but then the motion detecting security lights flooded the front of the house dispelling the cozy appearance, but imbuing her with a sense of safety. She fumbled with her keys, balancing both bags of groceries on one knee while her briefcase hobbled her key hand. When she finally unlocked the front door and flipped the switch, the light revealed a maelstrom of belongings, strewn, torn, discarded. Every one of her CDs and tapes were pulled from their cases and tossed in a heap. Through the open bedroom door, the destruction continued. Boxes, drawers, cabinets, anything that could be opened, was. The shock of the scene immobilized her.

A sound in the bedroom. A heel hitting the windowpane? An instantaneous fury short-circuited any common sense Audrey may have possessed, and propelled her into the bedroom. At the window she screamed at the top of her lungs:

"Come back here, you asshole!" But all she heard were footsteps running across loamy earth, then hitting pavement and sprinting off. She tried to weigh the footsteps in her mind. A large person? Not loud enough. A large athlete? Perhaps someone who could muffle a footfall with practiced joints. She searched the darkness.

"A fine mess." Fred's voice spun her around.

"You again." She put her fingers to her temples then looked up. "Did you see anything? Who was it?"

He wandered around assessing the damage. "How would I know? I'm with you."

"This is nauseatingly familiar," she said as she surveyed the mess.

"The cabin," he said. Audrey replayed the tape of that night and felt the same indignation, the same invasion she had felt looking at Fred's and her possessions littering the room. Someone had touched everything. Touched her sheets, her clothes, her undies. She thought that she wouldn't be able to wear one article of clothing until all of them had been disinfected. A shiver nearly convulsed her.

"They didn't find what they were looking for that night…So what is 'it'? And who are 'they'?"

Fred shrugged. "Don't look at me."

"Then what good are you?"

"You've got a little crisis at judgment central. I'm just here to help with that. So call the cops," said the deceased.

"I could've figured that out."

⋙⋘

Later, an efficient looking officer rounded the house holding a flashlight. He shined it on the outer reaches of the front yard that didn't have the full benefit of the security lights. Audrey watched from her perch on the steps.

Fred stood behind her leaning against one of the porch supports. He nodded toward the curb. "Here comes the cavalry."

Carl's car screeched to an abrupt stop. He hopped out and loped toward Audrey. "You all right?" She nodded. He sat down close to her.

"Find out who rang his dinner bell," Fred ordered. Audrey looked around and up at Fred, then back at Carl.

Prompted by this odd head movement, Carl asked again. "You're sure you're all right?"

"Positive. How'd you get here so quickly?"

"The jungle drums," said Carl.

"You heard about my problems up north through the grapevine. Now it's the jungle drums. Are you stalking me?"

"Ah, there's such a fine line between stalking and worship." Audrey narrowed her eyes at him. "Okay, the dispatcher's a friend of mine."

"Small town," observed Fred.

"True." It was out of her mouth before she realized it.

"True?" Carl looked concerned.

Oh, God. She'd crossed the line, responding to Fred as though he were really there. She scrambled to cover. "True that she's a friend of yours. I, I was just thinking what a small town this is...here in the middle of a huge metropolis...what a small town."

Fred paced on the porch behind her. "You're going to have to learn to recover better than that." She couldn't help looking back up at him. This time Carl also looked around at the empty porch then forced Audrey to look into his eyes.

"Do you want me to get you something to help you to sleep? You've been under a lot of pressure." She shook her head. Another officer stepped out onto the porch, then down a few steps until she was at eye-level with Audrey and Carl. Fred continued to pace.

"Well, unless you can figure out anything that's missing, I'd say they were after something specific, 'cause they left plenty of stuff they could've hocked."

"Did you tell her about your problems up North?" Carl asked.

"Yeah." Audrey didn't want to get into it again.

The first officer came up from the edge of the yard. "No sign of a break-in anywhere, and there's too many footprints out back to get anything from them."

The second officer eyed Audrey skeptically. "You sure you didn't give your key to anybody?"

"I told you, it's a new lock and I have both keys...no duplicates."

The officer looked at her and shrugged. "Yeah, well, we'll let you know if the prints help."

"Thanks," said Audrey.

Carl shook both officers' hands. "Yeah, good job. Thanks." The officers moved off toward their squad car.

After a long silence, Audrey looked at Carl. "I'm calling it in," she said.

"Calling what in?"

"The I.O.U. What are you doing this weekend?"

"Vlade Divac asked me to sub for him at center for the Lakers, but I can let him down gently. Why?"

"I want you to go up to Mitchell with me."

"I don't know, asking for a weekend date on Friday night... makes me feel kinda cheap."

"Get over it." She finally smiled for the first time that night, but it faded as quickly as it came. "I've got to get some answers or I really will go crazy."

"As opposed to just thinking you are?" Fred put in. She glared up at him, a look not lost on Carl.

"I'm here for you. Whatever you need me to do." Carl's tone was patronizing, but at this point she didn't care what form it took. She just needed his help.

Audrey looked toward the duplex next door. Dark. She thought back to the first time she saw Fred, yelling at Street, that dangerous reedy man on the porch; thought about the laconic slow-talking stranger whom she had never really known. This new version of Fred was oddly familiar in the root-sense of that word. He felt like family. Was this the brother she had asked her mother for one Christmas? The anti-matter sibling who perhaps existed in a parallel universe and who now crossed over to help her? If she convinced herself he was a spirit of some sort, then she wouldn't have to face the crevasse of psychosis. Whom was she kidding? She was familiar with a number of the manifestations of psychosis. Mom had seen to that.

⌾

"Stay right here, 'cause these are the good old days." Her baby-sitter had wanted to be the next Carly Simon, so she played her albums and strummed her guitar all evening when Audrey's parents went out. Audrey remembered the song, but never really listened to it, never felt its meaning like she did that day. She was sixteen and looked back on the month of grounding after the motorcycle incident as a gift. In the preceding few years she had been caught up in school and her friends and resented even having parents to interfere with the absolute freedom teenagers crave.

During the first few days of confinement, Audrey stayed in her room without a telephone, a punishment she was sure the Supreme Court would consider cruel and unusual. But soon she began to come downstairs after doing her homework and her mom, dad, and she would play cribbage. Her mother was the most competitive of them, shrieking with delight when she won, moaning in anguish when she didn't. But tonight she was quiet, concentrating. They were all very nearly even, their little pegs neck and neck in the race along the track described by the tiny holes in the board. It was the thirtieth night of her grounding, and she had begun to think of all the things she would do with her friends in the next week. Only Katherine had been allowed to visit during the month and then only when the girls convinced Audrey's parents that their school work would suffer if they didn't study together. She was off in this daydream of freedom when her father laid down his cards and began counting excitedly.

"Fifteen-two, fifteen-four, fiftee..." He couldn't put the peg in the hole. His eyes widened, then one side of his body became rigid as a post while the other side seemed to shrivel, almost curl in on itself. Her mother sat there as Audrey screamed at her to do something. She continued to sit as Audrey called for an ambulance. Continued to sit as they took her father away, mask over his face. Continued to sit.

Audrey wanted to go back and savor each day she had taken for granted. She wanted to be grounded again.

The doorbell fought its way through a dream haze, briefly was incorporated as a dinner bell at Camp Fire Girl camp, then finally, its atonal, electronic din rudely dragged her up to consciousness, or a reasonable facsimile thereof. She dug herself out from under the pyramid of pillows and waded through the sweaters and undies on her bedroom floor. She opened the front door to Carl, wide-awake, perfectly pulled together, actually chipper at eight o'clock in the morning on a weekend. It was insulting.

"Good morning," he said, as he looked past her into the mayhem beyond. "How 'bout I give you a hand in here before we go?"

"Naw, if they come back, I want 'em to be able to pick up where they left off." She moved toward the bedroom, negotiating the minefield of books, pillows and pieces of Buddha statues, which she collected for no reason she could articulate. "I'll just cull some clothes and be ready in a minute. Coffee maker's ready to go, just press the button."

As she picked through the clothes on the floor, she looked up to see Fred hovering over her, a little sleepy looking but otherwise dressed and ready to go. It always struck her, each time she saw this apparition, how different he looked from the original model. Now he was always perfectly groomed and dressed in stylish, yet casually conservative clothes, nice shirts, sweaters and khakis.

"That shell doesn't go with that turtleneck," offered the dead man now fashion consultant. She looked at the two pieces in her hand, then selected a different sweater.

"I don't really care what I look like and since when would you know what a 'shell' is?"

"I'm a man of infinite wisdom. Your lack of attention to your appearance is all the more reason you should allow me to help with your judgment even on such mundane things. Besides, we need to establish a pattern of trust."

"Are you going to be around constantly, because if you are, I'll just have Carl drop me off in Camarillo and check myself in to the state mental hospital."

"Not for long. I hear they're going to close it."

"Great. Where are we patients supposed to go then, the library?"

"Listen, you have more immediate problems to deal with."

"Yeah, like you—"

"Like me, what?" Carl asked as he approached the door carrying two cups of coffee.

"Nothing...I was just singing to myself." It sounded lame the minute it was out of her mouth and Fred couldn't suppress yet another eye-roll.

"Singing? This early in the morning? That's a little out of character for you." Carl handed her a mug. "Milk and one blue, one pink thing, right?"

Audrey nodded and sipped the coffee gratefully. Her morning personality had been the source of jokes between the two surfer friends who thought nothing of being out on the water at sunrise. Miles invited her along on these outings when they first started dating, but soon realized that Audrey found the hours before nine A.M. as comfortable as scabies. Carl, on the other hand, found them intoxicating, and hence, usually joined the walking wounded around ten-thirty each night when Audrey was just getting her second wind.

"I've decided my whole character's out of character. Anything goes," Audrey said. It was a liberating thought.

"Don't get too far out of it. I sort of liked your character," Carl said.

"I can't get much farther out of mine than I am," Fred interjected, "but you don't hear me carping about it."

Audrey clenched her jaw and concentrated on the clothes around her to keep from responding to Fred. "Let's just get this show on the road. This place's depressing," said Audrey.

"I'm ready," Carl said a little too brightly. "If you don't need too much stuff, we can take my car."

"Where'll I sit?" asked Fred.

Audrey smiled up at Carl. "I'd love to take your little car."

When she first met him, Carl was driving a pickup so he could throw his surfboard into the back in case the waves were good on the way to work. Miles and Carl had been surf buddies since they were kids growing up in the margins of the wealthy coastal communities near Los Angeles.

Miles' grandmother had the foresight to buy a large cottage on Fourth Street just below San Vicente at a time when Santa Monica was a weekend beach retreat for the well-heeled of Los Angeles. When Miles' father decided to quit his job as an insurance salesman and join the ranks of Timothy Leary's hangers-on, it wasn't much of a stretch for him since he had always believed in "free love", or so it said in a note his more conventional wife found on the kitchen counter of their Mar Vista ranch style home. After a two-month depression, Miles' mother sold the house with little to show for it after paying the mortgage arrears. She had been ill-prepared for the workforce when her husband tripped out, but she landed a job as a cashier at Polly's

Pies, walking distance from her mother's house. Miles and his mom made the Santa Monica cottage their permanent home.

Up the coast a way, near the beginning of the nineteen mile ribbon that is Malibu, Carl lived in a small house perched on pilings driven through the sand, its eastern edges—well, technically northern—grasping ever so tenuously at the highway for some small purchase on terra (one hopes) firma. Carl's parents were perennial entrepreneurs. Each year they devised a new company, a new idea, a new scheme to keep them afloat and in their beloved ocean front home. Money came and went with the tides, now high, now low, and occasionally, a minus tide. Carl worried about money a good deal more than his parents knew, a great deal more than they did themselves. Before he was a teenager, he had opened a secret bank account and began depositing the generous allowance that flowed freely during the good times. When money was scarce, Carl would insist that his parents take the extraordinary sums he had earned from washing cars and mowing lawns. He did these tasks for the usual teenage fees and supplemented the amounts with withdrawals from his bank account. His parents always seemed to find success just before the foreclosure notices were tacked to the front door and then a high cycle would begin again.

Perhaps it was their common lack of disposable cash that paired them off at Santa Monica High. Perhaps it was their mutual love of waves. Whatever the reason, Miles and Carl became fast friends and were inseparable until after college–they both attended University of California at Santa Barbara. The waves were particularly good up there.

Miles never said why, but the friends lost track of each other before Miles and Audrey were married the first time, something to do with the cop to shrink transition. Carl popped up again near the end of that three-year marriage fiasco and Audrey took an immediate liking to him. They remained friends during the first divorce––well, until that little incident––and picked up their friendship where they left off when Audrey started seeing Miles again. Carl played a crucial role in the second incarnation of Miles' and her travesty. After Annabel brought them together again, Carl cemented the deal. Audrey began spending more and more time at Miles' place and one night she made a huge Indian feast. As was the rule rather than the exception, Carl was dateless. So as the three drank shandies and finished the papadam, Carl rose unsteadily to his feet.

"Time for the two of you to either shit or get off the pot." An apt expression thought Audrey as she looked back on it.

Miles had shrugged. "It didn't work the first time 'cause you weren't there to be my best man. So, let's go to Mexico and do it right. What'd'ya say?" Miles looked at Audrey through a shandy fog. What'd'ya say, was probably perfectly appropriate for a second proposal.

"Why not?" was probably not the appropriate response, but that's hindsight for you.

"You going to take my name this time?" Now that question shocked her. The first time she had kept her family name, James, without thinking, simply because it had been her identity for twenty-eight years. She hadn't believed it had made any difference to Miles, but perhaps it had.

"Sure," she said. But she never got around to changing it. It's not as though they hadn't talked about remarriage. They had discussed all the important things, fidelity, commitment, children. But they kept putting it off. Now Carl forced their hand and Audrey felt like she was being pulled along. Sucked back by the Bernoulli Effect, which assured that spit, if not forcefully hurled out the front window of a speeding car, would end up in the back seat. When she thought about it later, she realized that speed and physics had nothing to do with her decision, which had been made with a pathological disregard for history. The uniform motion of folly deposited the three of them at the Rosarita Beach Hotel where she remarried Miles in a margarita haze, with Carl in a sombrero as best hombre.

⌦⌫

Fred looked pretty miserable sitting on the trunk of the tiny Miata with his feet in the passenger compartment between Audrey and Carl. He held on to the back of their seats for lateral support when Carl accelerated into a corner, which he did often on the windy stretch of highway near Big Sur. Audrey and Carl had been comfortable enough in their friendship to allow an easy silence to prevail much of the trip. Now as they approached a particularly treacherous turn, which jutted out into the steep-cliffed shoreline, Fred grabbed the back of Audrey's seat in preparation for the curve. Audrey looked up at him.

"You just had to come," she said, then realized she had spoken to Carl as far as he was concerned.

"Hey, you invited me."

"I didn't mean it the way it sounded, I meant, you had to come with me because I need someone I can trust, someone who knows I'm not a nut case...at least I think you fall into that category."

"You can trust me. I'm on your side come rain or come shine."

"Notice he skirted the mental health issue," said Fred.

"Notice I skirted the mental health issue," said Carl at precisely the same time. Then when Carl saw the look of open-mouthed surprise on Audrey's face he added, "I'm just teasing you."

They arrived at Nate's in the late afternoon. He happened to be pulling into the driveway behind them in his large Chevy pickup with the legend: "Artful Construction" painted on the side. Fred strolled off to examine the truck while Carl and Audrey waited for Nate to step down from the cab. He greeted them with a look of concern.

"Hey, Audrey, how ya doing? Anything wrong?" Audrey and Nate fumbled a stilted hug.

"No, I just had to come back up and see if I could find out anything more for myself. This is Carl Rogers, you might have met him at the funeral." The two men shook hands.

"Nice seeing you," Carl said.

"Yeah, how ya doin'?" Gone was Nate's Labrador eagerness and in its place was an edgy approximation of it. He kept wiping his hands on his jeans, then noticed Audrey noticing. "I always feel like I got the day's grime on me 'til I get cleaned up. Come on inside, Skitch can throw another cup a water in the soup."

"Oh, we won't stay, thanks." Audrey had the distinct feeling that she was trespassing, toeing dirt clods in a field Nate had hoped to leave fallow.

"Ya gotta," he said leaving no room for dissent.

Dinner was hardly watered down soup. Skitch grew her own vegetables and deftly combined them in a lemon butter sauce over a gigantic bowl of capellini accompanied by what must have been a fifty-dollar chunk of parmesan cheese. Nate and Skitch presided at either end of the rough pine table. Audrey and Carl flanked Nate while their teenage boys, Ron, thirteen, and Jack, seventeen, sat on either side of their mother. Audrey smiled across the table at Ron as he piled his plate with the concoction and proceeded to inhale it.

"So you have any kids, Audrey?" asked Skitch.

"No. Maybe someday. My husband wasn't father material." Skitch smiled and shrugged, then looked at Carl.

"How 'bout you?"

"Nope."

"Haven't met the right gal yet?" she asked.

"Or haven't connected properly with the right lady."

Audrey marveled at the rate at which the teenagers inhaled their food. She had only taken a few bites when Jack, the more clean-cut of the two kids, directed a question to his dad.

"Can I be excused? We're going to practice at Duane's."

"I don't know why you guys don't shoot over here any more," Nate groused.

"How 'bout 'cause Duane's got a full court." Nate waved him off and the teenager was out of the room in a second.

"Can I be excused too?" Ron grasped at his chance to escape the boring clutch of adults.

Skitch looked at him knowingly. "If you go straight up and do your homework." His response was a tossed off nod. Once the boys had left the room, an uneasy silence descended.

"Your kids are great." Audrey felt this sounded generic so she added: "They're so polite." That was much better. Damned with faint praise.

"I think Jack could raise himself, but Ron's got a little responsibility problem," said Skitch. "We have to sit on him to get him to do his homework, chores…anything but his computer games." Skitch glanced toward the stairs which Ron had taken two at a time and shook her head. "Having Fred around didn't help any."

Audrey saw Nate shoot her a look. Was it for speaking unkindly of the dead or something else? Audrey directed her question to Nate. "Why is that?"

After a telling pause, Nate ventured, "Fred was pretty good with computers. Hell, he was like the Apple guy...what's his name. Well, didn't invent anything, but put stuff together from old computers. Now that guy—what's it been, ten, eleven years—he's a millionaire ten times over. With Fred it was more personal. He just liked tinkering with them. He made Ron's computer as fast as anything on the market and it's three years old."

"Practically a relic," said Carl.

"How long have you...did you know Fred?" asked Audrey.

"We grew up in the valley together. North Hollywood. Valley used to be a great place for kids, but now, well, you know about Frances and the drugs and all."

"Maybe it's just who she hangs with," said Audrey. "Fred said something about his friends getting her into drugs." Again, she thought she detected a look pass from husband to wife. "Who do you think he was talking about?"

Nate shrugged, shook his head.

"That's why we moved up here. To get away from all that stuff." Skitch didn't look up from her food as she spoke.

"Heard anything from the local police?" Carl asked.

"Not a word." Now Nate studied his food.

Fred suddenly appeared, leaning against the wall with his hands in his pockets. "Ask him how he knows Terry." Audrey searched her memory for a connection, then remembered seeing Nate speak to Terry at the funeral.

"Was Terry also from the neighborhood?"

"Terry? Terry what?" Nate still didn't look up.

"I'm not sure what her last name is. She lives next door to me and I saw you speaking with her at the funeral"

"Was I? What's she look like?" Now he looked at Audrey, but with darting, nervous glances.

"Thin, twenties, brown hair with a few blond streaks, medium height." Audrey realized she could be describing a large chunk of the female population.

"I talked to a lot of people at the funeral, you know, just swapping stories about Fred. Can't say I recall her in particular."

"And if he did, he's not going to admit it in front of his wife." Skitch's comment was tossed like a Frisbee rather than a barb. The lack of edge in her voice told Audrey that Skitch was secure in her marriage. A pang of jealousy became a physical charge that caused her abdomen to clench. Audrey wouldn't have dared such a comment aimed at Miles. It would have hit too close to home. Get a grip. Don't think about Miles.

"I hope you noticed that Nate thought there were a lot of people at the funeral," said Fred leaning over Audrey's shoulder. "It was a pretty sparse turn out as I remember. Just another example of things you should be noticing. Probe him about Street, the guy who was beating up on the other guy next door."

"The first time I saw Fred he was arguing with a man named Street...the guy I told Detective Penn about," Audrey said. "The man was thin, about your age, maybe a little taller, dark hair. Sound like any of Fred's friends you knew?"

"Was he at the funeral?"

"I didn't see him..."

"Most of his friends I know were there. We haven't been that close in the last few years...could be somebody he met recently. You know Fred...friendly type. Always one to talk to a stranger, right? Anyway, sorry, don't know him." Nate shook his head.

Too much information. Audrey flashed on the lesson Katherine had taught her in college when the two girls had been caught with an open tequila bottle in the car.

"Throw that in the back!" Katherine had ordered Audrey as the red light flooded the interior of Katherine's Rabbit. Audrey had, but the bottle remained in view. "Yes or no answers. Don't make up a story, don't elaborate. That's how they can tell you're lying." The officer ambled up to the Katherine's door and shone his flashlight around inside.

"Evening, Ladies. License please." Katherine complied without a word. "That bottle belong to you girls?" he asked as his flashlight beam caught the half-empty bottle.

"No," Katherine said with a straight face. Technically this was true. They had stolen it from her ex-boyfriend's room in the dorm. She called it her friendly parting gift.

"Illegal to have an open liquor bottle in a car."

Audrey looked at Katherine out of the corner of her eye, but neither girl moved.

The policeman grabbed the bottle. "You got a broken tail light. Some folks don't know that's illegal. Most everybody knows that drinking and driving is illegal. You girls know that, don't you?"

"Yes." It was a simultaneous response.

"Well, I won't cite you for the tail light this time, but get it fixed. Since the bottle isn't yours, I'll just confiscate it till we find the rightful owner."

The girls had skated through on Katherine's street smarts and a sympathetic cop, but Nate didn't have the benefit of this early lesson and he had been too positive about not knowing Street based on the vague description she had offered. Fred strolled around the table then stopped behind Nate.

"Ask him about Florida," the dead man instructed.

"Do you have any idea what Fred was doing in Florida?" This time Nate's features seemed to relax, as though he had been waiting for a punch that had been pulled. "He had a pretty bad habit for awhile. I think he went down there to put together a buy with some other losers, but it didn't work out."

"What went wrong?" Carl asked.

"He didn't say. He knew I didn't approve of that stuff. I sorta think Florida was what came back to bite him in the ass. Figured that's why he came up here looking for work."

Now Fred crouched down next to Nate and looked into his eyes as Nate picked up a dropped napkin, then Fred shook his head like a disappointed parent.

"And exactly how did the cops know to call him when there was no I.D. on the body? The wallet was on the floor, remember?" the dead man asked.

Audrcy wondered why the thought hadn't occurred to her before. "Why did the cops call you? Fred's wallet was still in the motel room."

Nate shifted in his chair. "Everybody knows everybody up here. The cops knew he worked for me."

Fred sat in the chair, previously occupied by Ron, stretched his legs, and rested his feet on the table. "He's too guarded. He's not going to give us anything."

chapter **II**

AUDREY PULLED HER parka hood tightly around her head against the chill of the night air as Carl drove to the front of the large check-in cabin which dwarfed the row of smaller structures comprising the Cabin Motel complex. They approached the front entrance where a portion of the neon sign glowed in the window: Vaca___. Audrey's high-school Spanish registered that the sign, thus truncated, advertised a cow. It seemed a natural part of the surreal terrain that characterized this particular location for her. Did it happen? Was it all an actual nightmare? Had she really been in a situation she normally never would have considered: A motel room with a man she barely knew? She still held out some hope that she would wake up––maybe in a psych ward somewhere––and find it had all been just a bad dream.

Audrey followed Carl into the reception area where he rang the ancient plunger bell on the counter.

"You rang? Fred appeared next to her. She couldn't contain the indrawn breath of surprise.

"You okay?" Carl asked, concerned. She nodded.

"Sure, just a chill." Carl put an arm around her. After a few minutes, an elderly man opened the door at the back of the reception area allowing the din of a television to pour into the room, an over-loud commercial for a disposable razor.

"Sorry, had to see what those Bonanza boys were up to." He approached the desk, eyeing Audrey suspiciously, then pointed at her when recognition dawned. "The lady with the dead man." Audrey felt herself nod and step back, actually shrink from this harmless old man.

Carl sensed this and took over. "Is number nine available?"

"Sure thing." The old man handed him a key from a board checkered with numbered squares most containing keys hung from cup hooks.

"And another one close to it?" Carl continued.

"You want separate cabins?" the old man asked the obvious.

Fred looked at Audrey indignantly. "Damn straight separate cabins. You're still a married woman," said the dead chaperone.

"Jeeze," she half-sighed.

"That's what you want, isn't it?" Did Carl's voice sound disappointed or hopeful?

"Of course. That was just a tired sound, just tired."

"There ya go." The old man placed the key to number ten on the counter.

"I'll stay in number nine. You want to do this now or wait 'til morning?" Carl asked.

"Might as well get it over with."

Number nine was bright in the glare of the large new lamp fixture that bounced light off the recently painted ceiling and freshly scrubbed pine walls. Audrey looked around and wondered what she had dreaded about reentering this room. She felt nothing at all because every trace of that night had been expunged. Even the raggedy quilt had been supplanted by a homey looking chenille bedspread.

Carl studied her. "You okay? What can I do?"

"It's been completely cleaned and painted. I don't know what I expected to find here, but this doesn't even feel like the same room." She wandered around trying to get a sense, anything that might help her remember something useful. Finally she walked to the fireplace. The ashes hadn't been cleaned out. At the edge lay a piece of Fred's mug. They had scrubbed, painted and replaced nearly everything in the room but had left these ashes. While her mind was contemplating how something so basic could be overlooked, her emotions shanghaied her body. She burst into tears. Carl was next to her in an instant, putting his arms around her, letting her cry into his shoulder. She wasn't sure why she was crying, hadn't felt it coming, was ambivalent about even letting Carl comfort her. Her only certainty was that she felt safe for the moment, no tapes, no ghosts or psychoses, no fear for the moment. She supposed that she was crying because there had been so much she wanted to cry about but hadn't. She only knew that she felt comfortable, for the moment, safe, for the moment. As if that were his cue, Fred appeared leaning against the fireplace behind Carl.

"I wouldn't get too comfortable there if I were you." Audrey's eyes opened and looked at him over Carl's shoulder, though she made no move to end the embrace. "The guy's your husband's best friend, but if that doesn't bother you..." Fred shrugged as if to say that it didn't bother him either. It bothered her. It most definitely bothered her. She pulled away.

"Thanks, I'm okay now. I just got sort of overwhelmed."

"Let me help. Talk to me." Carl looked at her earnestly.

She smiled up at him and noticed, not for the first time, that his face could be the picture of compassion. It could also be intimidating in repose, so this look always surprised and pleased her. She took his hand in both of hers and hoped it conveyed the friendship she felt for him.

"Thanks, I would if I knew what to say."

"Try," Carl pleaded.

She shook her head, bemused. "I'll be fine, really."

Fred followed her to the door. "See how easy that was?"

⌁

Audrey opened the door to cabin number ten and dropped her bag on the floor. The similarity to the original look of number nine shocked her. Fred sauntered in and looked around casually. Audrey moved to the bed and ran her hand along the shabby old quilt then retreated to the lumpy chair by the fireplace where she sat stiffly.

In her mind's eye she saw a shard from his mug. Saw its triangular shape, pictured it, spike–up atop a wall in Macao or Caracas, let her mind drift to the sadness she felt for a society imprisoned in their homes, lamented that it was beginning to happen in her own country. Then the floor was covered with shards of a thousand broken mugs.

She grabbed her bag and dashed toward the door, treading as lightly on her feet as she could, fearing the thousand spikes that she knew didn't exist.

Carl took a moment before he answered her knock. When he did, he was naked except for a towel wrapped at his waist. Before he could say anything she rushed in.

"I can't stay in the other room. It looks exactly like this one did that night. Could we switch?"

"Sure. Just give me a sec." Carl flew around collecting things he had removed from his bag. He ducked into the bathroom, then reappeared in his jeans, threw on his sweatshirt and started toward the door. He stopped and turned around. "Are you sure you'll be all right in here...you know, alone?"

"Carl, Carl, don't even think of going there," Fred said, though only Audrey could hear him.

"I'll be okay," said Audrey. "And thanks." Reluctant to leave, Carl moved slowly toward the door.

"If you're sure."

Audrey nodded her response.

"She's sure. Take the hint." Fred helped Carl close the door. Audrey kicked off her shoes, pulled off her sweater and jeans and donned a flannel nightgown. She jumped into bed and curled up on one side.

"Want me to rub your back?" Fred sat on the other side of the bed.

"No thanks."

"You've gotta start trusting me."

"Good night." Trust. She'd tried that with her future-former-husband.

⌐⌐⌐

The images flooded back. The hotel room. The shower. The towel. Audrey remembered in minute detail the first time she knew for certain that Miles had slept with another woman during their first marriage. He was on location in San Diego and she flew down after she returned from a courier trip to Japan. The trip was supposed to include a two-day stay in Tokyo followed by a pickup she was to have brought back with her. When she learned that the second document delivery had been cancelled, she came back a day early and surprised Miles at the Hotel Del Coronado where the cast was staying during the filming of a low budget horror film. When Audrey arrived at his door, Miles seemed genuinely happy to see her, if a little nervous. They made love, and he paid particular attention to her needs over his own.

Stepping into the shower, she felt the jet lag steam away, felt infused with the invigorating force of optimism. No one in the world could be as happy as she was. She almost felt guilty about it. The feeling lasted throughout the shower but was blasted into hell when she wrapped herself in the damp towel and smelled the distinct aroma of Georgio perfume. Nerve gas couldn't have immobilized her as completely. She couldn't even breathe because at that moment she believed that the fumes would kill her. At some point she managed to drop the towel. A few minutes? An hour? Did she stand there naked, dripping for a day? Finally anger began to pool--like hot oil in her abdomen--then to expand, rising through her chest, then to boil over. She threw open the bathroom door and crashed it against the wall.

"You fucking bastard!" Audrey flew around the room throwing things into her suitcase.

"She paid a maid to let her into the room. I mean she was here, naked. It's not like I went looking for it or anything." That was one thing about Miles; he couldn't lie to anyone's face. His were the sins of omission. He omitted telling her about the women he had slept with since their marriage, and since she hadn't asked directly, who could blame him for not volunteering it? Miles tried to put his hands on her shoulders, but she threw them off as if they were still covered by the swamp slime the special effects people had provided for that day's shoot.

"Room service. How convenient." She pulled on her jeans and an oversized sweater.

"Look, it won't happen again. I'm sorry."

"I'm not. How could I ever've trusted anyone who would fuck someone who'd wear Georgio?" Not a sensible exit line, but the one that flew out of her mouth as she left the room, the marriage, the first time.

The only nod the town of Mitchell made to recent history was the inclusion of an electric tavern sign touting Coors beer because the mayor, at the time of the permit request, felt that too much had been made of the brewery's Anglo-centric, anti-gay proclivities and he wanted to show his support for the maligned company. Even so, the incandescent plastic rectangle had been required to be smaller than the bowling alley's coffee shop sign, which had been fashioned from local bark by the original owners at the turn of the century.

The Mitchell police station occupied the second floor of the only masonry edifice in the row of four buildings lining the main street that constituted the town. The lower floor housed store fronts with tenants which included a hardware store, a State Farm insurance office, a bakery which sold coffee and sported a sign displaying the word cappuccino encircled in red with a line crossed diagonally through it, a satellite dish sales office, and a tea and bait shop, owned by a husband and wife who split the space down the middle.

Carl and Audrey walked into the large main room of the station where a deserted reception desk looked like it was designed to discourage non-employees from invading the few desks fanned out behind it. Audrey nodded toward Detective Penn and the two marched up to his desk.

"Hi, I'm Carl Rogers, late of the Santa Monica police department. You remember Audrey James?"

"Sure, the girlfriend." The detective used the same dismissive tone he had used the night Fred died. He studied her a moment then turned back to Carl. "Why're you late of the force? Got a better offer?"

Carl clearly didn't want to get into it with this man who wore his hostility like a lawyer wore his Armani, in equal parts for vanity and intimidation.

"Something like that. Ms. James and I would like to talk about the progress you've made on the Frederick Engel case."

"Great progress. We closed it."

"Did you bother to investigate at all?" Audrey couldn't hide her contempt.

"Hey, you saw me out there in the middle of the night. We investigated and so did an accident specialist from the CHP." He threw a four-page report at Carl who caught it deftly then studied it.

"Can I get a copy of this?" Carl asked.

"That's my personal copy, 'n since the case is closed, I don't need it. It's all yours."

"What about our room being ransacked?" Audrey folded her arms in front of her defensively.

"You want to report something missing?"

"I can't be sure what of his was missing."

"But nothin' of yours was." Audrey reluctantly shook her head. "So maybe it wasn't a robber at all. You went out in a hurry, maybe left the door open, maybe some animal comes in looking for food."

"Oh, the mattress was slit by some knife wielding raccoon?" Audrey's tone defined sarcasm.

"Or it was a bear 'n he used his index claw." The detective found himself amusing. Carl fumed at his attitude.

"Listen detective—"

"Hey, I give everybody a hard time. Nothin' personal. Fact is the guy had an accident. The CHP agrees, even your pal Nate agrees."

"When did you talk to him?" Audrey dropped her defensive posture.

"A couple a days ago when I told him about the report."

⌘

The Miata parked at the curb, looked innocuous enough to most people, but Audrey could see Fred reading a newspaper while seated on the hood. Carl and she entered the car and sat for a moment lost in thought. Fred studied them.

"Bad news?" he asked. Audrey glanced at Fred then at Carl.

"Why would Nate lie to us about not hearing from the police?"

"Maybe he meant he hadn't heard anything good or significant. Then again, they were friends. He might be feeling some guilt for not taking the murder theory as seriously as you do. You know, not wanting to discount it for fear of looking disloyal, yet unable to really

believe in it himself." Audrey imagined that Carl was probably iden-
tifying with Nate.

"That doesn't account for all the tension during dinner last
night," Fred said.

Audrey paused then directed her statement to Carl. "There just
seemed to be something going on at dinner last night. I can't put my
finger on it."

"I know what you mean. For a guy who lives away from urban
stress, he seemed wound as tight as a commodities trader. I'll ask
some of the guys on the force to do a background check on him."

"Yeah. Check on Street, too."

"Okay."

"Thanks. 'Cause right now, we got 'fried nothing', as my dad
used to say." What would her dad say about her speculation that
someone she knew was murdered? Would he understand, or would
he worry that she was her mother's daughter?

In the daylight the highway at the hairpin turn appeared benign,
almost inviting. Luscious pines loomed near the drop off and looked
as if they could have caught Fred mid-flight if only their boughs had
blown a little lower. The sea, too, looked as if it could have caught and
held him in the soft gentle waves below. Only the rocks looked their
part: cruel, unforgiving of hurtling human flesh.

The rubber skid marks from Fred's screeching tires had faded
somewhat but were still easily discernable near the shorter, more
curved tracks left by those who managed to successfully negotiate
the angle. Fred's rubber continued into the guardrail, now temporarily repaired with wood and protected by two huge plastic barrels filled with sand. A bouquet of flowers tied with a yellow ribbon
rested atop one of the barrels. Audrey wondered if it had been left
by someone who knew Fred--Nate? Skitch?--or simply by someone
who had heard or read of the accident. She walked the skid marks as
she had that night, but this time with Carl beside her studying the
CHP report as he compared the notes to the physical evidence at the
site. The post-dead Fred strolled on her opposite side. Both men wore
khakis with cotton shirts and sweaters, though Fred's sweater was

tied casually around his neck. Hallucinations must be less affected by the cold.

"It all looks fairly cut and dried," Carl mused, more to himself than to Audrey. "He had to be doing at least sixty to lay that kind of rubber." He considered the other tire marks. "And there aren't any other recent skid marks to suggest that someone was chasing him-- at close range anyway."

Audrey looked out over the cliff, the craggy rocks, the undulating sea that was as majestic in its peril as in its capacity for tranquility.

"Maybe they weren't chasing. Maybe they were waiting for him." Saying this, Fred hoisted himself atop one of the sand barrels and perched there looking down at the earth-bound couple. Audrey tried to imagine how someone waiting could have forced Fred off the road. A memory tape played: the image of the car parked just beyond the curb when she was on her motorcycle at sixteen. She couldn't see it until it was too late to avoid.

"What if they parked a huge van or truck just where you couldn't see it until it was too late? Your choice would be to slam into a vehicle or take your chances with the cliff. Remember, he didn't know how much of a drop there was."

Carl tried to hide his skepticism, but it sounded as a base note in his otherwise carefully modulated reply. "I suppose that's possible."

"Now that's enthusiasm." Fred scrutinized Carl. "What if all the pertinent information didn't make it into the report?"

Audrey translated for the spirit. "What if there was more evidence but someone excluded it, then covered it up?"

"It's difficult to pull off a cover-up as demonstrated by our recently departed thirty-seventh president. Unless you're acting entirely alone, there's always the potential for betrayal." This time Carl's voice carried an unrecognizable quality. Guilt? Warning? Personal knowledge? Audrey studied him intently. "Come on," said Carl. "It's getting late." He held out a hand to her and led her back toward the car.

Fred jumped down from his perch. "And that, ladies and gentlemen, is why I'm here: to point out the obvious to the willfully blind. The guy's hiding something. His tone wasn't clinical; his eyes weren't talking to you. He was thinking about something he feels guilty about and you're letting him off the hook."

Audrey looked at Fred, gritted her teeth and took a deep breath. "Are you speaking from experience?"

"About what?" Carl's question sounded ingenuous.

"You know. Cover-ups, betrayal."

"I guess I think about it. What constitutes betrayal of friendships, betrayal of professional ethics, betrayal of personal integrity. Yeah, I've thought about those things."

"And cover-ups?" she asked.

Carl took a long moment opening the door for her. "Other than those things you gals throw over your bikinis, I haven't given a lot of thought to cover-ups."

"He's lying," said the dead man.

⚶

Audrey stuffed her bag down by her feet in the tiny car. Carl had gone to return the keys and to check out. Fred appeared, sitting on the sheered horizontal face of a tree trunk the size of a table for twelve just next to the driveway.

"I'll be there if you need me, but I think I'll skip the scenic ride back. I trust you won't blow anything."

"What's that supposed to mean?" Audrey asked irritably.

"It means get all the information out of him that you can, but don't reveal anything you don't have to."

"We're on the same side."

"You don't know that. Go through his glove compartment while you're sitting there."

"I can't just—"

"Of course you can. He may think he's withholding information for your own good."

She thought about it a moment and acknowledged the possibility. "What am I looking for?" Audrey opened the compartment and removed a plastic folder with the car manual. Inside, she found hastily stashed receipts for gas, groceries, car repair, and a duplicate deposit receipt showing the transfer of $600 from one account to another."

Fred looked over her shoulder. "Stick that in your purse." He nodded his head toward the deposit receipt.

"I will not."

"Then at least copy down the numbers of the accounts." Audrey thought a moment, glanced around furtively, but then entered the account numbers into the notes section of her Day Runner.

The late afternoon was glorious but Audrey didn't look at the view as the Miata neared San Simeon. Her face was a picture of consternation. Why would Fred question whether Carl was on her side? Of course he was, always was. When she found the checkout slip from a downtown hotel with Miles's signature on it, it had been Carl she had called. He calmed her down and convinced her to talk to Miles before she made any rash moves. She had. Miles admitted having had an expensive lunch there, figuring no one would remember him. Not a rational thought for an actor, even one of his less-than-stellar magnitude. But no one would say one way or the other whether he had been a guest in the hotel rather than just the restaurant, so she dropped it. Expensive hotels are nothing if not discrete.

Being the wife of any kind of a celebrity was a thankless position. Fans and the baser press would often overlook, look through or trample the hapless spouse in order to get to the object of their desire. Audrey kept herself apart from the reflected limelight as much as possible, and luckily Miles hadn't actively courted it or things could have been even more difficult. Still, there were times when, no matter what positive forces were in effect in her life, she would feel diminished by the casual disregard of her as a person by fans, the media, her husband.

They were walking together through the Denver airport after a celebrity ski invitational when a well-dressed woman crossed in front of her and handed her card to Miles.

"Call me any time. Collect if you like." She smiled what Audrey presumed was meant to be a seductive smile and moved off.

Miles smiled back and said, "Thanks." Audrey glared at him, but he continued to walk with the card in his hand until the woman was out of sight. He then made a grand gesture of tossing it into the trash as he said: "Wouldn't want to hurt her feelings."

Audrey wondered now why she had never said anything, why she hadn't said it hurt her feelings when he accepted the card, the scrap of paper, the room key? She had sat on the little things and had blown only when the irrefutable evidence was on the towel. Still, the little things ate away at her. She felt it was somehow beneath her to confront him on them. If he couldn't figure out that it hurt her, it wasn't worth her risking ridicule to tell him. Besides, she always felt that he had let her go too easily. When she slammed the door at the Hotel del Coronado, she imagined she heard him exhale.

Now when she thought about Miles' most recent escapade--the one that caused her such grievous personal angst that she was now consorting with a dead man--she realized that Carl hadn't been forthcoming about his best friend, hadn't warned her that Miles was up to his old tricks. And he must have known. Maybe she couldn't trust Carl.

"What're you thinking? Asking as a friend not a shrink." Carl studied her face. She hesitated, then switched to the subject she had pondered earlier.

"That while I've been playing detective on this field trip, Frances is probably getting further into her drug haze."

"Try not to dwell on that, 'cause there's not much you can do."

"Maybe there's something you can do."

"Like what?"

"Use your psychological expertise."

"I happen to know you're not a fan of the profession."

"When all else fails..." she said. "I'd like you to talk Frances into going to rehab."

Carl couldn't contain the single spontaneous "Ha!" But then, when he saw that she was looking at him quite seriously, he said: "No sweat. It's done all the time. You find yourself a druggie, walk up to her and say `You're a drug addict and I've got a place that'll cure you.' Generally, she'll throw her arms around you and pledge undying devotion." Audrey crossed her arms in front of herself defensively, but let him continue. "There is that rare exception where she'll tell you she's in control of her life and to fuck off."

"Well, since the odds are in your favor, I'll be that much more disappointed if you fail." She didn't have to look to know that his eyes were rolling.

The remainder of the ride was pleasant. She thought about how it had been sometime since any of the tapes had impinged on her conscious mind. On some level she realized that Fred's presence kept the tapes, the clutter, at bay. But then, why would anyone need an aspirin when morphine coursed through the system?

chapter 12

WE WERE SUPPOSED to be emerging from the recession thanks to our fervent spending. After the savings and loan debacle we learned that greed wasn't good. But that didn't stop us. A lot of people Audrey knew still had mundane fears: Would there be a job tomorrow? Would the mortgage fight with the grocery bill for dominion over the shrinking paycheck? Would the system ever correct the egregious wage disparities? Audrey thought that everyone should be required to know the price of a quart of milk.

She had weathered the national fear-storm relatively unscathed. So why was her central fear surfacing now? She had learned to live with it inside her, become inured to, yet not unaware of, its existence. It had been shoved deep in some mental layer beneath the never-used analytic geometry. Now the fracture in the mantle of her judgment had unleashed the slow magma flow of fear, glowing orange hot, spilling over into her conscious mind, as though it had been preparing for this breach, for this fissure in her person-crust since her father's death.

For months after her father died, Audrey had hidden her mother's plunge into silence from everyone except Katherine. Audrey was fully aware that the authorities would take her mom away and throw her, Audrey, into foster care. It was more than she could bear after losing her father. She tried to understand the bank statements. Tried to pay the bills. Wondered what would happen when the money in the accounts ran out. She was sixteen. She could get a job. Take care of her mother during the day...and what? Lock her in a room while she waitressed at night?

Her mom had sat for days in that same chair without saying a word. Audrey would help her to bed every evening but every morning, when she came down for breakfast, she would find her mother back in the chair, having replaced the pegs in the cribbage board precisely as they had been on the night her father died. Her mother would sit, looking at the board, trying to divine the exact move that would bring back her husband.

Audrey's mom had been beautiful, high cheekbones below large heavily lidded eyes. Her dad loved those eyes and would say so often. Her mother would take the compliment with a lilting laugh that meant she knew she was a beauty, but was too elegant to admit it.

Audrey's parents had grown up together during World War Two in Redlands. Her grandmother died giving birth to her mother near the end of the depression and her grandfather never made it home from the war, though he hadn't been compelled to go, because his advanced age and young daughter could have exempted him. A maiden aunt, as they were called in those days, stepped in to supply the necessities of daily life to the five-year-old. And though this aunt was known throughout the neighborhood as the savior of small birds, rescuer of lame animals and tireless worker for the elderly, she couldn't extend the same compassion to her niece. Her aunt's home was a solitary and lonely place, and Audrey's mother found her world increasingly desolate...until she entered grade school and met her best friend, Audrey's father.

Her father was the youngest of six children born to Quaker parents who ran a small produce market in Redlands. He had been a great disappointment to them as an adult because he left the faith, but he supported them financially until their deaths from two heart attacks––two weeks apart––when Audrey was six.

Both of her parents attended the University of Redlands, her dad in business, her mom on an English scholarship. Her mother had briefly considered switching to drama, but didn't because her aunt explained that the words actress and harlot were synonymous and that neither was to be uttered in her home. On his graduation, Audrey's dad was offered his junior broker position in the Glendale brokerage of Saylor, Holloway and Associates. He persuaded her mom that marriage to him would afford her a secure base from which to study drama, after they started a family, of course. Audrey was born the requisite nine months to the day after their wedding. They were delighted because both had an idealized notion of family: the conviction that, though neither had experienced it in their homes growing up, a happy family was something two like-minded people could will into existence, if the desire were strong enough.

Long before other people had noticed, Audrey's father was well aware of her mother's "eccentricities" as he called them. Symptoms began to assert themselves in her late teens, but far from putting him off, they made her all the more fascinating.

Once when the three of them had gone to the zoo, Audrey's mother began talking to the chimps, maintaining that they were talking back to her. Her father noticed how Audrey, at ten, looked around, embarrassed. He took her hand and walked her toward the seal pool.

"Honey, does it upset you that your mom talks to the chimps?"

Audrey nodded sheepishly, knowing it wasn't the answer her father wanted.

"Why?" he asked.

"Because everybody knows that chimps don't talk."

"What if they do?"

Audrey shrugged and looked away.

"Do you think they can talk to each other?" her father continued.

"I guess," said the young girl reluctantly.

"Well, what if your mom happens to be the only human who can understand them?"

Audrey seriously thought about this for a moment, then dismissed the idea. "You know she can't."

"Well, we really don't know because we're not experiencing what your mother is. She's a very special person. Not like anyone else in the whole world. If you don't appreciate her eccentricities, at least try to find the humor in them. It's the difference between being able to enjoy her gifts and being sad for her."

"Are you ever sad for her?"

"No, because she's my counter-weight." Young Audrey's face was the picture of confusion so her dad continued. "You know how when you're on the seesaw and you're both about the same size. You can balance in the middle."

Audrey nodded. "But you're bigger than she is."

Her father laughed. "Good point, but she can make me lighter, just by being who she is. I'm your mom's anchor and she's my hot air balloon. She's an exceptional person, Audrey, and we're very lucky to have her. Do your best to enjoy the ride."

Once after receiving a particularly frivolous gift, her mother reminded her father of the maxim, "A penny saved is a penny earned".

Her father responded with his own credo: "Life's uncertain. Eat dessert first." Audrey hoped that he had. Her dad had been raised to conform to the expectations of family, of propriety, of his own exacting inner conscience. And he did. Her mom on the other hand was incapable of conforming to anything. Her life was his spice, but in his role as her keeper, did he have time to enjoy the dessert?

By the time they came for her mom, Audrey realized that she had mentally traveled too far from Glendale to hold out any hope of bringing her back. The rescue fantasies had played out in myriad scenarios, but all with the climax of Audrey effectively drawing her mother back into the real world the way her father had.

Her mom finally spoke after a suicide attempt. Well, that might overstate the case. It had been a confused attempt at suicide. Audrey had cancelled all her extra curricular activities and was in the habit of stopping by the local grocer's for over ripe fruits and vegetables and day old bread. Mr. Genova had always admired her mother and now gave the two women bargains unheard of in the corner grocery trade that survived on such a thin profit margin. So it was while she was holding two brimming bags of squishy peaches and slightly fuzzy strawberries that Audrey found her mother in the garage, inside the Mustang, motor running, with her eyes closed. The image that stuck in her mind was of the bags dropping to the ground and all the fruit melding together in a gooey self-compote. It was the lost fruit that was the final straw rather than the suicide attempt because the fruit had been real and her hope that her mother would suddenly snap out of her own little world had been fantasy. Audrey's mother had retained a wispy recollection of the properties of carbon monoxide, as being integral to a method of suicide, but her mind couldn't follow the sequence to its effective end. She sat in the car, motor running, with the large garage door open and even the small back door and side windows flung wide. She later explained that she had opened them because the fumes irritated her throat, which accounted for the first words Audrey heard her mother utter in three months: "If this is heaven, why is my throat sore?"

Though Audrey was thrilled to hear her mother speak, she knew it was time to make the call. Speaking and speaking meaningfully, Audrey learned, were distinct experiences.

Joie de vivre must have been coined for her mother in one of her past lives. It summed up for Audrey all of the good moments she could recall. Her mother had had three incarnations in this life: Eccentric, crazy, medicated. Though Audrey held out little hope that her mother would return to her in anything resembling her former self, she did cling to the possibility that newer drugs would make her more alert, more accessible and might have fewer side effects. So far, none had been able to unlock her former personality. And though Audrey treasured those rare snatches of coherent though impersonal conversation, the drugs had left her mom little more than simply breathing for years. Audrey decided that she would rather be crazy than medicated. To lose that spark, that essential energy was, for her, to die without the benefit of burial.

<hr />

Early on the morning after her return from Mitchell, Audrey pulled her Jeep into Katherine's semicircular drive behind a row of parked cars. She jumped out and started for the front door, but a fragment of an old tape threaded through her gray-matter VCR. She turned and walked toward the garage while she replayed her redesigned version of the night her father had died. Instead of faceless paramedics thumping on his chest, instead of a mute immobile mother, instead of the riptide of helplessness she felt caught up in, Audrey took matters into her own hands. The moment that gruesome death-stare formed in his eyes, she whacked her father on the back and, in some perverted Heimlich result, he choked up a pistachio nut. They finished out the game--she could tell he let her mother win--and Audrey didn't even mind losing. She had won the day. Audrey then recommended some fresh air, so the three of them hopped into the Mustang and drove through the desert with the top down, moonlight bouncing off the stark topography. She preferred this image of the three of them happy in the car to that last image of her mother seated behind the wheel, forlorn, frustrated in her momentarily lucid bid for release.

Now, Audrey tugged the side door open and peered into the garage. There, on the far end next to Katherine's Mercedes, was her dad's Mustang, tireless, perched on four concrete blocks. It still retained most of the greenish gold original paint, but even the yearly wax jobs hadn't been able to keep the rust from grabbing hold in places where there had been a chip in the paint or where the chrome had been scratched. She was glad she hadn't sold it, but by the same token, she couldn't think of driving it. It was still too painful. What was the half-life of the loss of a family? Would the Mustang ever be safe to drive or would it radiate painful memories for years to come? Would the fallout rain down on her for the rest of her life?

Inside Katherine's home, a wall of glass exposed the Pacific in all its splendor. On this stretch, the sea was skirted by little dots of houses perched on the highway. The view could have been a massive painting hung low in the cavernous room; just another work of art blending seamlessly with the other elegantly displayed unique pieces from around the world. Katherine had the taste to compliment Coburn's money.

And money was something Katherine had become accustomed to. She saw financial security as, well, security. Something she had little of as a child. Still, Audrey had envied Katherine's large family. Not that her own childhood was lonely—her mom was companion and playmate--but she also longed for that lost-in-the-shuffle, surrounded by a sea of siblings feeling that Katherine tried so hard to escape. The two girls had been neighbors growing up in Glendale, that middle-class 'burb stuck between the more famous Burbank and Pasadena. In the sixties and seventies it still maintained the small town feel and even had the attendant city center decay which awaited, in Sleeping Beauty repose, the kiss of corporate largess.

Katherine would flee to Audrey's home to escape the cacophony of her four younger siblings and commensurate stench of diapers as well as her mother's incessant requests for help. She found refuge in the James' house. In her own home, Katherine had to be the responsible older sister, but in Audrey's, she could design her own world with the enthusiastic encouragement of Audrey's mother. It was Katherine who dubbed Audrey's mom a fairy princess. Her mom took that ball and ran with it, playing with the six-year-olds for hours, dressed in an old chiffon formal she had scrounged at a second hand clothing shop on San Fernando Road. She helped the girls make costumes, build forts, design castles. Far from being frightened or derisive like some neighborhood children, Katherine, like Audrey's father, had been enchanted by her mother's peculiarities.

Katherine suggested that she had been dropped by the stork down the wrong chimney, that she really should have belonged to Audrey's family where she felt special, very nearly singular. At her home there were always too many people and not enough of anything, thanks to her dad's spotty employment record.

Though fighting for truth and justice had won out over the lure of financial gain at a high priced law firm, Katherine had allowed Coburn to sweep her off her feet with his high rolling art dealings. Their relationship afforded her a shot at having both of her non-human passions: a moral crusade and cash.

Coburn found in her a beautiful, practical woman who lent some temperance to his excesses. The problems began when his excesses became excessive. Katherine was working for the Federal Prosecutor in Los Angeles when a D.E.A. agent she knew called her to come to the site of what would soon be a particularly large cocaine bust. Coburn had been poised to enter the home of a major player in the art world who was rumored to have financed some of his acquisitions with drug money. Coburn was there ostensibly to sell him art, but the undercover agent said he had seen Coburn sample the cocaine in the past and questioned whether he might also be involved in dealing the illicit wares of his host. Katherine was able to warn Coburn off before the bust went down. She felt compelled to resign from the Federal Prosecutor's staff because of her, probably illegal if tangential, involvement. She had cited a need to be closer to home because she wanted to start a family. That the sordid details of the bust could eventually come out, haunted her. The only person she had confided in was Audrey.

After much screaming and shouting on Katherine's part, and more remorse and apologies on his, Coburn checked into an exclusive drug treatment program. Upon his release, couple counseling seemed to mend the tear in the fabric of their marriage caused by his cocaine addiction. Katherine threatened that if he didn't get his act together, she would leave him. Luckily, that ultimatum hadn't been tested so far. Audrey often wondered which side of her friend's personality would prevail if Coburn were to go back to his old ways: The hold-that-line prosecutor or the woman who could forgive a loved one almost anything? Katherine had become used to Coburn's money, but at the bottom of her soul, she loved him to distraction.

The intervening years had passed without further incident and Coburn had diversified into mid-range art as the bottom fell out of the high end of the market. He supplied upscale chain stores with trendy objects that could be mass-produced and shown in their catalogs as the next necessity for the well dressed home.

Now, in the beautifully appointed home that Coburn's money built, Audrey acted as Lamaze coach to the frantically breathing Katherine. The overstuffed furniture had been pushed to the walls and the lush rug was occupied by seven "couples" in the middle of a class. The militarily gruff instructor moved in and around the couples as she barked her encouragement.

"That's right. Now move on to the "hee hees". Coaches, be there for them." She walked by Audrey and Katherine who "hee heed" together. Katherine always chafed at anyone telling her what to do.

"Okay, already, we got it." She put her hands behind her head and lay back. "I'm still fuming that Coburn didn't get back from Guyaquil."

"Where the hell's that?"

"Ecuador. He found some local artisan who makes pre-Columbianesque pottery." Katherine made her voice sound like a radio commercial. "For the discerning but budget-minded collector." She resumed her normal rapid-fire speech. "At least I hope that's what he's importing." This last was said wryly, a sign that she really wasn't worried at this point.

"Well, that's why you've got me. Ready to pinch-hit at a moment's notice."

"I drove out to see your mom yesterday." Katherine tried to sound casual, but both women knew the ritual attendant upon the subject. "Knew you were up north but just got the itch for a drive."

Audrey supplied the required response. "Yeah, I've got to get out there to see her, it's been awhile." Both of them wanted to leave the subject, but felt too rapid a transition would only point up the estranging nature of it. Audrey inquired after a strained moment. "Did she say anything coherent?"

"No. But that doesn't mean that she won't."

"Hope springs eternal." It was the only subject where the two switched optimist/pragmatist roles. Katherine was sure Audrey's mother would come back to them one day and Audrey knew she wouldn't. But even in that firm belief, she found no peace. No ability to let go. Of what? Her mother as she had been? Or of the resentment that she wasn't that person any more?

Katherine mercifully segued. "You get everything cleaned up?" She grabbed Audrey's hand to help leverage herself into a sitting position then wrapped her arms under her knees in an effort to maintain it.

"Couldn't face it. I just left the mess while I was gone, then didn't have the energy last night. I feel pretty good today, though. I'll clean it up when I get home."

"Now I really feel guilty. You've got all this coming down on you and I make you get up before dawn just to hold my hand."

"I don't mind getting up for a good cause. I just popped two brownies, chased it with an espresso and rocketed out the door." Audrey felt that if breakfast was the most important meal of the day, it should also be the most enjoyable.

"Brownies and espresso, breakfast of champions," Katherine said. "Listen, there's one other thing. I've had a couple of requests for documents on my hard drive at work, and I'd rather not have Roland poking around in my computer. Can I come in with you this morning and show you the security stuff? He can take care of it after you get it for him."

"Sure, honey," said Audrey.

"So how's Opal? She giving you any breathing space?"

"She's trying...You know how she is."

"Yeah, I know," said Katherine

"Achievement's as important to her as chocolate is to me."

"Right, achievement, appearances, style over substance," said Katherine.

"Style over substance—"

"Oh, please. She was so excited about marrying the blue-blood Nichols name that she had him adopt her kids when they were teenagers. And I'm sure she knew he was a major slime ball, always hitting on the clerks."

"Hey, give her a little credit. She had to fight for every inch. Put herself through law school."

"No, I put myself through law school. She was a Judge Nichol's nurse. He put her through law school."

"Okay, I may have misunderstood. Maybe she put herself through nursing school. Who cares? I think you guys just got off on the wrong foot. She can be a very sensitive person. She's been trying to help me get a murder investigation opened in Mitchell."

Katherine grabbed Audrey's hands and continued to hold them as she looked with concern into her friend's eyes. "Stop and think a minute. A guy has a motor cycle accident. A motel room that two people leave in the middle of the night is robbed..."

"Nothing was really taken," Audrey put in defensively.

"Nothing of yours. You don't know what he had." Audrey glanced away, but Katherine moved her head to force eye contact again. "Then your place is hit. You probably scared them off before they could take anything. Odd coincidences? Yes. Impossible? No."

"But there are more elements than just those coincidences. Nate said Fred went to Florida to set up a drug buy. Something went wrong. If I can find out what that is, I'll have a motive."

Katherine looked at her friend and recognized an earnestness that wouldn't be tempered by logic. She sighed. "I've still got friends at the DEA. I'll make some calls…but meanwhile, think about what's important to you. You were finally getting some direction in your life. Only a year left of law school. You've got enough on your plate. Don't get side-tracked with other people's problems."

Audrey focused on her friend's words. Katherine had always known what she wanted and had gone for it. Audrey had been content to let her life follow the path of least resistance, to wait for circumstances to force her into action rather than make a decision herself.

"Except mine, of course. My problems are important and you'd damn well better be there when I need you," Katherine added needlessly.

"I'm there, babe." The instructor spotted the slackers and descended.

"If this baby shows up tomorrow, you'll wish you'd have paid attention." Audrey looked properly chastised, but Katherine remained rebellious.

"Hee, hee." Katherine curled into a fetal position and Audrey rubbed the small of her back. She marveled at the way Katherine's skin stretched around the enormous baby ball in front. How could a body do that? Travel that incredibly far from normal and ever return? It was done all the time. The distance from normal traversed and returned. It was a comfort to see this physical proof of it.

⫷⫸

"Okay, here it is." Katherine sat at her desk and stretched her arms full length to reach the keyboard over her impossibly large stomach. She had always been conscious of her beauty and Audrey wondered how she was handling this distortion of her usually petite figure and normally oval face. It was one of those subjects she wouldn't think of broaching unless her friend did first. Over the years they had developed ritual patterns of approach and avoidance of certain areas of their lives.

Audrey looked over Katherine's shoulder at the maze of numbers on the screen. "And how am I supposed to make heads or tails out of this?"

Katherine hit a couple of keys. A file opened displaying a series of numbers followed by three letters. "This is the code. The numbers correspond to the first four letters of the case name. You know, like if the name were ABCD it would be: one, two, three, four. Okay, James Bond it ain't, but it'll keep out the merely curious. If anyone needs information that I haven't already left for them, you get it, okay?" You're the only one in the world I trust."

"What about your family?"

"Maybe my mom. Certainly not my father...and the sibs are questionable."

"What about Coburn?"

"Right now he's still in the sibs category."

chapter 13

For years the Santa Monica Pier had been a wonderful mixture of grunge and magic where trashy arcades and greasy food joints ruled. It called to mind every county fair that didn't have the funds for continual cleanup. Now it's much cleaner, more refined, more Disneyesque than the carnival sleaziness that once evoked a nostalgic charm. The new amusement park was not designed to be a state of the art draw where each ride must be bigger, faster, higher. Rather it was ostensibly designed for families with younger children: a roller coaster which wouldn't dislodge a lunch, bumper cars which wouldn't dictate a visit to the chiropractor, and a Ferris wheel which sported closed carriages that an acrophobic could ride. The new pier was designed for aging boomers who wanted a place where they could relive what they recalled as their history; share it with their late-in-life-children. But the boomers' recollection of a kinder, gentler childhood didn't really exist even at the time—though their childhood was certainly easier to navigate than the mine fields children faced today--and the fantasy of Beaverville where problems were solved by two loving parents was a rarity at the time and remains the treasure of a very few. So where is the magic in rose colored hindsight history? In the expectation. People expect the pier to be more than its reality, and it becomes that if only during the pretense.

But no pretense is needed for the genuine article: The Santa Monica Carousel. A delightful piece of folk art fashioned by the Philadelphia Toboggan Company in the early nineteen twenties, it had been restored a few years back, horses and frame painted to a glossy newness which eclipsed the sense of history and buried much of the charm under, of all things, auto paint. Expedience trumped art since the bright shimmering colors could withstand the assault of vandals who would scratch their initials into the prancing figures. But even the high gloss, high tech paint couldn't dispel the history of magic which reached back through the ages to the first device which flung a man in a circle, the centrifugal force squeezing a smile from the most taciturn. Circle after circle, smile after smile.

Audrey and Carl sat on a bench outside the building watching the nearly empty carousel spin. Audrey found comfort in its predictability. She glanced at Carl and thought the same of him. Comfortable. Predictable. Fred seemed to be trying to make her suspicious of everyone, but why did he harp on Carl in particular?

"What's that look for?" Carl's question made her realize she had squinted enough to give herself a unibrow.

"Stress," she responded. "And waiting. Two things I don't do well. Frances is supposed to be at work at one and it's five after."

"Fred's sister works here?" Carl asked incredulously, indicating the carousel.

"At Dave's Organic Diner farther down." She waved a hand toward the end of the pier.

Carl glanced in that direction then turned back toward the carousel. "There's something mesmerizing about carousels. I loved this one as a kid...They still make me, I don't know, peaceful," said Carl.

"If you were any more peaceful you'd be in a coma."

"Hey, I work at it. I've studied my fellow surfers for years to get that perfect laid-back quality."

"Well, you mastered it. You're the Grand Lama of cool."

"I can't believe you grew up in Southern California and didn't learn that cool and laid-back are like oil and water...like booze and cards, like—"

"Margaritas and wiener schnitzel?" she offered.

"Exactly. They're not the same, and they don't go together. Cool takes a lot of effort to look like you're not caring if people think you're cool, while laid-back is truly not caring what people think about anything."

"You can pretend you're the grand poobah of laid-back, but I think you have more invested in what people think of you than you're willing to admit."

"Well, certainly of what some people think of me." Though he was smiling, he looked at her with an intensity that embarrassed her. She was relieved when her gaze could be naturally drawn to a child of about five, on roller-blades, who careened around the corner near them. Simultaneously, Audrey and Carl saw a small maintenance vehicle on a collision course with the boy. Both sprinted toward it shouting at the top of their lungs.

"Hey, look out!"

"Stop!"

The small truck did its best to avoid him, but the child slammed into the side panel. Audrey and Carl raced to the little boy's aid. Though more shook-up than injured, the child wailed. Carl knelt down and cradled him, speaking to him in soft reassuring tones.

"It's all right...You're okay...Where's your mom?" As Carl looked around, his face became a mask of rage. He railed to no one in particular. "Who's supposed to be watching this child?"

Audrey was shocked at the magnitude of his anger. A youngish man, also on roller-blades, skated over with an ice cream cone in each hand. Though the man's face was a picture of concern, Carl lit into him.

"Where were you? You can't leave a kid alone like that. Anything can happen. What were you thinking?" Audrey simply stood and stared. She had never seen Carl lose it before. As the father shrank from Carl's rebuke, he also positioned his son behind him as if to protect him from this frenzied lunatic. She took Carl by the hand and led him away.

"Come on, Carl. The kid's okay. "

"That just drives me crazy...parents not paying attention or not giving a shit what happens to their kids."

Audrey felt disoriented, that prelude to seasickness which hits your head before you realize that it's about to hit your stomach. Disoriented, because it was the first time she had seen Carl in a situation where he wasn't the absolute master of it. It wasn't that he had to control or to win, but he always was certain of himself. Now, he was raw, exposed, unpredictable. Then she thought of the brick. At the time, it struck her as uncharacteristic of him to have thrown that brick down the street, but she hadn't given it another thought until now. Maybe she didn't know Carl as well as she thought. Audrey couldn't have been more surprised by his over-reaction than if she had seen the carousel horses stampeding down the pier. He rambled on in a loud voice, more to some unseen audience than to her.

"Parents should have to pass a test, get a license. Nobody should be able to have a kid unless they can prove that they desperately want one and know how to take care of it."

Audrey worried about her scheme. Carl would need all his faculties when confronting the bright and feisty Frances. She was about to voice her misgivings when she spotted, in the parking lot below, the early eighties Ford Fred's mother, Margaret, had described to her on the phone.

"There they are. Are you up to this?"

Carl seemed to return from his mental sabbatical. He nodded. "Yeah."

They both watched as Frances emerged from the car and slammed the door. Wearing her security-blanket leather jacket, she mounted the stairs and walked along the pier. When the Ford pulled out of the parking lot, Audrey and Carl angled to intercept Frances. She didn't spot them until they were right next to her. When she did, she made no effort to hide her contempt, but Audrey proceeded as if they had just parted friends.

"Frances, how are you doing? Listen, I'd like you to meet a friend of mine, Dr. Rogers."

"Hi, Frances." Carl extended his hand. The teenager looked at it disdainfully, then glared at Audrey.

"Like, what are you doing? I won't go to rehab, so you drag rehab to me? You're, like, so pathetic." Audrey stepped back slightly at the onslaught. "If I need Mr. Roger's help, I'll, like, watch his TV show."

Carl moved in front of her. "Can I just talk to you a minute?" He looked toward Audrey and a tilt of his head indicated she should make herself scarce. She moved away from them but glanced back now and then. When she neared the carousel, she let the Skater's Waltz blaring from the band organ sooth her, take her back to a time when things were at once more momentous and yet somehow less weighing on her spirit. Everything new in her child's world seemed supremely important, fraught with an irrevocability which she learned to discount as an adult. Yet adult knowledge of the mutability of life holds its own set of terrors. Adolescence, which she hoped Frances would survive, was by far the most perilous because it was the confluence of the belief in ones immortality and the most anxious questioning of one's worth.

She watched the ill-matched couple from a distance: Carl in his casual yet beautifully cut sports coat, Frances in her retro-seventies baby dress with her leather jacket and jack boots. Carl's hand movements indicated appeal while Frances stood with her arms crossed in front of her, hips thrust forward. At least they were speaking. As if this thought some how jinxed the process, Frances positioned her face very close to Carl's and yelled.

"Go fuck yourself!" The girl turned on her heel and trotted away from the deflated Carl, who watched after her. Audrey joined him, put an arm around his back, and felt a welling of love for this good man who always could be counted on to pitch in regardless of the level of futility.

"I'm sorry I put you through that," said Audrey. She had the idea that she could feel, through her hand on his back, the compassion released in his deep sigh.

"It's all right. She was just one of those rare exceptions," said Carl.

⌘

Audrey felt empty. If things had gone better with Frances maybe that victory would have filled the gaping maw she imagined was visible between her solar plexus and the bikini tan line that she had cultivated before an extra five pounds chased her into a one piece swim suit. She knew people were just being kind by not staring at this cavity. She would cast sidelong glances at passersby to see if she could catch them gawking at her. So far, they'd been too cunning. Work was the answer, and she threw herself into it with a vengeance. Work and humor were usually her retreats. And where was her sense of humor, her sense of the absurd, which had helped her through some of the rough patches in her life? It was probably with her judgment, and that, she believed, was still being held captive by Miles in Canada. She wouldn't put it past him. He probably had her sense of humor and her judgment handcuffed together in his hotel closet in Calgary. So they were gone. Quit whining. Deal with it.

Since she returned from lunch she had plowed through file after file and had come up with an excellent take on one of the threads of the Sitwell case, the one Opal was so keen on winning. Audrey was ready for something to go right. She knocked lightly, then opened Opal's door. Her boss looked up from the file she had been studying, and motioned her in.

"Here are the initial pleadings. I think I've found a way to keep them from introducing the Carter depos, but I'll take them home tonight so you can have them first thing in the morning if it turns out you'll need them."

"That Carter can give 'How-to' seminars on perjury. We just can't prove it. Good job. Sit down a minute." Audrey pulled a chair closer to the desk. Her boss took off her glasses and rubbed the bridge of her nose. "I'm afraid I haven't had much luck with the police up in Mitchell. They seem convinced your friend's death was an accident." Opal frantically twirled the half-glasses by one temple until Audrey feared she would spring it.

"I know. And I guess I'm beginning to agree with them." This information made Opal pause, made her brows knit forming deep crevasses which appeared to extend the line of her nose north into her forehead. Audrey wanted to warn her about that particular expression lest the lines get any deeper on her account.

"Since your break-in, the police down here seem to have taken an interest," said Opal.

"I think that's just Carl calling in favors."

"Well, if you do come up with anything else, bring it to me and I'll try to keep it from getting stuck in the pipeline."

Audrey smiled at her boss. "Listen, thanks so much for everything you've done. I'm going to refocus my energy on doing my job here and getting Fred's sister into that rehab program, though I haven't been very successful so far."

"Yeah, well, I've told you what a long shot that is." Opal looked at her as she twisted a lock of hair behind her ear. "I hope I'm not prying, but if you believe in something strongly, why would you abandon it?"

"The problem is I'm not sure I believe it myself any more. Also, I guess I worry that I'm going to get a reputation for being a kook."

"Well, that I certainly understand. Reputation's everything and, though it would be nice if we were known only for our actions, we have to be careful about how things appear. I've tried to drill that into my children's heads."

Audrey smiled slightly to herself, remembering Katherine's reference to Opal and her "good name". "Well, it seems to have worked. You've got a couple of great kids. Isn't your daughter about to graduate law school?"

Opal threw up her hands. "She wants to quit and marry her boyfriend with only a semester left...have kids as soon as he gets his JD. I've told her she has to finish even if she doesn't want to practice right away. A woman has to have something to fall back on when people let you down. Well...you know that." Opal's look was one of concern, empathy. "It's why you're in law school, right?"

"Well, I'm not enrolled this semester..." The admission somehow embarrassed her in front of this driven woman.

"You'll go back," Opal said, more like an order than a statement. Audrey nodded, but suddenly wasn't as sure that she would. Opal put her reading glasses back on signaling the close of the conversation but added: "When this Engel family thing gets sorted out, I'll expect you to work 150% of the time, but until then I'll try not to pile it on too heavy. You've got enough to think about with the trial coming up."

Audrey saw Opal's use of Fred and Frances's family name as testament to the attention she had given to Audrey's problems. It pleased her. But that didn't keep her from reflecting that, as much as she admired her boss, she would certainly be expected to make up for any time spent on outside activities. Quid pro quo was Opal's mantra.

She worked late again, not wanting to face the wreck that was her home. On her walk to her car, escapist fantasies presented themselves in her head theater. Earlier in her life, the tapes had been a warm place to retreat. A place where the outcome was always perfect whether the fantasy was about sailing around the world or about restoring her mother to her former vivacious self. She had always realized that they were just that. Fantasies. She realized too, that, though they had been a source of enjoyment, they had nearly ceased when she had become caught up in work, law school, and her ill-advised remarriage. She had indulged in them more often when she had been a courier. More mental free time? Does it follow that you're more mentally healthy if you don't have the time to be crazy? Workaholism as a cure for the borderline personality?

But the tapes had become less enjoyable and more obsessive as with the revenge fantasies about Miles. And those tapes were worlds apart from her real-time interaction with Fred. She didn't need to be told by anyone that this went beyond "normal". But that word was so fluid in regard to anything human. To Audrey, mental health was a continuum. Most people stayed somewhere in the middle, but anyone could gravitate to one side or the other depending on prevailing life circumstances or chemistry. Her mother had whizzed back and forth along this continuum like an icon in a video game. Audrey felt that she herself traversed the middle ground for the most part, but now and then, ventured toward the extremes. She remembered that if you think you're going nuts, you probably aren't because you have the capacity to question. She questioned that.

<hr>

Audrey slowly mounted the stairs of her front porch, enervated by the thought of the task ahead of her. As she stared at the front door, she recalled the chaos within: scattered pieces of Buddhas sprinkled on spine-broken books. Just reuniting her tapes and CDs with their covers would take an hour. Heaving a sigh, she entered the house and switched on the light. Her eyes widened in disbelief. The room had been perfectly cleaned and organized. She threw her things on the couch and moved to the bedroom. The bed was beautifully made with a dust ruffle and her dozen pillows. The boxes were gone.

Only the plywood floor remained unfinished. She opened a closet and found all her clothes hung in perfect order, just where she would have put them. Fred walked through the door behind her, put his arms around her. She wrapped her arms over his.

"You can move things."

"I can do anything you need me to do." Could she have done all this last night or this morning and blocked it? She didn't think so but the other explanations were too complex to consider. She reached up and stroked his face, then lightly ran her finger along the still un-healed cut above his eye.

"With all the broken bones and gashes you got on your flight down that cliff, why do you only have this cut?"

Fred held her hand to the cut. "It's a sign that we're soul-mates, just like the one you had."

"I never had one."

"Hmm."

"Why doesn't it heal?"

"It will." As he said it she almost heard the added word: "un-fortunately". A sad look crossed his face. He turned her head to kiss him. They continued to kiss as his hands explored her body. She kissed him more hungrily as he removed her clothes. She tore at his garments and with each article thrown, they took a step closer to the bed. He held her head in both his hands lacing his fingers through her hair as he lowered her to the pillow.

This time, their lovemaking was sweet, passionate and thought-ful. It was everything she had longed for from Miles, the unques-tioned devotion, the caring conveyed by the tender touch, the unity of two bodies that had scaled the heights together. She had only been this sexually high once before, so it shocked her when they climaxed together and she burst into tears. Fred held her as she sobbed on his chest.

"Come on, I know I wasn't that bad."

She shook her head. "It's not that."

He held her away from him slightly and ran the back of his hand down her cheek, then her arm, as he spoke. "It's that I'm perfect for you. You're the only one who can see me...the only one who can touch me. More importantly for your particular wounds, I can't touch any-one else. Beats the hell out of your marriage doesn't it?"

She turned away from him and burrowed under the covers.

"Hey we've got to talk about him sometime. You act like he doesn't exist." He uncovered her head and stroked her hair. "Be care-ful, he'll come back to haunt you."

She pulled a pillow over her head, but couldn't keep Miles from invading her thoughts. She could handle thinking about why she hat-ed him. The feeling was prickly and invigorating, the hot feeling of dry ice, yet nurturing in some perverse way. What she couldn't stand was remembering why she loved him.

At the height of their passion, just before they were married the first time, they had gone camping north of Santa Barbara. A small tent and a Coleman stove completed paradise for Audrey on the windy stretch of campsites just off the beach. Miles wanted to camp in the wilds farther up the coast, but Audrey liked to rough it with the hot showers and modern plumbing that the campground afford-ed. She put in a request for a B&B so there would be room to negoti-ate on the campground. The first night they lay in their sleeping bag outside the tent, under the dome of stars that sank into black ocean. Audrey finally got the courage to ask the question that seemed too intimate even after having known each other for three years.

"Why do you love surfing so much?"

"Because of the waves."

Audrey released an exasperated breath.

"I mean it literally," he said. "It's because waves are the one con-stant thing in the world."

"But they're not. They change, grow, diminish. How many times have I heard you bitch about the ocean being flat for days. They're anything but constant."

"They're constant. They're there even when it's flat. They're waiting. Waiting for the moon or a storm to rouse them. Waiting for me to challenge them. That's why the ocean will always have it all over people."

"How's that?"

"It's there. It can't leave."

"I won't leave. Unless you want me to."

"Sure you will. Whether I want you to or not." But his kiss said otherwise. And their love making filled her with the sense that they would always be together. Both being blond with blue eyes, they would have a couple of toe-headed kids who would be bright and athletic. They could take them camping. She would show him that he could trust her. He had been hurt by his father's abrupt departure, but she could fix him.

Early in their relationship, she had felt as exclusive as a Jovian moon. There were always others in his orbit. When he chose her--all right, when he chose to marry, rather than to lose her--she thought she would feel the weight of the world lift from her with the prospect of her dream future. Instead, she came to understand that life with Miles was ephemeral; It obtained a quality of theater and the foundation of their relationship turned out to be a mere set, buildingless store fronts of her own device.

⇥⇤

A murky dawn found Audrey snoring lightly as she spooned with Fred. The phone rang. Audrey grabbed for it groggily and pulled it under the blanket that covered her ear.

"Hello?" Fred leaned over and pulled the receiver away from her head slightly so that he could hear. The voice on the other end sounded like it had been electronically altered.

"We've got the girl. You know the drill. Give us the brother's disc. You've got forty-eight hours or she's dead. We'll call at four a.m. Saturday and don't even think about police. We'll know."

Then sounding at some distance, Frances' unmistakable voice. "Audrey! Help me!"

"Frances? Frances!" Audrey screamed into the phone. But a click on the other end halted further pleading.

chapter 14

AUDREY'S M.O. was to save people, primarily her mother and Miles, but also sundry strangers who likely weren't aware of her gift of vigilance on their behalf. She was the rescuer of fallen rollerbladers, the flinger of newspapers when two in a driveway revealed an absent family, the sneaker of bills into a shoe clutched by a sleeping homeless woman. Saving was her M.O. and the fact that she had yet to succeed on other than the smallest scale, didn't register a blip on her radar. She would save Frances.

So, down to business. What kind of disc was it and what was on it? Was it the "insurance" Fred had talked about for Frances? Where was the disc now and where could she even begin to look? She remembered the bubble pack Fred had in his hand when he came to the office the day before he left for Mitchell. She was sure he must have mailed it somewhere, since whoever was looking for it, found it neither up North nor when they trashed her place. But where and to whom would he have mailed it?

"I say we start with the mother," said Fred as he handed Audrey a cup of coffee in the bathroom.

"You mean your mother?" Audrey hastily threw her clothes on.

"Whatever. We'll find out if they called her, too, and we can search her house for the disc," said the apparition.

"How're we supposed to do that? 'Hi, we dropped by for tea and to inspect every inch of your property.'"

"You'll manage. Let's get over there."

"After I see Katherine."

"You heard what they said. Keep your mouth shut."

"I need her help," said Audrey with more than a soupcon of cayenne in her tone.

"We don't need any help."

"This isn't up for a vote."

As they drove up to Katherine's house, Audrey was more convinced than ever that she needed her friend to know about everything. Needed her counsel, her support. She needed her best friend to know about everything except Fred.

He was. She no longer questioned his existence. She made no judgment about what he was. She, again, speculated that he might actually be from some source other than her head, but it didn't really matter what that source was. Spiritual energy? Some cosmic projection? A chimera, part nightmare, part savior? An angel? And if he were one of these, perhaps she wasn't as near the brink as she had imagined. A further thought suggested that perhaps all people who believe in anything other than the tangible world could be considered nuts. She shoved these speculations into the attic of her cluttered mind because they really didn't matter. He just was.

Audrey and Fred approached the house together, but before she rang the doorbell, she stopped and put a hand on his shoulder.

"Please don't say anything when I'm talking to other people. It's too distracting."

"Hey, it's hard to keep my mouth shut when you're missing something...or actively ignoring it," said Fred.

"Yeah, well, do your spectral best."

Coburn Dale, fifty, handsome in an angular way, answered the door dressed in his Ralph Lauren bathrobe and slippers. His eyes were bright, animated, not a trace of sleep in them despite the early hour.

"Audrey, come on in." She hugged him, then followed him into the living room.

"Morning Coburn, sorry to come by so early."

"It's cool. I've got a tee off time at seven." He headed down the hall toward the bedrooms, then stopped, turned. "Want some coffee?"

"No thanks." As he disappeared through a door, Fred inspected the eclectic art pieces.

"Does she know he's snorting again?" asked Fred as Audrey folded herself into a comfortable overstuffed chair.

"Right now I'll be happy if he's only doing it, not dealing it." Audrey responded automatically, though under her breath.

Katherine waddled into the room wearing a long cotton nightgown, holding the small of her back with one hand. "What'd you say?" asked Katherine. Ignoring the question, Audrey put a finger to her lips and motioned her friend forward to sit in the other oversized chair, which Katherine did with no little difficulty.

"Nobody can know, not even Coburn."

"He's already on the phone. Can't hear a thing. What is it?"

"Promise? I'm not even telling Carl."

"I promise," Katherine said with a note of fatigue in her voice.

"Frances has been kidnapped." Katherine looked at Audrey blankly.

"How do you know?"

Fred couldn't keep his mouth shut as advised. "Oh, she believes you."

Audrey looked at him with disapproval, a look not lost on Katherine. "You don't believe me?"

"It's not that—" Katherine started, but Audrey jumped in.

"Somebody called me an hour ago and said if I didn't get them Fred's disc in forty-eight hours, they'd kill her."

"Disc? What disc?"

"I don't know! Except I think he might have mailed it somewhere."

"Why'd they call you? Why not his mother?"

"Who knows? Maybe they contacted her too. I'm going over there next. Listen, did you turn up anything on that Florida connection?"

"Haven't heard back yet, but one way or the other, you've got to go to the cops."

"They'll kill her if I do."

Katherine looked down momentarily. "This just all seems too fantastic."

Fred headed for the door, again Audrey's eyes followed. Katherine noticed Audrey's odd head and eye movement. "She thinks you're nuts. We're out of here," Fred said.

"Yeah, well, it does sound fantastic, doesn't it?" Disappointment weighed on Audrey. She had been certain Katherine would accept everything she said without question. Katherine struggled forward in her chair.

"I didn't mean it like that. Tell me what I can do to help."

But the disappointment in her friend made Audrey loath to press the issue. "Just follow up on that DEA business if you can... and don't try to get out of that chair until your muscles are properly warmed up." Audrey forced a smile, kissed Katherine on the forehead and strode to the door, fleeing the unvoiced questions hanging between them.

It was only the second time in their friendship that Audrey felt let down by Katherine, felt that her best friend hadn't been there for her one hundred percent.

The first time had been when Audrey had wanted to talk about her father. She had talked to her mother's psychiatrist about his death endlessly, but she never shared it. Audrey, who had such an abhorrence of talking about deep emotional issues, ached to talk to her best friend about it. They had discussed everything in their lives: Katherine's family, boyfriends, hopes and dreams. But when it came to her father...

What had caused his stroke? Besides the patchwork of platelets and plaque that formed the obstruction in his brain, was there a certain stress level that became the catalyst for that cohesion? Was the thought of having to monitor the movements of yet another human being finally too much for him? Had the burden of his wife and, then, of his rebellious, motorcycle-riding daughter worn him down until just the slightest irritation triggered a deadly chain reaction?

Audrey wanted to talk to Katherine about these speculations, but she realized that the disintegration of her family had been as hard on Katherine as it had been on her. In the end it came down to the fact that neither could stand to witness the other's pain.

⧊

Having grown up on the margins of the valley, Audrey had sworn never to live in the area again. When she looked back on her days at Hoover High, she thought it was quite a nice school, quite a nice town, for that matter, nice people. All very nice. She never wanted to live there again. So it was with the slightest touch of nausea that she drove down a perfectly respectable, perfectly average, perfectly middle-class street in North Hollywood. Her Glendale home on Kenneth Road had been slightly more upscale, but it had exuded the same closed-in feeling that she was experiencing driving down Beck Avenue where Fred grew up. Though the houses sat one atop the next, they were all well cared for, with particular attention to the lawns and gardens.

Audrey and Fred mounted the stairs of the front porch and she pressed the button which produced the muffled sound of church bells chiming.

He looked around curiously. "So this is where I lived." Margaret Engel appeared at the side of the house, shading her eyes with her hand in an attempt to identify her visitors.

"May I help you?"

"Hi, Mrs. Engel. It's Audrey James."

"Oh, hello dear. I was just doing some gardening...It helps calm the nerves."

Audrey joined her, shadowed by Fred. "I don't mean to interrupt, but may I ask you a couple of questions while you're working?"

"Of course."

As they rounded the side of the house, Audrey was astounded by the English country garden that lay just inside the fence. Roses abounded as well as blowsy, spaghetti-thin daisies, bowing in floral obeisance to the slightest breeze. Here, in what Audrey had charac-

- 161 -

terized as a stultifyingly ordinary place, Margaret had created the sublime. The sad woman pruned as Audrey and Fred admired the lush retreat.

"I'm afraid I wasn't very successful with Frances the other day," said Audrey. "I was wondering if she might be around."

Margaret didn't look up from her work. "She's run off again. That's part of the reason I've been out here since sunrise. That and Frederick, ya know."

"You haven't heard from her?"

Margaret shook her head. "Oh, it's happened before, but mostly when her father was alive, and she'd done something wrong and didn't want to get a lickin'. She's at one of her friends. She'll be back in a few days. She always comes back."

"I'm sure you're right." Margaret attempted a smile at Audrey's assurance, but the uplifted corners of her mouth couldn't mask the pain radiating from her eyes. She returned to her roses, her refuge.

Fred sauntered over to Audrey. "Get into my old room."

Audrey briefly cupped a dahlia in her hand, her mother's favorite. She contemplated the magenta glow that lit her palms as she cradled that organic explosion of color. "Do you mind if I look in Fred's room? He borrowed a computer disc from me and I thought maybe he might have left it here."

Fred patted her on the back. "Good thinking," said the illusion. She tried not to look at him, but couldn't help turning her head slightly before meeting Margaret's gaze again.

"Of course, dear. Though I don't know what he would've done with it. They took his machine after all the trouble."

"Trouble?"

"Oh, I never understood it all, but the police said he'd somehow gotten into somebody else's computer over the phone lines. Can you imagine?"

Margaret led them through the back door and down some stairs. When she opened the door to his room, she stopped abruptly. "That girl! What on earth was she thinking? Look at this mess."

Almost a separate apartment, Fred's room easily could have been tossed by someone without Margaret's knowledge. The destruction appeared less menacing here; the search seemed to have been perfunctory. His Eric Clapton posters of various vintages and magazine cutouts of Harleys had been ripped away from the walls, but left dangling by one or two corners. His bed was torn apart and the small desk with a dated monitor and keyboard had all the drawers pulled out.

"You can bet she was looking for something to sell," said Margaret.

"Well, it might not have been Frances. Sometimes when someone dies, crooks will hit the house during the funeral. Have you been down here since then?"

"No, 'spose I haven't."

"So, Fred didn't have a computer here?" asked Audrey.

"Well, the police left these things." Margaret indicated the monitor and keyboard. "Only took the square gizmo." A sad expression played on Margaret's face as she ran her hand along the top of the monitor. "He'd spend hours down here. Nothing but trouble came of it, though. One time he changed Frances's grade in the school computer so her father wouldn't give her a lickin'." Margaret shook her head at the memory. "I had to talk to the principal myself so's he wouldn't find out. They both would've got it good."

"Yeah, I got the sense that Fred felt protective of Frances," said Audrey.

"Oh, yes. He loved his sister. He'd always be stickin' up for her. When he was here."

Audrey watched Fred inspect the room; He seemed actively to observe everything as one would displays in a museum. A wave of Audrey's hand indicated the posters. "Looks like he was fond of motorcycles and rock music."

A light blazed behind Margaret's previously resigned-looking eyes. "You know that rock music's the reason they got into drugs." Audrey and Fred looked knowingly at each other.

"Yeah, that rock music'll give you a lickin' every time," Fred said. Audrey felt again the ambiguity that colored her feelings about Margaret. The woman clearly wanted the best for her children, loved them, yet let them take "lickin's" from their father. Was it out of her own fear of her husband or the belief that extreme discipline was simply part of child rearing?

"Sometimes it's a combination of things," Audrey offered Margaret in response to her assertion. Margaret's shrug allowed for their difference of opinion as she moved toward the door.

"If you need anything else—"

"Has Fred received any mail here in the last month?"

"Not as I can say." Margaret seemed to search her memory. "Some high school reunion flyers and the like."

"No packages?" Margaret shook her head. "Did you know any of Fred's friends?"

"Just his school friends, Nate and Street."

"Street? Is that his real name?"

"Street McClean." Margaret nodded. "A family name if I recall. A little wild for a while in high school, but I guess he's settled down now. Fred said he got real rich, I forget what line of work…Anyways, he's got himself a construction business now."

"Don't you mean Nate?" asked Audrey.

"Well, both. I'm sure he said they're in business together. Partners, you know. I always hoped Fred would maybe go in with them instead of drifting around."

"Do you think either Nate or Street were into drugs?"

"To tell the truth, I just don't know anymore. Seems like they're everywhere, doesn't it? Poisoning our children." A look formed on Margaret's face, which defined depression. Audrey thought of her own mother's passive face and wondered if Margaret would like to change places with her emotionally anesthetized mother. Is feeling worth that pain?

"Thanks for your help. We'll be out in a minute." Audrey noticed the older woman's fatigued gait as she shuffled out. Margaret hadn't even noticed Audrey's use of the plural pronoun. Audrey looked around the unkempt room and began what she projected would be a futile search. "Not much chance of finding anything here if they've already gone over the place. At least we know Street's full name and the fact that Nate lied to us about him. But I don't know how we'll find him if Nate won't help.

"Get the corporate records for Nate's company, "Artful Construction", then see if that's the company Margaret was talking about." Fred picked up a pair of leather motorcycle riding pants and held them up. "I had interesting taste, didn't I?"

Audrey dismissed the comment with a look. "I can do a title search on the duplex next door. Maybe we'll come up with Terry's last name."

"Carl knows more than he's telling you."

"What's that supposed to mean?"

"Just what I said."

"He's my friend. If he had any information, he'd share it." Would he? Or would he hold back if he found something that he thought would endanger her? "Okay, I'll pump him. I'll invite him for a picnic at the house, give him a couple of beers, and take advantage of him." Fred shot her a reproving leer. "Not that away. I'll take advantage of his loose lips—". Now Fred added a raised eyebrow. "Oh, never mind," said Audrey.

"Run a credit check on those bank account numbers you got out of his glove compartment," added the spirit.

"What for?"

"For information. Lots of things can be learned from credit histories."

She watched as Fred looked around his old room. "So, does seeing your mom give you any, you know, pangs?"

Fred smiled and put his arm around her. "You still don't get this. I have more connection to your mom than to mine."

"That's not unusual. Everybody liked my mom." Audrey thought of her fragile yet stunning mother and immediately felt guilty for not having visited her for so long. Was she worried that she might find her mother perfectly recovered having passed the torch of psychosis to her daughter?

<hr>

During her last visit with her mother, Audrey had fancied that she, herself, should have been put in restraints. Her level of frustration had been so great that she imagined doing something wild like running down the hall and setting free the crazies; inciting her own

Cuckoo's Nest rebellion. She fantasized about doing anything that might evoke a response from the summer squash that masqueraded as her mother. Dressed in an institutional looking bathrobe, spittle clinging to the corner of her mouth, her mother sat on the edge of her bed staring at the ever-present cribbage board. Audrey picked up the board and placed it on a nearby table, then sat in the precise spot where it had rested on the bed, hoping her mother would look at her, would make, if not eye contact, at least eye-body contact, hoping that she would do anything at all, anything that would indicate to Audrey that there was still someone in there, still some vestige of the woman she had been in awe of, had been ashamed of, had loved fiercely. She wondered fleetingly whether experiencing this level of frustration could actually cause one to go off the deep end. She swore that she would never return to this institution of the damned. Announced to herself that sitting with a person who didn't know her from a burrito was a futile if not masochistic effort and therefore unnecessary at the very least and, more likely, destructive.

chapter 15

THE DECEASED FRED sat in the "guest" chair opposite Audrey and rested his feet on her desk. Her new desk. Her newly cluttered desk, piled as high in her little ante-chamber office as it had been in the bullpen. Fred clasped his hands behind his head in a pose meant to convey his ennui. Audrey was listening to a synthesized version of Sting's "Englishman In New York" while waiting to speak to a bank manager.

"Tell them you're a yacht dealer and that you don't want to embarrass your client, but you need to know how much is in the accounts and—"

"I will not. I feel bad enough that I ripped the numbers out of his glove compartment," snapped Audrey.

"How'll you get the information?"

Audrey thought a moment. "I don't know...Maybe I'll say he's a prospective tenant."

"If you're going to lie, why do it badly? He'll just tell you that Mr. Rogers can afford etc, etc." A deep female voice came on the line.

"I'm Ms. Packard, may I help you?"

Audrey looked away from the reclining spirit. "Yes, I'm with Fairweather Yachts and a Mr...let's see...Carl Rogers...is considering financing an eighty-six footer with us. He gave us the number of two accounts and said we could verify the amount in them with you. Could you possibly help me with this?"

"I'll need the account numbers and the figures Mr. Rogers gave you."

"Well the account numbers are zero-six-eight-zero-one-three-six-two and five-two-triple-seven-four-one-three. I'm still looking for the amounts. Listen, all I need to know is whether they both belong to him and if at least one averages a balance of over ten-thousand."

"His own checking doesn't keep anywhere near that amount, but his SandCastle Trust account certainly would meet your criteria."

"Could you possibly give me the exact figures?"

"I'm afraid not."

"Well, Ms. Packard, you've been most kind. I'll call if I need any further verification."

"Please do."

Audrey hung up the phone and looked at Fred. "Over ten thousand dollars in one of those accounts that she called SandCastle Trust."

"Maybe that's the account where he keeps his blackmail money."

"Only if he's blackmailing himself. The deposit slip was a transfer from his checking into the SandCastle account. It's probably just a tax thing."

"Or a cover-up thing," said the persistent figment.

Audrey entered Opal's office and placed a stack of papers on her desk. Opal nodded an absent-minded acknowledgement, but didn't look up from her laptop's screen.

"Opal, during my lunch hour, could I possibly use your priority code to get into Sacramento's corporate records?"

"For Sitwell?"

"No. It's, um, personal." Audrey felt as if she were asking if she could pilfer Post-it notes or paper clips.

"Something to do with your dead friend?"

Audrey managed a guilty nod. "But I assure you that I'm well ahead on my Sitwell work and—"

"You're preaching to the choir. I'm a firm believer in following your hunches. Of course you can use it. Here's my password. I know you won't abuse it." She scribbled the word "judgment" bracketed by capital X's on a piece of paper then handed it to Audrey. "In fact, go ahead and use my computer. It's a good deal faster than yours."

"Thank you." Audrey could barely frame the words she was so grateful. "You seem to be the only one who doesn't think I'm tilting at windmills."

"I don't know whether you are or not. I just know it's important to put your mind to rest about it. Do whatever you need to. I know you'll get your work done. That's why I chose you." Opal stood, picked up her purse and started for the door. "I'm going to Hal's. Want anything?"

"No, thanks. I just had a sandwich at my desk."

"I'll be back in an hour or so."

"Thanks." Audrey sat down in front of Opal's sizable monitor. The computer was more than twice as fast as Audrey's and could access the most arcane information in a matter of seconds with the click of a mouse or a couple of key strokes. On a shelf behind her desk, hard drives, linked one to the next, contained the entire Penal Code of California.

She logged on to the central repository in Sacramento and began a name search for Artful Construction. It was indeed a California corporation that dated back to 1986 when Nate first filed his Articles of Incorporation. Nate was both president and treasurer. Skitch Bower was vice-president and secretary. Currently, they jointly owned forty-five percent of the stock. The other fifty-five percent was owned by another corporation called Roadworks. When Audrey tried to find out who the principals of Roadworks were, she became entangled in a maze of partnerships and other corporations. She jotted down the names of the officers of each, but didn't recognize any of them. Nate's company barely broke even for five years, but then he showed a huge leap in profits without a commensurate jump in construction jobs. The only difference from the previous years was the sale of a portion of the company to Roadworks which took the lion's share of the paper profits for the succeeding years. If what Fred told Margaret was true, regardless of the other names or partnerships, Street McClean was Roadworks.

The title search of the property next door to hers wasn't as tedious as it used to be in the days before computer access, but Audrey still had to get a link into the county records bank, then find the owner of record. Easy enough, but she found that she was running up against the same problem she had experienced with Artful Construction. The owner of record wasn't a woman named Terry something, but rather a limited partnership called "Failsafe". After more searching, this time back into the state records, she found that the limited partnership, Failsafe, was comprised of one limited partner and one general partner. This time something looked more familiar. "Roadworks" was the limited partner and the general partner was a man named Ernest Block, her real estate agent.

Fred tried to keep the gloating note from his voice: "Didn't your friend, Katherine, recommend him? Without responding, Audrey picked up the phone.

"Hi, Doll, how're you doing?"

"Worrying myself nauseous about you," said Katherine. "How are you doing?"

"I'm good, don't worry. Listen, off the subject, but, how'd we find Ernest, the real estate guy?"

"Some friend of Coburn's recommended him, why?"

"Somebody was asking about an agent, no big deal."

"Audrey, I think you should go to the police."

"Can't. Not yet."

Audrey strode into the Sands of Time real estate office; a single large room with twenty-foot ceilings supported by five oddly angled walls, two of which were glass. Huge plants sectioned off the six comfortable areas and disguised the natural fiber backed partitions that gave each office some measure of privacy.

In the spacious cubicle, identified by large pewter letters as belonging to Ernest Block, Audrey presented herself, arms crossed in front of her. The young man looked up from his absorbing phone conversation and covered the receiver with his palm.

"Do you have a quick question? This is a really important call."

"Real quick. How deep into Roadworks illegal activities are you?"

"I'll call you back." Ernest couldn't get the phone down fast enough. "I'll tell you right up front. You're under the wrong impression here, but I think we'd better get this cleared up in a hurry. I'm not involved in anything illegal."

"How do you know Coburn Dale?"

"We, uh, have some friends in common. I've done him some favors; he's done me some."

"And did you trade him some white stuff for my referral?" asked Audrey with sarcasm laced sweetness.

"Listen, I don't know what you're talking about."

"I'm talking about your company, Failsafe, and in particular your limited partner, Roadworks."

"I have nothing to do with Roadworks. I just file the papers and get a couple of grand a year for my troubles."

"But as the general partner you assume the liability."

"That's why they chose me. I'm not worth anything. If something goes wrong with the company, I just file for bankruptcy."

"So, technically, you are Failsafe."

"No. No, not really."

"And Failsafe is essentially a sham partnership fronting for Roadworks, a money laundering corporation." Audrey stated rather than questioned. Ernest cringed.

"Ask him what Roadworks ostensibly does." Fred appeared next to a potted palm.

Audrey's jaw clenched in irritation. "And what above the board business is Roadworks engaged in?"

"Oh, I don't know anything about—"

Audrey shot out of her chair. "I think I'll find someone more interested in getting to the bottom of this...like my boss, the D.A."

"Hey, I'm trying to help here. I don't know a lot, just that they bid on roads, public works, anything where there isn't a municipal maintenance crew."

"I happen to know that's not the only business Roadworks is involved in."

"That's all I know about," said Ernest, eyes darting around the room.

"You keep the books?"

"Not for Roadworks, just for Failsafe. All I do is take care of the stuff that has to be done for the duplex next door to you. You know, pay the mortgage, insurance..."

"Where do you get the money?"

"Terry gives me cash. I deposit it into the company account."

"Don't forget Terry's last name," Fred prompted. Audrey shot him a dirty look, then turned back to Ernest.

"My currently absent neighbor, Terry?"

"Yeah."

"What's her last name?"

Ernest paused a moment before saying: "McClean."

Audrey nodded thoughtfully, though she was inwardly excited about the connection to the nebulous figure of Street McLean. "How much a month does she give you?" Ernest had to think a minute and Audrey realized it wasn't because he didn't know the amount.

Finally he responded in a low mumble. "Twenty grand."

"Twenty grand? I know mortgage and insurance can't be a quarter of that. What happens to the rest of the money?"

"I transfer it into a Roadworks account."

"Where's Street McClean right now?" shot Audrey as she concentrated on his eyes. Ernest did a very bad job of trying to look like he was searching his limited memory bank.

"I swear. I don't know where he is. I only deal with Terry."

☙❧

Audrey marched across the parking lot to her Jeep. Fred caught up with her. "So Terry's Street's wife or sister or cousin or something."

"Or something, though I think I'll rule out his mother. Old Ernest obviously knew more about Street, but was either too scared of him or not scared enough of me to cough it up." Audrey's words were clipped. She outpaced the shadowing figment.

"So the cash from Terry gets—"

"Laundered," Audrey cut off the dead man. "With all their corporate screens, Roadworks has to be a company set up to clean drug cash. Nate's Artful Construction most likely does the same thing since we know Roadworks is his partner, too."

Audrey got into the car and backed out of the parking space. She noticed that ahead of her, three cars waited to enter the busy main street. She put the Jeep in four-wheel drive, drove up over the cement block in front of her then up on to a grass berm which separated the lot from the one next door. With studied nonchalance, she drove out the adjacent lot and onto a side street.

"Good work. Bend those rules."

Audrey didn't respond. She wasn't sure why she was so irritated with Fred, but it had been building within her. Finally she let it out. "Why would you have to prompt me to ask what kind of a company it was. That was going to be the next thing out of my mouth. It's annoying."

"Sorry, thought I was helping out."

"Well, you weren't. You were just...annoying."

"So you said."

"If I start to walk out a door and I haven't covered something, you can prompt me, but otherwise, lay off. You got that?"

"Got it. You blow it. I prompt. Enough said."

She shot him what should've been a withering look, then realized that ephemera were probably less disturbed than most by looks that would ordinarily kill.

Right now, Nate Bower was up there with okra on Audrey's list of things that did not please her. She had called his house a number of times over the past week and left her home number but the messages were never returned. Now she called the number for Artful Construction and got a recording that referred her to a pager, which she then called and keyed in her office number. In about five minutes, she received a call back from a leery Nate.

"Yeah, this is Nate Bower. You page me?"

"Hi, Nate, it's Audrey James."

"Yeah? How you doing?" His greeting was forced.

"Not great, Nate. You're a hard guy to reach."

"Yeah, well, I've been real busy—"

"Can we cut the crap, Nate?" She took his silence as assent. "Why didn't you tell us that you'd talked to the detective up there about closing Fred's case?"

"I, uh, figured you needed to find out for yourself, you know, not take my word for it."

"Well, that's logical since you're such an inveterate liar. I know it's been a while, but I want you to stretch your truth muscles here. I'm looking for a disc that Fred might have mailed to you or to somebody you might know."

"I swear to God, I don't have it."

"But you know what I'm talking about." Silence from the North. "What kind of a disc is it?"

"A disc. You know, a computer disc." Nate sounded both desperate and frustrated.

"What's on it?"

"I, uh, I don't know."

"You're lying and doing it badly. You'd think with all your practice you'd be better at it." More silence. "Who else would he have trusted?"

"You. That's the short list of who Fred trusted in the end." The information stalled Audrey's momentum. It depressed her in a way that was usually reserved for the misfortunes of friends or family. She forced herself back on track.

"Who owns your partner in Artful Construction, Roadworks?" Now the silence was of the active variety, like after someone's stomach growls in an elevator. "Besides Street McClean, that is," Audrey added.

"Look, Audrey, I'm warning you as a friend. Don't get mixed up in this."

"Who's Terry McClean to Street?"

"His sister. Listen, don't ask about him. Don't look for him. Just stop."

"Why?"

"'Cause he's your worst nightmare. Keep away from anything that has anything to do with Street McClean."

"He's made that impossible."

Audrey finished the last of the documents for the Sitwell trial which would begin the following day. Opal encouraged her to do some of the reading at home, which she took as license to leave shortly after the lunch hour that she had worked through. Making a picnic for Carl now seemed frivolous. If he didn't have any concrete information for her, it wouldn't be worth her time. She was beginning to feel that weighed down feeling of incipient depression. No time for one, she thought. Her mental state had been clearer, less fragmented as she had focused on the Frances problem. She knew she had to lower her head and plow through, stopping for anything could mean stopping period.

On her way home, Audrey dropped by the Wednesday farmer's market which always lifted her spirits, probably because of her love affair with food. Any food. It didn't have to be chocolate, although that helped. The outdoor produce market sprang to life at the intersection of Second and Arizona and spread for a block or so in each direction. It reminded her of countless street markets in countless cities she had visited around the world. When she thought of how she missed her globe trotting, she was mollified by the fact that much of the world was coming to her. On one corner she could hear Japanese, Spanish, French, Farsi, and sundry eastern European languages spoken among the shoppers, all of whom took buying vegetables very seriously. Fresh out of the ground, off the tree, no wax, organic; eggs gathered before dawn, flowers picked near sunrise, and fish—Fresh From The Sea This Morning. The hand painted signs lent an air of authenticity to the earthiness that characterized the market. Not for us, the hermetically sealed, fresh frozen, canned, boxed, bagged, all for the convenience of the over worked and under enjoyed major segment of the population of modern American cities. It was important to Audrey, the closeness to the source: one hand picked it, one sold it, she cooked it. Not picked hard so as to weather the journey, no hours in a refrigerator truck, no precise pyramids in the supermarket, no prepackaged quantity. Two hands, sometimes one, then into the pot. She ached for the children who, due to the necessity of working moms, knew only ready made, microwave food. Her mom had purchased the entire Time/Life series of cook books from around the world and had faithfully circumnavigated the globe through food. Often she would pull together a costume that resembled the picture in the encyclopedia of the native garb worn in the country where the food had originated. Her father would laugh and promise that one day the three of them would visit every place her mother had cooked, but they never did.

⌧

Back at her house, she peeled and deveined fresh shrimp. The physical intricacies of this task fostered thought. She mulled the growing estrangement from Carl that she felt as a result of Fred's suspicions. She also experienced an uneasy feeling tied to fixing a meal for him. In the past it had always been the three of them at the dinner table. Miles and Carl would have a beer and re-shred old waves while she would marvel at the way the same waves grew with each re-telling. She smiled now at the memory. Realizing she had been dwelling on an image of Miles, she frowned.

Audrey carried an elaborate picnic basket and a small cooler out to the recently finished patio, a ten by ten section of two-foot, prefab bamboo squares. In what remained of her small yard, an iridescent green fuzz promised a lush lawn. Tiny would-be rose bushes lined the fence where they could soak up the most sun. In the corner stood a gift from Katherine: a multi-citrus tree which had grafts from an orange on one bough, a lime on the next, lemon and tangelo on the final two main branches. A tree with multiple personalities. The perfect gift for the possibly deranged.

She set the redwood table with place mats, silver and napkins, all the while making a concerted effort to supplant the contemplation of her sanity with musing about all the new pieces of the puzzle she had discovered.

"Anybody home?" As the top of Carl's head appeared above her freshly painted fence, Audrey's knitted brows un-knit themselves and a Pavlovian smile forced its way to her lips. Seeing Carl could do that. She opened the gate and hugged him as he entered. He held her slightly longer than the usual friendly hug, then released her and looked around, taking in all the new improvements.

"Very nice. You're a handy one, aren't you?"

"Very handy indeed," she replied.

"Have you finished the inside?"

"All except the hardwood floors. I may need help there."

"I'll be happy to lend a hand."

Audrey looked at him skeptically. "I didn't think you were handy."

"Not in the least handy…but I've got a lot of heart."

"True, you are hearty. How about a beer?" She led him toward the inviting table.

"My drug of choice."

"Nothing harder?" He raised an eyebrow and began a response, but Audrey cut him off. "Sticking to the subject of drugs."

"Not my cup of tea––sixties euphemism intended."

"I always thought it odd that with all of Miles' indulgences that he never got caught up in drugs."

"We got busted in high school. Pretty much stuck to drinking after that." He smiled at her. "Figured I was already close enough to the edge anyway."

Audrey immediately flashed back to the incidence of his rage at the father who hadn't been watching his child closely enough at the pier. Carl, uncomfortable with the admission, looked toward the roses and saw that the root bulb of one of the bushes was partially buried in loam. He bent and spread the dirt away from it with his hands as he spoke with nervous haste.   "So, why are you bribing me with food? You must want something badly."

"Cynic. Why do I have to want something? Can't old friends just enjoy a meal together?" She rummaged through the cooler while he clapped his hands together to rid them of the dirt.

"Of course they can. So, what do you want?"

"Well, I wouldn't mind knowing what the police down here have come up with."

"Hey, if I'm going to lie down, at least pay me. Where's that beer?" She pulled out a frosty Corona, opened the cap and handed it to him.

"I can ask somebody else. I have friends in the department, too."

"I'd be horribly hurt if you used someone else." He took a long pull on the beer before speaking. "It seems your boy, Fred, got into a local dealer's computer, copied most of the files to a disc, then crashed the hard drive."

"Crashed? Like, can't retrieve the data'?"

"Crashed as in 'bashed with a sledgehammer'."

"When'd you find this out?" She didn't bother to conceal her irritation.

"Few days ago," said Carl as nonchalantly as he could.

Fred suddenly materialized on the bench beside her. She had learned to tone down her surprise at his comings and goings, but her eyes were still drawn toward him, particularly when he spoke.

"With friends like him..." said the spirit. Carl noticed her odd head movement, but Audrey recovered and looked him in the eye.

"Why didn't you tell me sooner?" asked Audrey.

Carl took another long swallow of beer. "'Cause I think it's something you should let the police handle."

"And why is that?" Now there was open hostility in her voice. Carl leaned toward her and put a hand on her arm.

"It turns out this guy, Street, has a rap sheet 'til Christmas, and not just drugs, assault and a murder arrest, though the material witness vanished before they could get that case to court."

Audrey ran both hands through her hair, an excuse to pull her arm away from Carl's hand. "He's also a partner in Artful Construction which probably launders money through a corporate shell called Roadworks," she said in a forceful staccato. "Fred, our friend Nate and Street were high-school buddies." Audrey felt she had to bludgeon Carl with these facts to show him she could glean her own information and didn't need his patronizing, overprotective attitude.

"I told you not to tell him anything he doesn't know," Fred snapped. "Just get information from him."

"How did you find all that out?" Carl asked, a note of admiration in his voice.

"Corporate computer search on Artful Construction." Her look, meant to be read as coy, actually veiled increasing anger. "So what else aren't you telling me?"

Carl's smile was sheepish. "Street used to be a high roller in the modern art world. He'd speculated heavily with his supplier's money, which produced a chunk of change until the bottom dropped out of the art market. Left him holding a couple of million in devalued paintings."

"So has anybody brought him in? Anybody talked to him? The guy proves my case by existing."

"There are people working on it. They haven't been able to locate him yet, but give them time."

"I don't have time." Audrey had tried to keep the urgency from her voice, but it filtered through.

Carl put a hand on her shoulder, then moved it up to caress her neck as he spoke. "I know you're not going to feel safe until we have him locked up."

"It's not that. I'll go find him myself—"

"Promise me you won't. This guy isn't some petty criminal. He's dangerous. I couldn't handle it if anything happened to you." Carl looked into her eyes and Audrey felt that she could see in his some unattainable ideal of compassion. World peace? She felt a disconcerting electrical charge course from her neck where his hand rested, down to her feet.

"Give me a fucking break!" Fred shouted. "I'm telling you, don't trust this guy."

Audrey looked down, pulled away slightly. Carl removed his hand, unnerved by his admission. Embarrassed by pulling away so noticeably, Audrey tried for a light tone to reestablish their companionship.

"I may be emotionally challenged right now, but I'm not a fool. I won't do anything risky." Carl didn't respond, but finished his beer as Audrey took a bowl of guacamole from the picnic basket and set it on the table next to a bag of chips. He stood and nodded toward the house.

"May I wash my hands?"

"How fastidious. You know where it is."

He moved toward the door, then looked back over his shoulder. "Me and Lady Macbeth."

Fred looked after him disdainfully. "Sounds like a confession to me."

"What, that he killed you?" Audrey asked incredulously.

"He feels guilty about something otherwise the parallel wouldn't have occurred to him. Or is he just trying to impress you with a literary reference?"

Audrey shook her head. "It's pretty obvious you don't like him, but your suspicious rants are getting tedious. He's a very dear friend."

"Yeah? I don't believe that men and women can be 'just friends'. Not if they're really close."

Audrey studied him. Where was this leading? She smiled as it dawned on her. "You're jealous."

"He can't hold my jock strap."

"He has one distinct advantage. He's breathing." The finality of her gibe pleased her.

Fred leaned over, cupped her chin in his palm and looked into her eyes. "For you in particular, not breathing is my most attractive quality."

Her smile vanished. She pulled away from him.

chapter 16

AT THE CONFLUENCE of the Bow and Elbow rivers sits the grown up cow town of Calgary, Alberta. Though in the mid-nineties oil and natural gas industries dominated, Calgary still retained much of the cattle flavor that was the original economic base of this modern city stew. The town still has a yearly gathering called the Calgary Stampede, which a minor, but well connected, producer thought would make a good backdrop for a film. He hired a twenty-year-old writer/director out of film school and instructed him to incorporate roping, riding and sex. Beyond that, he let him give full vent to his creativity, which had hitherto been tested only on a twenty-minute student horror film. The director's parents put up much of the money and received a small profit participation based, of course, on that accounting Shangri-La, the net profit.

Miles had asked Audrey to read the script, which she did and pronounced it abysmal. He had always asked her opinion about prospective projects, and she was always honest about their merit or lack thereof, which was usually the case. The truth was he never received decent material, a common complaint among actors, but quite genuine in his case. In his few acting stretches, mostly on stage, he had proved to be a wonderful comic in the bemused style of Cary Grant. He was also terrific as the supportive friend and chilling as the covert villain. But his Robert Redford good looks cast him forever in the role of leading man, a role which fit him like a tutu on a linebacker.

Taking Audrey's advice, he turned down the project and was promptly offered twice his considerable going rate for the two-month assignment. No moral dilemma there. It paid for at least a year of waves.

Audrey arrived in Calgary and was met by a limo, since Miles was working most of the fourteen-hour days required for a quick shoot. The company was filming interior scenes at the St. James studios near the heart of the city. The building was a converted sawmill that had been gutted to accommodate offices, wardrobe storage, sound and lighting equipment. On the sound stages, walls "flew" to accommodate shots from various angles. Above these mobile walls were myriad lighting fixtures crisscrossing the upper reaches of the flying walls in place of a ceiling.

Audrey walked through the cavernous, bustling building toward the active sound stage. A nice looking woman in her late twenties strode up to her.

"Hi, I'm Lynn Rinofsky, the co-producer. You must be Audrey. Did everything go okay with the limo I set up for you?"

"Yes, thanks. Nice meeting you." Audrey took her outstretched hand.

The co-producer led Audrey to a chair emblazoned with Miles's name on one side and "Stampede" on the other. Audrey sat while Miles and his co-star, a highly recognizable television actress with the single name of Marsella, shot a scene where she was supposed to be seducing him. It clearly wasn't working and the director yelled "cut" then gave everyone a five-minute break. Miles came over and kissed her.

"Everything go okay? Looks like you found us all right." His casual manner seemed forced but it could be the alien territory--work, not Canada.

"Piece of cake," said Audrey. "Your co-producer sent a limo for me." Audrey nodded toward the woman who was now in conference with the director.

"Oh, yeah? She's real tight with the producer." Miles didn't usually offer asides on other people's lives. In fact he was one of those rare individuals who didn't believe in gossip of any stripe. The director called for another take of the scene and Miles returned to the softly lit set. Makeup and hair professionals fluttered around both actors, then the assistant director shouted, "Roll 'em", the sound man yelled, "speed" and the director followed with, "and action." Miles looked bored while Marsella sidled up to him and let the strap of her slip drop from her shoulder seductively. Before she even said a line she shouted at the director.

"Jesus! I'm not getting anything from him."

"You're not supposed to be, that's the character," Miles shot back.

"Cut!" the director yelled.

"Where does it say you're supposed to be a fucking log?" Marsella screamed.

"It just shows what a great actor I am. Who in real life would be able to resist the fabulous Marsella?"

At this point, the co-producer stepped in and tried to pull Marsella away, but the actress wheeled on the girl and nearly spat at her.

"Of course you're on his side...in fact from what I've heard, there isn't a side of him you haven't been on."

"That's enough of that shit. You're fucking with my marriage here," Miles attacked, cognizant of the best defense being a good offense maxim.

"No. You're fucking with your marriage," the actress responded with obvious satisfaction.

Audrey observed the proceedings as though they were part of the script. She was waiting for the obligatory scene at the end of the second act when it was provided by the guilt stricken co-producer who turned to her with a passively good reading of the line: "I don't know what she's talking about." Audrey immediately knew that she did.

Marsella looked at Audrey with what may have been the barest morsel of regret. "Look at it this way, honey, the truth will set you free."

And so it had. Audrey didn't believe in killing the messenger, but she did hope that the actress would end up in that particular hell usually reserved for people who put wood-handled knives in the dishwasher.

Audrey didn't have the furious reaction she had the first time; actually she experienced that ever so temporary rosy glow of vindication. She knew he couldn't be faithful and now he had confirmed it. She turned to the co-producer and spoke without rancor. "I hope you surf."

Audrey left the studio, Calgary and the marriage. The second time.

⌐|¬

Now, Audrey felt the pressure of all that she didn't know, felt the pressure of the twelve hours that had already elapsed since the kidnapper's phone call. She had pushed the few pieces of comfortable furniture against the walls so that the large central area of her living room was clear. Now she crawled around and scribbled notes in colored chalk on her unfinished plywood floors.

Fred paced beside her ever-increasing list of questions:
- Where the hell is the disc?
- Street top candidate?
- What is Florida connection?
- Was Street the midnight caller?
- Is Nate more than just money launderer?
- What was "insurance" for Frances? The disc?

"Don't forget to add Carl's reluctance to share information with us," said the illusion. "Also, note how nervous he was and add that suspicious trust account."

"Shall I add the possibility of a shooter on the grassy knoll as well?" But she scribbled the question:
- Why withhold info & how much is C concealing particularly re: SandCastle Trust account?

"Joke about it. But while you've got your head in the sand you'll be hit by a tank if you don't look at the people you think you can trust."

"Fine." The word telegraphed Audrey's displeasure. "Who were you talking about that night in the motel when you said 'If you fuck with her, I'll kill you?' Frances? But if they had her once, why'd they let her go? And why'd they kill you if they didn't have the disc? Why not just kidnap you and force you to tell them where it was?"

"You're forgetting that I can only speculate about this stuff, too."

"So speculate. Why would you've gone up to Nate's if you knew that Nate was still tight with Street after you'd copied Street's files and beaten his computer into quantum particles?"

"Maybe I'd burnt all my other bridges. I might've counted on an old friendship being deeper than business ties. Maybe I thought Nate would empathize about Frances being into drugs 'cause of his own kids. Who cares? I think you're spinning your wheels with all these 'what ifs'. You need to face something that you know."

"And what's that?" A note of irritation crept into Audrey's voice.

"That nobody broke into your house. Somebody had access to your keys and made a copy."

"Or they were practiced enough to pick the lock. That doesn't mean anything."

"Picking a lock leaves traces the cops would've found. What about Coburn, Katherine's husband?"

"What about him?"

"If you're going to be defensive, you'll never put this together. Write this down. 'Does K's husband have knowledge or connection?'"

Now Audrey's body language was openly hostile, but she wrote the question on the floor. "Even if he were dealing, what are the chances he'd be in the same group or gang or whatever they are as Street?"

"It'd depend on how high up he is. Ranks get thinner at the top. And don't forget, he doesn't have to be dealing. He could be connected to Street through the art world."

"And the disc holds valuable secrets about where he can find perfect replicas of pre-Columbian fertility Gods."

"Just write it down," said Fred.

Audrey remembered the DEA bust Katherine kept Coburn out of but as quickly as the thought surfaced, she forced it back down. "Why can't it just be Nick the Nose or Joey Bagadonuts? Somebody I don't know."

"Because the kidnapper called you and not Frances' mother. It has to be somebody who's aware of your personal relationship with Frances."

"Well, that's Nate, maybe Terry, Skitch for that matter," she said.

"—and Carl and Opal and Katherine and by extension, Coburn."

"Wait, now we're throwing in Opal? Why not my mother?"

"I'd have added her but you haven't been to see her since you got your keys."

Audrey flinched. The last thing she needed right now was guilt impinging on her already rebellious brain. "Get back to Opal. How do you figure?" she asked.

"Husband was a slimeball judge, maybe there are skeletons in the closet."

"Dead slimeball judge. You're reaching."

"You've told her everything."

"Not everything."

"She goes on the list," said the cynical spirit.

She shook her head and began to write, but stopped abruptly when a knock at the door startled them both. They exchanged a look, as if the other should know who it was. She moved silently to the door and peered thought the peephole.

"It's Katherine." Audrey glanced around, hesitated, then finally opened the door. Katherine looked forlorn in her cape that easily could have hidden the entire Cirque de Soliel troop beneath her swollen belly. Audrey hugged her. "Hi, Darlin'. You look great in that—"

"Tent. Just call it a tent. I know what I look like."

"Whatever it is, tent or Dior gown, it looks fabulous. How's my half of the baby?" Katherine felt her stomach, then pointed to an area high on the beach ball that protruded from her mid-section.

"Nudnick's upside down so your bottom half's up here." Audrey laughed and felt where Katherine had indicated.

"Better stand on that question about her husband," Fred warned. Audrey tried to glance causally at the floor as she moved to the chalk "K" and obscured it with little movements of her foot. Katherine noticed the list but didn't seem to notice the intentional blurring.

"What're you doing?"

"I was just trying to organize my thoughts. Everything I know related to the kidnapping."

Katherine nodded as she read the list. "Obviously you searched everywhere you could think of for the disc."

"We tore the place apart."

"We?"

Fred couldn't restrain himself. "Good going."

"I mean, I did...and whoever ransacked the place."

Katherine looked down, motioned her aside. "Move a little... Whose husband might be involved?"

"Think fast," the dead man said.

"Uh...Opal's."

Katherine looked at her incredulously. "From the grave?"

"Are you on drugs?" His question pushed her perilously close to shouting at him, but she maintained her composure and didn't glance in his direction.

"He adjudicated a lot of drug cases and probably shared information with Opal. I suppose I should've just put her name...just, you know, to ask if she knows anything about Street."

"Oh, yeah. A big word'll convince her you knew what you were talking about," Fred taunted. Finally Audrey couldn't help but glare at him. Katherine noticed, studied her friend, but made no comment.

"Actually, I wouldn't put anything past the old goat himself, if he were alive. A lot of whispers about the venerable Judge Nichols. He never hit on me. Liked the vulnerable type. His seat's still open because of budget cutbacks. I'll bet she tries for it."

"Yeah? Listen, I'm thinking about filling her in on Frances," said Audrey.

"Your call, but as chief deputy D.A., how could she not go to the police?" Katherine continued to read the list. "What's this about Carl? Why would he keep things from you?"

"I don't know, but he didn't tell me about Street until this afternoon, and he's known for days. Have you ever run across the name Street McClean in any cases you've seen?"

"Don't you think I would've said something?" asked Katherine with a touch of annoyance in her voice. She erased the "Florida Connection" question with her foot. "You can take this one off. Fred was involved in a minor drug transaction in Florida, but got off because of problems with the evidence. Just small time stuff, local stuff."

Audrey smiled warmly at her friend. "Thanks for checking. You're a pal. Always have been." Audrey took Katherine's hand and looked into her eyes. "Remember when we were kids and we could count on things."

"Like?" Katherine asked.

"I don't know. Like our parents. Like leaving our bikes on the front lawn and knowing they'd be there the next day. I miss that. I miss the certainty."

"Yeah right. My dad left when we were in junior high and my bike was stolen right out of our garage." Audrey had forgotten about the bike and since things were patched up between Katherine and her dad now, had forgotten how painful his leaving had been for her.

Katherine picked up her purse. "You've got selective memory." She patted her stomach. "And I've got two weeks left to be nothing but miserable, so let me do some of the leg work. I'll see what I can get on Street. Mean time you get some sleep."

"Does it show?" Audrey hadn't thought of how she looked in weeks, but imagined that her recent schedule had taken its toll.

"It's not that you look bad, it's that you get, I don't know, distracted. Same thing happened to me when I was cramming for the bar. You get fragmented."

Audrey looked at her watch. "A little over a day left to find that disc."

"You'll find it."

"I'm not sure how at this point."

Katherine smiled at her, the serious smile that conveyed a depth that she allowed few people to see. "By the power of your good intentions."

"What happened to the road to hell?" Fred interjected.

Audrey hugged Katherine as close as she could, given her friend's stomach. "Nice to have someone who believes in me."

Although they had disappointed each other in the past, and would continue to at intervals throughout their lives, the knowledge that Katherine believed in her gave her strength, comfort and clarity amid the clutter. It derived from an unshakable belief in the eternity of true friendship.

⚜

When the child welfare people searched for a guardian for Audrey, they finally unearthed her father's sister who lived in Dayton, Ohio. "Aunt Bonnie" had been thrilled to sign over guardianship of the sixteen-year-old to Katherine's mother who figured she wouldn't notice one more in her brood. Whether Aunt Bonnie would have been as hasty had she known about the substantial life insurance policy her dad left, Audrey would never know. No one would have known if Katherine hadn't dug around like a forensic accountant. Even at her tender age, Audrey knew that her mother would need the entire sum if she were ever to avoid the depressing mental hospital she initially had been thrown into by the court. Later, Katherine set up a trust to pay for her mother's care in a home more salubrious than that which the State of California provided.

Being part of Katherine's chaotic clan enabled Audrey to keep busy, to keep herself from thinking. She felt useful, needed. Audrey's main duty was to help with driving the younger ones to their games, practices, lessons and friend's homes in her mom's station wagon. Her father's Mustang remained in the garage, dutifully washed and waxed, but never driven.

Katherine had an interesting reaction to the disintegration of her second family. She began to study. Both girls had been decent, though rather directionless, students, but now Katherine threw herself into her schoolwork to the exclusion of all else.

When Katherine's father walked out on the family a year after the last child had been born, the thirteen-year-old Katherine had sworn never to speak to him again. His marriage to a woman who was in fragile health baffled everyone, but he seemed content. And that rankled Katherine more than his absence. He had abandoned them and was happy. Now the rug had been pulled out from under her for the second time in her young life by the loss of Audrey's parents. But rather than the aimlessness the demise seemed to engender in Audrey, Katherine threw herself into being the architect of her own security.

If Katherine had a blind spot, it was where friends and family were concerned. She, like Audrey, only wanted to believe the best about them. The difference was that Katherine would change circumstances or history in her account to accommodate her original belief. Audrey simply accepted people's inherent shortcomings or temporary failings because she could always change them in her fantasy tapes.

In her business life, Katherine wasn't against bending a rule now and then; she was a strict adherent to the spirit of the law. The letter of the law was an opportunity for creativity. Audrey, on the other hand, couldn't bend rules because her mother did. She followed the rules. Well, except for the motorcycle. And look what happened.

Audrey mused that she had been without parents for as long as she had had them. The Jesuits say, give me a child until six and I'll give you a Catholic for life. She took that to mean that she should have been cooked by six, should have had the essential emotional tools to survive because she had been given the love of two wonderful people until she was sixteen. Whose fault was it that she was now falling apart? Her parent's? Miles'? Her own? What could she have done to prevent it? What was she doing now? Playing detective with a hallucination.

When the phone rang this time, Audrey snapped to a sitting position, immediately awakened from her light sleep.

"Hello?"

"Audrey? It's me." Frances's voice sounded small, tentative.

"Frances, are you all right?"

"Audrey, please get them what they want. I'm scared."

"Tell them I'm trying. Tell them I'll give them money—"

Again the voice with the odd electronic timbre. "One more day. We'll call you." She jumped out of bed and stalked around the room.

"What can I do? What else can I do? Should I give up and go to the police? I'm so ineffectual."

"If we get down to the wire and still don't have anything, you can tell them that you just need a few more hours. Then go to the police. But right now, we follow up on the questions we put together last night. First thing you do is get into Katherine's computer and find out anything you can about the SandCastle trust."

"What makes you think Katherine has anything to do with SandCastle?"

"Because she didn't ask you about it. It was right there on the floor. She asked about everything else." Audrey remained silent. "She didn't ask because she already knew about it."

"Why are you after Katherine?" The question sounded plaintive even to her own ears.

"I'm not after anyone. I'm here to keep you from letting your emotions get in the way. I'm here to make you question everything."

"And that's doing me a favor?" He didn't answer her, nor did he nod or shake his head. He stared at her with a slight smile on his lips.

⚜

Audrey dashed around her kitchen in the minimum movements necessary to produce a cup of coffee. She stood in her running clothes, mug under the machine's filter holder and prayed to the coffee god for a speedy cup. The sun was just rising and stark beams slanted through the blinds throwing stripes on her hand holding the mug. Through the slats, she saw Terry slipping out of her duplex next door. Audrey raced after her. Terry carried a large suitcase on the way to her twenty-year-old Beemer which sported a dent or scratch for every year. Audrey nearly tackled her.

"Hello? Terry?" Terry glanced back at Audrey, but continued toward the car. Audrey helped her put her suitcase into the trunk, a gesture not appreciated by the woman in a hurry.

"Sorry, like, I don't have time to be neighborly."

"You know, we haven't been formally introduced. Can't really count the night you warned me not to talk to the police about the beating. My name's Audrey. Fred said you were a friend of his so I thought maybe you could help me. I'm looking for your brother, Street."

"Can't help you."

Audrey slammed the trunk and grabbed the keys. "That's too bad because I was going to promise not to tell the cops I found out you're on the board of a company that launders money for drug dealers."

"Hey, gimme those," said the skinny woman as she lunged for the keys.

Audrey kept them just out of reach. "See, I happen to think Street killed Fred and kidnapped his sister just to get a disc."

"Whoa, like, you are so off base. My brother had a lot of reason to be pissed at Fred, but he wouldn't've killed him. Fred burned his own bridges. Had a real meth jones for a while. Now give me the fucking keys."

"Tell me about it," said Audrey, as she kept Terry at bay. Terry glared at her.

"He goes down to Florida to try to setup his own buy and uses Street's name to undercover cops and gets busted. Fred comes back all born-again crusader and threatens to clean Street's clock if he doesn't quit dealing to Judy, or Frances...whatever she calls herself now. Street blows him off until he finds out that Fred has copied files then crashed his computer."

"Why wouldn't Street quit dealing to Frances?"

This actually made Terry stop and think for a moment. "I don't know." She sounded convincing.

"So where's Street?"

"He said, but I can't remember. I think it might be in South America."

Fred appeared leaning against the car's hood. "Give her some options."

Audrey sighed before complying. "Colombia, Venezuela?"

Terry thought for a moment. "I can't remember. Some weird country...not like Columbia or any of those."

"Ask her if it's Ecuador," Fred prompted.

Audrey looked at him sternly. "No."

Terry was naturally confused and not a little pissed herself. "No, what?"

Audrey's resistance dissolved. "No? How about Ecuador?"

Terry nodded thoughtfully, then shook her head. "I can't be sure..."

"Did he ever mention cities like Guayaquil? Quito?"

"Could be. First one sounds familiar."

"I'd bet on it," put in Fred.

Terry held her hand out for the keys. "Listen, I gotta go." She looked around furtively. When Audrey handed her the keys, Terry hopped into the car and sped off.

Audrey glared at Fred. "Street's the one were after no matter what his sister says. And just because Coburn bought some things in Guayaquil doesn't link him to Street even if he does happen to be in Ecuador. Why won't you let this Coburn thing go?"

"You know why. Because you have to get down to the heart of the matter sometime. It's ultimately up to you, and hey, I never claimed hundred percent accuracy."

She studied him. She had been so willing to let someone else make her judgment calls that she had simply presumed accuracy. Presumed it, probably because she didn't want to question whom or what she was letting influence her decisions. Her confidence in herself was at such a nadir that she figured anyone's decisions were likely to be better than her own.

It led her back to considering what he was. If he wasn't infallible, that let out angels, or so she supposed, not having given the fallibility of angels a great deal of thought. If he were some astral projection from another solar system or universe--they say even that massive state isn't singular--then his information should be accurate. He would have access to the future, having had to manipulate time to get here. That left the most likely explanation: he was an invention of her recently malleable mind. Why now? She had never considered herself capable of traveling to the true extremes, glimpsing them perhaps, but she hadn't felt that she had been injured enough by life or chemistry to truly approach the abyss. She had hoped that, having seen her mother do it, she somehow had been inoculated. That notion was in constant battle with the more primal fear of a hereditary tendency.

Audrey jogged along the bike path as the sun continued its ascent. She needed something to clear her head and, since sleep had become elusive, running had to substitute. In her travels, she had found that exercise mitigated the effects of jetlag, had invigorated rather than enervated her when sleep was scarce. As she breathed in the salt mist, she could almost feel her mind clearing. The familiarity of movement warmed her, reminded her of jogging along some eastern seaboard or European coast. As she passed early morning moms with strollers, her step lightened. Focused runners passed her, heads down in concentration, bodies slightly forward for momentum. She could feel herself relaxing. The world continued and that amazed her, continued to spin on its axis while individuals like Frances careened out of control. But what about the kidnapper. He was certainly out of control. What information was so important that a life had to be taken, that another hung in the balance? Or was this his daily bread? Was mayhem as much a routine for him as her deposition reading was for her? She imagined some shadowy figure pondering his Day Runner and worrying that he might not be able to fit in an extortion between Thursday's murder at noon and the five o'clock kidnapping. Yes, running lightened her spirit. She was beginning to feel almost human.

The vision was at a distance, yet so intimate to her that her breath caught. She thought of turning around but the figure drew her like a magnet, like an electromagnet with the power to transform her coppery glow of ephemeral contentment into the dusty verdigris of renewed doubt. A transient stood on a jungle gym in a children's play area and spoke in angry tones to the wind. The wind evidently answered, since the transient's side of the conversation acknowledged the other party. Her childhood eagerness to see what her mother had seen surfaced and melded with the present. To whom was he speaking? Was it his own personal Fred? She tried to force the scene through her intellect. What a travesty our mental health system has become. This man needs help. His clothes and emaciated body speak of chronic neglect. His personal hygiene hasn't crossed his ravaged mind in days. Someone should help him. As she moved closer, a tightness which had begun in her throat now seemed to reach around and constrict her chest like a boa squeezing the life out of its prey. The vision was leaking into her soul. His tapes had taken control of his reality. He needed no private moment to indulge in his fantasy. The tapes had sucked him into theirs.

She pulled a twenty from her running pouch and flung it at the man. He looked at it, seemed fascinated by the arc of its flight but not even a glimmer of recognition of its value lit those eyes, which were sunk in bony sockets. When the bill landed, it no longer held his interest. He returned to his oratory and she, to her fears.

Keep it together. Stay focused. Fantasy tapes of her rescuing Frances threatened to halt her momentum. She knew she was slipping, knew it would take an increasing amount of strength to hold herself together. She would have her hereditarily ordained, richly deserved nervous breakdown after she found Frances.

chapter 17

AUDREY GLANCED AROUND the D.A.'s bullpen casually to be certain no one was taking any undue interest in her. She ducked into Katherine's office and fired up her computer. A dizzying array of numbers that made up the directory of Katherine's case files flashed on the screen. It seemed like months rather than days ago that Katherine had shown her how to retrieve files from her hard drive. She didn't even know if the file would be called SandCastle or some acronym. Recalling that Katherine had told her that the letters corresponded to their numerical position in the alphabet, she worked out that the first four letters, "S,A,N,D", would correspond to the numbers: nineteen, one, fourteen, and four. She entered the file code and was rewarded with the corporate paper work for the SandCastle Foundation. Within the legalese of such documents, Audrey gleaned that the president was Carl Rogers, the vice-president and treasurer was Katherine. She read that Katherine also held absolute power of attorney over all transactions without Carl's approval, an odd provision Audrey thought.

Fred appeared and looked over her shoulder. "Well, that's interesting. They're into something together and neither of your dear friends mentioned it to you."

"Probably because it's none of my business what either of them does," replied Audrey sharply. "It doesn't prove anything."

"It proves that your friends keep things from you."

Audrey continued to peruse the documents while the increasingly annoying dead man looked over her shoulder. The stated reason for the foundation was to engage in investments to benefit a person, Damien Calloway, and a company, Pool Fund. The incorporation was dated two years earlier and the initial investment had been twenty-five thousand dollars. Within each of the past two annual reports Audrey learned that the sum had grown by fifteen thousand each year, and yet there was a slow, steady drain that amounted to about a thousand a month.

"Steady payments," said the spirit. "Couldn't be blackmail though. Don't even think about it."

"It could be anything." She closed the file and glared at him.

"Could it be enough to make you question your blind faith in your friends?"

"No." But even as she said the word, she saw the myriad things Katherine and she avoided: her father's death, the reality of her mother's condition, any discussion of Coburn's current drug use. The person closest to her in her life was at a distinct distance.

Court days were always the worst. Opal was a bitch. Not to Audrey necessarily, but on court days, her boss was so testy that her staff trembled as furiously as the opposition. Which was why Audrey ran up the walkway toward the Santa Monica court house, no mean feat considering she was trailing a luggage cart which held two bulging legal-sized storage boxes. Just as she began to mount the stairs, she turned to check her load and spotted Carl moving in her direction from the parking lot. He stopped a few yards away, hands held out in a helpless gesture.

"I'm sorry. I didn't want to be part of this."

"Part of...?" But she froze as she realized what "this" was. Miles alighted from a limo that was parked behind Carl's Miata. Her expression hardened as Miles strode toward her carrying a large envelope. Her anger rose at the sight of him and not just because of the infidelities. It was galling that he looked younger than she did, though he was in his mid-forties, a decade older. She had always accepted without bitterness that he was more attractive.

Audrey's eyes shot daggers at Carl. "Brutes. What are you, psycho? This is the last thing I need right now." She stormed past him,

Miles in pursuit of her. Carl remained rooted to his spot, his head bowed. When Miles caught up with her, he spoke as though continuing a conversation only momentarily interrupted.

"Low blow."

"What?" Audrey asked irritably.

"Calling Carl a psycho when you know he was in the loony bin for a while."

She missed a step, but caught herself and tried to pretend it hadn't happened. "You never told me that."

Miles shrugged, as though he had just related the surf conditions at Zuma Beach. "I didn't? Hmm...Anyway, what are these papers?" He waved the sheaf of papers at her.

"They're divorce documents. You've seen them before, only the dates have changed."

"I mean, why did you send them to me?" Audrey marveled at the breadth of his ego. He truly couldn't conceive of the notion. It was as though he had been handed a calculus final without ever having taken the class.

She opted for the tone of the patient teacher. "Because you were unfaithful after we agreed that you wouldn't be. Is that clear enough?"

"Alright, I back-slid. I admit it. It's something I've got to work on. And I will. But you've got to be able to put this behind us."

She took a deep breath and put a patronizing hand on his shoulder. "I know this is going to sound harsh, but sixteen strikes and you're out. Sign the papers." She turned and continued toward the courthouse.

The tone of Miles' voice became less assured, even insecure. "I don't want to not be married to you."

She stopped. He had just summed up their life together. "Perfect."

"I meant..."

She faced him again, this time with real rage in her eyes. "Exactly what you said. You don't want to not be married, but you don't want to be married all the time."

"I only rarely want not to be married," Miles said, head lowered in deserved embarrassment.

"Sign the fucking papers!" She started up the stairs, angrily pulling the cart up each one with a satisfying thud.   "You can't leave me. I won't let you," he shouted as he returned to the car.

"Too late," she shouted back with a note of satisfaction.

"I promise you, you'll regret it." Miles stood next to his limo for security. He could be forceful when he was working. She reached the top step and looked back down at him. Carl had marched up to him and the two of them were having a heated exchange, none of which she could catch. To hell with them both. She flipped them the bird. The uncharacteristic gesture made her feel at once powerful and demeaned.

How had they arrived at this point? The point at which love and hope had mutated into anger and blame. How had she chosen someone who couldn't remain faithful? How had Katherine chosen someone whose dealings were so questionable? The two girls had their share of boyfriends before either of the future husbands appeared on the horizon. Katherine had nearly married an investment banker but she said he had no "soul". Coburn, she claimed was a soul who had made numerous appearances on the planet before. Audrey wondered how someone supposedly evolved could endanger his marriage with drug use and possibly drug dealing.

As for Audrey, Katherine had renamed all of her potential suitors. "He of the high-rise" was Katherine's name for Harold who happened to own property in Manhattan and "Will ski for food" was her name for Bill, a fireman who had shushed his way into Audrey's heart.

The friends had married within three months of each other and had worn the same maid of honor dress to the other's wedding, partly because they had both disposed of a closet full of "you can wear it again" bride's maid dresses and partly for the bonding nature of the gesture. Katherine had pulled a celadon silk crepe flowing dress from the sale rack at Barneys.

"Perfect. You're height'll take up the length. My fat'll take up the width," said Katherine.

"You mean you're boobs'll pull it up and it'll hang where mine aren't," said Audrey.

"Exactly. We'll be perfect maid-of-honor material for each other. I'll look slightly dumpy, you'll look slightly frumpy." Arrow straight to the heart of the matter. How could she even think of doubting Katherine? Their friendship was enduring, forged by life's uncertainties. Perhaps it was lasting because Audrey didn't try to fix her friend. Katherine wouldn't allow it. She knew she wasn't broken.

Even with the time pressure bearing down on her, Audrey couldn't help but feel the thrill of her first time in court as an assistant at the prosecution table. She looked around at the prospective jury pool and figured Opal would get a sympathetic group. Herman Sitwell had defrauded hundreds of working class people out of their homes by using a loan scam which made them think they were taking out a second mortgage when in reality they were signing over the deed to Sitwell's company who then leased their own homes back to them. Until he evicted them.

Opal looked crisp in her navy suit and starched white blouse. Only the circles under her eyes revealed how hard she had been working on the case. Audrey had seen her haggard before when she had been preparing for court, but now she looked both tired and peeved.

Behind the defense table sat four expensively suited men, but Audrey couldn't guess which was Sitwell.

The judge entered.

"All rise," said the bailiff. All did, and then sat in unison with the judge. Judge Crowe was a youngish looking man with a no-nonsense face. Audrey decided she wouldn't like to be on the wrong side of the man with that penetrating stare. One of the defense counsels rose and addressed the court.

"Your honor, my client is currently indisposed under a doctor's care for extremely high blood pressure."

Opal sprang to her feet. "Your honor—"

"Thank you for your objection, Ms. Nichols. Counsel your client will be in this courtroom in two hours or he will be tried in absentia. We will reconvene at three o'clock." Judge Crowe slammed his gavel down then rose and left the court, not a happy man.

Opal looked at Audrey. "Give me the hard copies of all the leases. I want to be able to point to the stack during the voir dire. He thinks he has high blood pressure now?"

Audrey's face betrayed her panic. "I don't have them. They weren't on the list of documents to bring."

"The case hinges on those leases. I didn't think I'd have to tell you to bring essential evidence." Opal's voice was harsh with a jagged edge to it.

"I have the hard drive. We can attach it to the laptop—"

"Great. I'll just hold it up, hit "page down" and flip through it for twenty minutes. That'll give them a real sense of magnitude." Opal sat back down and held her forehead in one hand.

"We have time. I'll go back and get them right now," said Audrey as she rose to leave. Opal grabbed her hand and gently pulled her back down into her seat.

"I'm sorry. I just hate it when these little boys think they don't have to play by the rules. I'll get the leases. You're right. They weren't on the list. It was my responsibility to put them there."

"Really, let me—"

"No. I insist. I just started out frazzled today...my damn car wouldn't start...had to be towed to the shop. Think you could give me a lift home?"

"Of course. And I'll get those—"

"No. You go take a walk, relax. I want you back here fresh in an hour and a half."

Audrey walked along Palisades Park, the bluff above the Pacific Coast Highway. She noticed that a particularly large, fresh chunk of earth had joined the terraces below. One day, Santa Monica would be lucky to even have a sidewalk on the ocean side of the avenue. Entropy. The universal tendency toward chaos. Is it the natural state of everything the universe holds? The natural state of the human mind? Is the natural tendency toward mental chaos so strong that only constant vigilance can keep it in check? Is that what was happening to her? On a minor scale, was it happening to Opal today? It seemed Carl hadn't been vigilant enough. He had let entropy have its way with his mind and the result had been a stay in a mental hospital. At least he had gotten out, hadn't become a permanent fixture like her mother. Was that the cause of his abrupt switch from cop to shrink? He never spoke of the time when Miles and he had "lost track" of each other. Neither of them spoke of it.

She had eighteen hours left to find the disc. Figuring out that Street was the kidnapper didn't put her any closer to that goal. The disc wasn't at Fred's mother's house, wasn't at hers. Nate was the only other option, no matter what he had said.

The boxes of the hard copy leases weren't in the corner of the office where Audrey had left them. Apparently Opal had been there and gone. Audrey extracted her Day Runner from her purse and looked up Nate's home number. After a couple of rings, Skitch answered.

"Hello?"

"Hi, Skitch, it's Audrey James."

"Oh...Hi, Audrey."

"Is Nate around?"

"No. I don't expect him back for sometime."

"Where can I reach him? It's important."

"He's...He's gone fishing in Mexico." Conveniently, Audrey thought. Was he with Frances right now?

"I really need to talk to him," said Audrey, but Skitch remained silent. "It may be a matter of life and death, Skitch."

"He can't be reached," she responded a little too quickly. "I mean, he might check in. I'll tell him you called." A click, then silence.

Back in court, Mr. Sitwell slumped next to a doctor who wore a white lab coat and had a stethoscope hanging around his neck. Audrey was surprised Sitwell hadn't opted for an I.V. drip on wheels.

Opal draped a protective arm on the two-foot stack of leases on the prosecutor's table as she waited to question the first prospective juror during her voir dire. She addressed an elderly woman who wore a somewhat frayed gray suit.

"Juror number three, would you have any problem sending the defendant to jail for the forty plus years the cumulative counts of fraud would require—perpetrated on home owners like you—even if it meant that he would most likely die in prison?" Before the nodding woman could answer, the head defense counsel was on his feet.

"Your Honor, may we have a conference in chambers?" Opal's incisive attack had secured a white flag on the first question out of the gate. They would deal. But a deal with Opal would never be considered a victory of any sort. Opal was known for extracting her pound of flesh.

⌖

You made five dollars a day in the mid-nineties on jury duty and for that princely sum you were guaranteed a cramped jury room containing peers you would never equate yourself with and a TV blaring the waning years of the Donahue Show. If you were lucky enough to get on a case quickly, you might actually see daylight within the thirty days you served, but if you were selected the last day, you were doomed to jury purgatory. Put your life on hold.

Audrey spoke into the pay phone near the jury room where potential jurors milled about generally looking as bored as prospective jurors must.

"Hi, you. Whatcha doin'?" Audrey asked Katherine.

"Lying on my side to give my kidneys a break."

"How's my half of that kid?"

"Kicking the hell out of my gall bladder, thank you very much. You'll never guess who flew in a week earlier than I asked."

"Your mom's here? Put her on."

"You know better than that. She barely put her suitcase down before she took off to buy a slew of organic vegetables. Come on over for supper." This was the familiar Katherine, wasn't it? Why couldn't she shake the feeling that something wasn't right between them?

"I can't tonight, but soon. So what've you got for me?" The question felt abrupt even as she asked it.

"I got copies of Street's file from the feds. And, Audrey, there's something we need to talk about, but not on the phone. Remember, any of this gets traced back to me and I'm a pregnant manicurist. They'll disbar me."

"Don't worry. No one else on this planet will see them."

"What're you doing tonight?"

"I'm giving Opal a ride home. Her car's in the shop. She's in chambers right now with Judge Crowe working out a plea bargain. I almost felt sorry for old Sitwell. She'll nail him." Audrey knew she was blabbering to cover the growing sense of estrangement.

Katherine's voice sounded tired. "I'll bring it down there. Parking lot at six?"

"Only if you're up to it," said Audrey.

"I'm fine. By then I'll need a break from Mom anyway."

Audrey noticed a man with a bushy mustache in a baseball cap and dark glasses taking particular interest in her. "You're the best," she said to her friend.

"Got that right," said Katherine who paused for a moment before adding, "Are you okay? You sound, I don't know, distant."

"I'm just, you know, frazzled. Nothing a week or two of sleep won't cure." Audrey's eyes became glassy with tears. Great. Now she's getting allergies. She's not losing it. She is not losing it.

"Okay, see you in a while." Katherine hung up without saying goodbye.

Audrey ducked a melee that had broken out in the line for the pay phone behind her and walked down the crowded hallway. The thin man with the Groucho mustache followed her as a crush of people emptied into the hall from one of the courtrooms. Within a few yards the thin man fell in step with her, but didn't turn toward her as he spoke.

"You gotta help me out." Audrey recognized him immediately. His reedy body was echoed in the thin nasal quality of his voice. Fear shot through her like a current, but she remained composed.

"You're Street McClean," she managed to say without a crack in her voice. He nodded as he glanced around nervously. "I think you're the one who needs to help me out."

"You've got it, like, so wrong. Keep walkin' and don't look at me."

"I can't help it. You couldn't find a phonier looking mustache." Audrey felt safe insulting him. What could he do with all these people around? The crowd jostled them both as they moved toward the stairway. She stopped. "And why should I go with you?" Street looked back at her, annoyed. He glanced around nervously again.

"'Cause I'm, like, the only one with the answers." As he said this, an interesting group of people surged forward, as if someone behind them had tripped: among the more normal looking people were a woman in a head scarf that concealed her face, a bearded man, a woman wearing heavy makeup and a dated bouffant wig, and an androgynous person wearing a muumuu. Did they still make those? As a group, they lurched into Street who careened into Audrey. Street grabbed his lower back, uttered the word: "Fuck," then fell into Audrey's arms, knocking her to the floor.

Wait a minute. Was this happening? Or was she now making up entire scenes rather than just resurrecting the dead? And was that a woman or a man in the troweled on makeup and wig? Was Street McClean really on top of her bleeding from the mouth all over the only conservative suit she owned? She would need to get another jacket before she could appear in court for sentencing. It wouldn't look right, blood in the courtroom. She screamed.

⌖

Audrey exited the police station wearing Carl's jacket since the investigators had taken hers into evidence. Carl had seemed to materialize next to her in the court house. He had pulled her away from Street and held her until she calmed down. He had remained with her throughout the questioning. At first, she appreciated it, gave herself over to being taken care of, but then it felt intrusive. Concern on his part was natural, but now when he took her arm she imagined him attaching himself to her like an abalone to a sea cliff.

She had nearly told all to the police, had come within a hair's breath of revealing Frances' kidnapping and the electronically altered voice. She had been so certain that Street was behind everything that she hadn't allowed herself to seriously consider others, people she knew in particular. If not Street, who? Fred had pointedly told her to suspect everyone. And where was that ephemera?

She subtly pulled her arm from Carl's grasp as they walked toward the parking lot in the early evening. Carl, realizing she was brushing him off, dropped his hand self-consciously.

"Why were you in the court house?" she asked.

"Our team was closing in on Street."

"'Our' team?"

"The police. I asked them to keep me in the loop where Street was concerned." Carl stopped at a lamp post. "Listen, Audrey, I don't think you realize what you've gotten into. I talked to a friend who's a forensic toxicologist. His best guess is that Street was injected with rattlesnake venom."

"Hey, I grew up here. A rattlesnake bite doesn't usually kill you and certainly not that quickly."

"It does if it's a combination of the Mojave venom which shuts down the nervous system, and the garden variety which causes hemorrhaging. I know a guy in Hesperia who milks both types for research."

Irritation seeped through her attempt at control. "A toxicologist, a rattlesnake farmer, is there anyone you don't know?" He looked at her with a bemused expression. "I'm sorry. Okay, it was snake venom. Please don't worry, they weren't after me." Was that fear for her or pain that she saw in his eyes? And what was it about Carl that roiled her mind? Carl shoved his hands in his pockets and inhaled deeply, obviously stifling a retort.

"Good night," said Audrey as she kissed his cheek.

"'Night." He watched her as she walked off.

A cold sea breeze kicked up and Audrey pulled the collar of her borrowed jacket tightly around her neck. She felt a presence behind her, thought it might be Fred, but found that it was Opal who was walking double-time to catch up with her.

"I wanted to take the Bleaker file home, but I couldn't find it," said Opal.

"I'll get it. I'll just be a minute with Katherine." Audrey stopped to wait for Opal then placed her keys in Opal's outstretched hand. "Just hit this button twice to turn off the alarm. It's the black Jeep at the end of that row." She pointed to it as she hurried toward Katherine's Mercedes.

Katherine was asleep, her head resting against the window. When Audrey reached the car, she tapped lightly on the windshield. Katherine awakened with a start before lowering the window.

"Almost gave up on you. If you get caught with this, my tit's in a wringer." She handed Audrey a bag full of neatly folded towels.

"Linen service?"

"The envelope's at the bottom. I didn't want Opal to ask you about it."

"I'll be careful," said Audrey.

Katherine looked closely at her friend now. "Geeze, you look awful."

Audrey hesitated, unsure whether to tell Katherine. Finally she simply blurted it out. "Somebody killed Street while I was walking with him just after I talked to you."

"Oh, my God." Katherine's hand moved involuntarily to her mouth.

Audrey leaned her head on the roof of the car. "Have you ever had the feeling that everything you touch turns to shit?"

Katherine grabbed Audrey's hand. "Don't go home. Come stay with us."

Audrey contemplated doing just that as she looked off toward Opal who pointed the alarm mechanism at the Jeep.

There was a supernova. No, it was her Jeep igniting in a fiery sphere. Audrey's brain tried to file the scene under fiction. As with Street's death, she tried to convince herself that it was an invention of her over-taxed mind. But she recognized her bumper as it flew through the air and lovingly wrapped itself around a lamppost, felt the heat from a nearby sapling as it ignited like a roman candle, knew that it was Opal's body floating backward and landing on a grassy mound. It was all happening at a leisurely pace as if time had wanted to facilitate her observation. The orange ball of flame that had been her car reflected her own internal inferno.

chapter 18

NIGHTMARE? TIME DRIPPED like a Daliesque clock one moment, then the next, raced as if a tuck had been taken in the space/time continuum. Audrey wondered if she really had crossed over into one of her head tapes or a Dante's gruesome version of one. Was this the Inferno? Not knowing if you were seeing what everyone else was? Katherine was still here. She was a constant, a lighthouse whose beacon assured Audrey that she wasn't yet a wreck on the shoals of madness. Katherine the constant...or was she? Was Audrey just imagining that Katherine was steadfast? Would she ever believe in anything or anyone to a certainty again?

More police. More questions. More questioning. Like the crazy transient—was that just this morning?—who couldn't discern the edges of the real world: She felt like a hapless mime, hands futilely groping to define that boundary.

Katherine held her belly as she jogged while Audrey ran to catch up with the EMSs who wheeled Opal's gurney though the corridor. She looked down at her unconscious boss. Blood oozed from a small wound on Opal's cheek, but beyond that, she appeared to be sleeping peacefully. The woman had been blown off her feet. What kind of peace could she be experiencing? Any kind would help assuage Audrey's guilt. For what? Becoming embroiled in this nightmare of kidnapping and murder? Could she have avoided it? When? At what point precisely?

The two women tried to follow the gurney into an emergency operating room, but were waved away by anonymous pink and green clad figures. Katherine was now huffing and puffing from the strain of trying to keep up. Her stomach seemed to be half her entire body mass and Audrey wondered how she walked any distance, let alone jogged. Audrey placed an arm around her friend and steered her toward the waiting area.

Miles suddenly appeared down the hall walking in their direction. Audrey's sense of fatigue increased with each step her estranged husband took toward her. He looked both concerned and agitated. His body language was an odd combination of a bowed head with rigid shoulders that conveyed an underlying defiance. He spoke directly to Audrey, ignoring Katherine completely.

"You okay?" She nodded weakly. "Carl said I'd find you here," he continued. "We sorta got into it earlier...I called him to finish venting and he told me. You sure you're all right?"

"Fine," said Audrey.

Katherine rolled her eyes at Miles, who placed somewhere near Mussolini on her list of favorite people. She often wished Miles could share Il Duce's state of decay. "Sorry to have to leave you two love birds, but I've got to pee." Katherine plastered an obviously phony smile on her face. "Same level of pleasure as always, Miles."

Miles still didn't look at her. "Yeah, you too." He looked at the ground nervously as Katherine disappeared down the hall.

"What is it?" Audrey snapped. Her patience was like an electrical cord which had been yanked one too many times from its socket.

He looked off in the distance, then back at Audrey. "You don't need this right now. Besides, I gotta get back up to Calgary." He started to turn to go.

"Just spit it out. You and Carl got into what?"

"We just got into it, you know, about everything. About you, me, him." Audrey sighed and crossed her arms in front of her. Her stance annoyed Miles and he became less concerned and more agitated. "You wanna know why Mr. Perfect left the force?"

"Because he had a nervous breakdown." A rote sounding response from Audrey.

"Cause he shot a kid in a drug bust. Nearly killed him. Except there weren't drugs in the place until his partner planted them. They covered up the fact that they couldn't prove probable cause to be there and nobody ever found out. And there's a lot more you don't know about him." Miles looked at her accusingly. "Then again, maybe you do."

Even in her scattered state, this alarmed her. "Why are you telling me this now?"

"'Cause he's not the perfect person you think he is."

Audrey started to defend herself. "I never thought—"

Miles cut her off angrily. "I saw the way you compared the two of us: Mr. Virtue, Mr. Vice. I know what you were thinking."

A strobe went off in her head. Blinding, yet illuminating. "I, I didn't mean to–" said Audrey.

Miles rose, hesitated as if to say more, but instead moved quickly down the hall tossing a casual sounding remark over his shoulder.

"Take care of yourself. I mean it. You gotta watch your back around Carl."

The words echoed like the aftermath of thunder. Audrey had clung to the belief that Miles had been unfeeling, oblivious to all except his immediate wants and needs. That was why he was promiscuous. That was why he showed little interest in the things that were important to her. Now he had just, in as many words, admitted that he was jealous of Carl, that he thought she compared him unfavorably to Carl. And he was right. As she looked back, she realized that she did see her husband as frivolous and his friend as, well, not. What part had her close friendship with his best friend played in the undermining of an already injured psyche? Had her secret pessimism about his ability to remain faithful added to his own lack of belief in himself? And did he ever find out about that time while they were divorced? Now she thought of all the times she had let things slide, hadn't confronted problems, expected him to figure out what she needed. Even in counseling she hadn't brought up the things that really hurt her for fear Miles would see them as petty. And the name. Had it really been important to him that she take his name? She now viewed their relationship as two people wrapped in separate cocoons of self-protection.

The legal concept of contributory negligence popped up as if she had been searching for it in a deposition. She didn't want to examine her culpability because it brought their entire relationship out of Miles' corner where she had filed it under "fault" and left responsibility for its demise an open question, a pie to be apportioned more equally than she had been willing to acknowledge.

Perhaps if she had been able to commit completely, to truly forgive him for the past, to give him unconditional love…But as soon as the thought had taken shape, a voice said: that variety of love is for good parents and therapists. To be able to give truly unconditional love in a marriage, one would have to be a saint, and Audrey knew that she wasn't. Yet even with all the ill feelings between them, Miles was warning her that she was missing something. Something that he knew about Carl. Certainly guilt about shooting an innocent child could push someone over the edge. But how far over had he gone? And how close to the abyss had he ranged since his return? In her experience with her mother, she'd found that once you'd been there, it was easier to find your way back.

"You okay?" asked Katherine who carried her cell phone as she approached Audrey.

Audrey hesitated, then responded. "I'm fine. Don't worry." She slumped into a row of conjoined, plastic chairs and became aware of the cacophony emanating from the adjacent waiting area.

"I can't get a damn signal in here, not that I could hear if I did. I'm going to find a pay phone to call Coburn. He's probably frantic."

"I'll call him. You sit down."

"I'm okay and I need to talk to him anyway." Katherine waddled off down the hall.

Fred appeared in a chair next to Audrey. "She's got to keep him informed so that she can warn him about another mess."

"Perfect. You're nowhere to be found when I need you, and I can't get rid of you when I don't." Audrey didn't look in his direction. "She's a wife telling her husband why she isn't home."

"She stopped you from telling Opal about the kidnapping."

"All she said was that Opal would be obligated to tell the police."

Fred stretched his legs out and folded his hands behind his head. "She knew exactly when you'd be in the parking lot."

Now Audrey turned her full body toward him and could barely speak through anger-clenched teeth. "What are you saying? That she planted the bomb?"

"Or someone close to her..."

Audrey was about to unload on Fred, when a doctor exited the emergency room. She leapt up to intercept her.

"Will she be all right?"

The doctor hesitated before answering. "She was amazingly lucky. We'll want to keep her for observation. She'll be sore from the fall, a couple of sprains, possible concussion but beyond that only superficial contusions and abrasions."

Audrey sighed and bowed her head. "Thank God." As the doctor disappeared back into the operating room, Katherine returned.

"How is she?"

"No major injuries, but they want to keep her over night to be sure."

Fred leaned against a wall right next to Audrey. "Ask her about who she might've told, besides her husband, of course." Audrey looked at him then stumbled over the fuzzy line that delineated her reality.

"Shut up," she said aloud.

"Good one," said Fred sarcastically. She glared at him. He shrugged, then disappeared.

Katherine looked at her with something resembling resignation, then sighed and with the exhaled breath, communicated the exhaustion, which seemed to have overtaken her. "Shut up? Audrey, you're losing it."

Audrey struggled with the weight of the next question. She picked up her friend's hand, hoping the connection would soften the landing.

"Katherine, who else knew what time I'd be leaving the office?"

Katherine didn't immediately understand the implication of her friend's question. "How would I know...who'd you tell?"

Some part of Audrey knew that the boulder she had been pushing up hill was about to flatten her. "Did you tell Coburn?"

It took another moment to sink in. When it did, Katherine reacted as if struck, physically fell back, then caught herself and edged away as if Audrey were contagious.

"Wait a minute. What are you saying? That my husband had something to do with this? That he'd try to kill you, that he'd risk killing me and our baby for what? A fucking disc?"

Audrey was frightened by Katherine's contorted face. "I just don't know who to trust…"

"Oh, no…No. This isn't the person I promised half of my first child to." She shook her head, leaning against the wall for support.

"I don't mean you…" Audrey's response was unconvincing. Katherine's features hardened as she looked down at Audrey who felt like she was shrinking under her friend's gaze.

"You're my best friend. I've been there for you while you've been on some crazy roller coaster ride that's taken you farther and farther from reality. And I'll keep waiting for you, but down here. You're not taking me with you."

"Katherine…" Audrey grabbed for her friend as she turned away from her, but Katherine threw off her hand.

"When you figure out who your friends are, call me." She half jogged half-stumbled down the hall. Audrey held her head for a moment, hoping the physical pressure would contain what felt like an imminent explosion. She gritted her teeth and bolted after Katherine, racing past curious staff and visitors, noticing people staring but undeterred by any thought of hospital decorum. She had to mend this breach, had to staunch this flow of life force, which seemed to be draining out of her with each step her friend took. Katherine was nearing the door when she suddenly stopped and clutched her stomach. She seemed to be trying to get her breath as she doubled over and sank to her knees. Audrey ran to her and eased her to the floor.

Katherine lashed out at her. "Get away from me."

Audrey tried to cradle Katherine in her lap. "Let me help, please."

"Don't touch me. Just call Coburn."

"Like you said, I'm nuts right now. Just realize it and forgive me. Please." Katherine shook her head violently, but then, another contraction rocked her. Audrey held her hand until it passed. "Please, Katherine let me help until Coburn gets here?"

Katherine had no energy to fight: It was taking all her strength to get through the fiery pains. "Just 'til he gets here."

Audrey grabbed her hand and kissed it. "Thank you." People started to converge near them, but seemed reluctant to approach the women on the floor. Audrey looked up and shouted to no one in particular, "We're having a baby here. Can we get some help?"

They didn't get much of a chance to put their Lamaze studies into practice, except for some cleansing breaths before the anesthesiologist stuck a needle into Katherine's spine for her epidural. Audrey called Coburn who had jumped into the car after a futile three-minute search for Katherine's hospital bag—it had been in her car—but he didn't arrive in time to be of any pre-birth assistance. Everything had happened too quickly.

Audrey held Katherine's hand as they wheeled her toward a room on the maternity ward. Once there, two nurses began hooking her up to machines that were designed to monitor both her well being and that of the baby's. Audrey tried to get Katherine to breathe with her during the contractions, but the pains were fierce and irregular.

"Come on, how 'bout some cleansing breaths." Audrey felt focused, in control, though she suddenly couldn't remember a thing about the order of the various methods of breathing. She searched her brain for a cogent pattern. Katherine's face was contorted more from fear than pain.

"Don't patronize me. Something's wrong. I can feel it." Audrey looked toward the nurses who continued to hook up machines. A plump one patted Katherine's hand reassuringly.

"First child?" Both Audrey and Katherine nodded. "You'll be an old hand at this before long." She attached a disk the size of a big cookie high on Katherine's stomach and held it in place with a large Velcro tabbed belt. The machine next to the bed began to record Katherine's contractions. Audrey watched as her friend's face scrunched in pain in direct proportion to both the numbers climbing on the monitor and to the print out that looked like a seismograph recording the magnitude of her belly quakes. The Lamaze classes were coming back. She remembered the order of the different breathing patterns, but now had trouble gauging what stage of breathing was appropriate since the contractions were much larger than early ones should have been. The younger nurse maneuvered another metal disk around Katherine's stomach.

The nurse's brows knitted in concentration. "I can't seem to get the fetal monitor positioned properly. It's not reading." The larger nurse took it from her and moved the disk around on the taught skin covering Katherine's belly. After a minute or so, the heartbeat registered on the machine next to the bed. The number fluctuated between eighty and ninety and seemed to match the other monitor.

The nurse looked at her co-worker sternly. "I could be getting the mother's heart beat." The other nurse left the room quickly. Katherine looked after her then at Audrey.

"What is it? What's wrong?" asked Katherine. Audrey looked up at the large nurse with eyes that pleaded for comforting news. The nurse just kept moving the disk around on Katherine's stomach. Another contraction hit and this time Katherine grabbed Audrey's hand so tightly that she feared dislocated knuckles. The sound that escaped the expectant mother was less a scream than a growl. A doctor burst through the door and placed a stethoscope on Katherine's stomach, moved it a couple of times, then addressed the plump nurse.

"Prep for an emergency C-section." Katherine clutched Audrey's hand as the doctor turned back toward them. "There seems to be some fetal distress. We'll do the emergency C-section, but it's nothing to worry about; It's routine under these circumstances."

Katherine looked drained, but she was able to muster a look of skepticism for the good doctor. "If it were routine, they wouldn't call it an emergency C-section, would they?"

The doctor managed a smile. "Well, it's more routine for us than, say, a paramedic trying to get you here in an ambulance. When did the contractions start?"

Katherine shook her head, looked to Audrey. "I don't know," said Audrey. "Maybe about ten or fifteen minutes ago, but there was no warning, just a big one right away." The doctor continued to listen with his stethoscope as he spoke.

"You're lucky you were near the hospital." He then stepped into the corridor and yelled. "Come on! Come on!" All hell seemed to break loose after that. Half a dozen people prepped Katherine: drawing blood, shaving her, disinfecting her stomach. Katherine bore it all with the stoicism of a Buddhist monk.

Her mantra was a simple. "Just take care of my baby...Take care of my baby." Though never a fan of doctors or hospitals, she managed to turn herself over to them entirely in exchange for the unspoken promise of her child's health. Audrey remained beside her until she was wheeled into the O.R. Just before she left, Katherine grabbed Audrey's hand and squeezed it hard. It was just a look that passed between them, but the look encompassed the years of history the two women shared, the gamut from euphoria to despair, the unique bond of chosen family. And in that eye to eye exchange of love, Audrey knew that she had been forgiven.

※

She had been certain that it would be a girl, so when Y-chromosome toting Brent Austin was unceremoniously wrenched from Katherine's abdomen, Audrey figured it was par for her current course.

Now in the brightly colored room with the comfortable furniture, a half-dozen people milled around Katherine's bed in an atmosphere that was more like that of a home than a hospital. Katherine's mother, one brother and two sisters who lived locally, Coburn's parents and of course Coburn all doted on Katherine who lay holding the magical boy to her breast.

Katherine's mother beamed at Audrey and threw her arms around her. The other siblings joined in making it a large group hug.

"I can't believe our little girl's a mom," Katherine's mother remarked.

"I can now," said Audrey, looking over at her friend.

"I always thought you'd be the first. You were so good with the younger kids." Audrey just smiled, not knowing what to say to her replacement mother. "Still, you've got plenty of time, right?"

Audrey nodded. "Sure." She hugged Katherine's mother tightly again. "It's so good to see you."

"You too, sweetheart." Carl entered with blue balloons, and gave Audrey a perfunctory kiss on the cheek. Coburn moved quickly to shake his hand.

"You missed all the screaming and shouting. Come to think of it, so did I," said Coburn. "And actually, from what I hear, I'm glad I did."

Carl handed him the balloons. "I was waiting to find out what color to get."

"Sorry I didn't have time to cancel my appointment. I've been a little preoccupied," said Coburn, cocking his head toward the bed where his wife and child lay.

"I'll only charge you half." Carl put an arm around Coburn.

Audrey wondered if anyone else heard the loud click, like the final tumbler falling into place on an ancient safe. She thought not. It had been in her head. But it was so loud. She looked from Carl to Coburn. Therapist and patient. Pieces of a puzzle. But what did the whole look like? The men moved away from the bed and spoke in low tones off in one corner.

Katherine held Brent up to Audrey. Audrey took him and studied the perfection of his little hands, the wonder of his little face, all the while battling a dissonance which threatened to overwhelm her. If Coburn had something to do with the kidnapping, was Carl aware of it? Had Coburn let fall some hint during a session? And why hadn't Carl been more forthcoming about the information he had on Street? Was Coburn involved in Sandcastle as well as Katherine and Carl? And what the hell was SandCastle Foundation's function? What would Carl do about it if he knew Coburn was somehow involved in the kidnapping? Which of his professions would rule, cop or shrink? She shoved aside these discordant thoughts and looked down at the bundle in her arms. She nuzzled the top of his head to smell that sweetest of perfumes, infant nectar. She turned back toward Katherine.

"Thanks for letting me be a part of this...and I'm really sorry, you know—"

"You were there for me. That's what counts. Besides, I realize that you're just stressed out." Katherine smiled at Audrey's absorption in the child. "And, on the plus side, I don't think you blew up your own car."

Audrey hadn't considered that Katherine would have thought her that far gone. "You thought I'd been making it all up?"

"I considered a lot of explanations. Now I just want you to be careful. Don't take any more chances."

Audrey kissed the baby's head and handed him back to his mother. "You're right, as usual. I'm going to go check on Opal."

"Give her my best and tell her I'll be by to show her Brent as soon as they let me get up."

"Birth has suddenly made you magnanimous?"

"Let's just say it's made me realize life's too short to be petty."

Audrey had never thought of Katherine as petty. She thought her ill feelings toward Opal had been legitimate since Opal didn't like to share the limelight and in fact, actively kept Katherine from it when she could. Audrey kissed Katherine's forehead and squeezed her hand then walked toward the door. She glanced back toward Carl and Coburn, still in conference at the back of the room, then toward the more comforting vision of mother and child. As she left, the conflicting images generated conflicting emotions about the men but she had no doubts about Katherine.

⌁

Pausing in the hall, Audrey was unwilling to open the door to Opal's room. Unwilling to see the damage done to an innocent. Damage intended for her. How do you apologize for something of that magnitude? I'm sorry I got in beyond my depth and nearly got you killed in the process. Please forgive me for not seeing that I was in danger and for letting you walk into a conflagration. What could she say? Pardon my shrapnel?

Opal slumbered, small, fragile in the folds of the prosaic hospital blanket. A two-inch bandage concealed part of a cheek, another encircled her wrist. Audrey hesitated again inside the door, but marshaled her strength and tiptoed to the side of the bed. Opal stirred, then surfaced to full consciousness. Audrey smiled down at her.

"How're you feeling?"

Opal managed a weak smile. "I've felt better. Might not be too mobile for a while."

Audrey took a tentative step toward apology. "It's all my fault. I'm so sorry."

"You planted the bomb?"

"Well, no, but—"

"Then it's not your fault. First, let me tell you something I should have told you a long time ago. I presume you know about Katherine's husband and how he was excluded from arrest in a drug bust because she had a friend in the DEA?"

Audrey nodded, but was extremely surprised that Opal knew.

"I learned that Street McClean, was also in that bust and that someone got him off, as well," Opal continued. "I have no proof that it was Katherine, but I believe it was. I searched for the files but all the records have disappeared." Opal's look of sympathy met Audrey's look of devastation. Katherine had lied to her. She had said she didn't know who Street was. Audrey began to view her relationship with Katherine as a stroll down a Mobius strip: questioned, then vindicated, then suspected again ad infinitum. She needed guidance, someone to tell her where the truth lay. She needed her mother.

"Now start from the beginning and tell me everything you know." said Opal with just the right note of empathy.

Audrey experienced a lightening of her mood as though she had shucked off a heavy winter coat. She pulled a chair close to the bed. Opal reached for her hand.

⌦⌫

Now Audrey understood how people could become involved in cults. She felt drained. She had lost all faith in her own judgment, was beginning to doubt Fred's, and just wanted someone to point her in the right direction. If Opal formed a church tomorrow, Audrey would be the first to pledge eternal fidelity. Any belief was better than this uncertainty. Losing it. She was losing it. Just like her mother. She was questioning the unquestionable. Why had Katherine reacted so violently at her suspicion about Coburn? Why had she kept the secret that Street was the dealer in the bust Coburn had ducked? Audrey had been forgiven by Katherine, but something gnawed at her soul. She knew that Katherine could be a lioness when threatened.

chapter 19

KATHERINE AND AUDREY were about eleven when her mom decided that she was no longer a fairy princess, but Sheena, Queen of the Jungle. She caught the girls reading the vintage comic book and had been appalled.

"Why would you read something so ordinary when you could create and act out your own stories?" she demanded. The two girls had been excited at first as Audrey's mother fashioned short tiger print outfits from a sheet one of Katherine's little brothers had begged for then found too scary to sleep in. In their suitably jungle-like costumes, they prowled the back yard searching for the good and bad animals. In keeping with her mother's worldview of people being essentially good, animals too, were good. Like people, the bad ones were renegade individuals within species rather than any one single group. If pressed, her mother would have developed long psychological profiles for the "bad" animals with recommendations for their rehabilitation.

Perched on the verge between childhood and adolescence, both Audrey and Katherine were reluctant to go to the park in their costumes because they were just becoming aware of the importance of fitting in at all costs. Still, they faithfully followed Audrey's mother when she insisted upon a return to the wild.

Glendale's Brand Park was large by municipal standards with lush green lawns and a variety of mature trees. The three prowled toward the untamed foliage beyond the library and studios. They ignored curious glances as they acted out an intricate scenario directed by Audrey's mom. Katherine seemed oblivious to the stares, whole-heartedly giving herself over to the story. Audrey tried to slough off the self-consciousness she felt, tried to shrug away the feeling that everyone was looking at her, knowing she was related to the eccentric woman in the scant tiger costume. Yet the thought of deserting her mother never crossed her mind. The girls continued to follow her mom when she climbed a meandering oak whose branches then became her domain.

The young Audrey looked down from her branch, which was below Katherine's, below her mother's. Children had begun to gather around the trunk, giggling and pointing at the strangely clad woman in the tree.

"Mom," pleaded Audrey. "Mom, come on, let's go." But her mother didn't hear her. She was communing with the birds. "Katherine, tell her to get down."

"I don't think she wants to."

"Katherine, please."

"All right, I'll try." Katherine climbed up a branch closer to Audrey's mother. "Audrey wants to go now. We're going to go back home. Come with us, okay?" When she received no response, Katherine looked down at Audrey and shook her head.

"It's almost five. I'm going to go get Dad. You stay here, okay?"

"I will," said Katherine.

As Audrey passed the sniggering children, she looked back up at her mother and knew that she was no longer in Brand Park. She was in Africa.

Audrey's father brought a ladder and her mother's rain coat. It didn't take him long to cajole her down from her jungle lair. Audrey kept her distance as he walked her mother back toward the car. She was mortified yet guilty for the feeling. Billy McInty and Davey Schwartzwald drove by on their bicycles and shouted at her.

"Hey Audrey, your mom's out of her tree." Katherine took off after them as Audrey stood immobilized, every capillary in her face exploding in shame. Katherine picked up a handful of sharp rocks and hurled them rapid-fire at the boys. One opened a wound on Billy's cheek just above his mouth. Audrey watched in horror and satisfaction as blood oozed through the fingers of the hand Billy had placed over the gash.

⚜

Audrey was staring at her own hand as she walked down the hospital corridor. When Carl rounded the corner and nearly collided with her, she yelped, a sound that ranged somewhere between a cry and a shout.

"Sorry, didn't mean to scare you." He looked concerned about her reaction.

"It's okay. I'm just edgy."

Carl put an arm around her. "You look tired."

"Drained."

"Drained and edgy. Quite a combo."

"Number four on your menu." She said it flatly. Their normally easy banter had become colorless, forced on both their parts. An unusual tension charged the atmosphere between them. Something was different. Something that couldn't be explained by the estrangement she felt from him, from everyone right now. She realized that she was carrying his jacket and handed it to him.

"Thanks."

"Keep it. I'll get it later," said Carl.

"No, take it. I'll be fine. I'm going straight home." Reluctantly, he took it. He steered her toward the elevator, while pulling a bulky cell phone from his pocket.

"Take this."

"A cell phone on a public servant's salary?"

"That one's Katherine's. I've got Coburn's. The last number called is this one," he held up Coburn's phone. "All you have to do is press that green button and you can get me any time day or night."

"Why would I need it?"

"Don't play games." He handed her a small aerosol container. "And keep this with you everywhere. And I mean in the shower."

"What is it?"

"Mace. It'll disable an attacker long enough for you to get away but you've got to hit 'em with it."

"You mean grip it like brass knuckles and hook him with my left?"

"Audrey, I'm serious," said Carl. She nodded to him lethargically but accepted the mace. "You were in with Opal?" Audrey nodded again. "How does she seem?" His inquiry sounded rhetorical.

"Fine. Why don't you go see her?" Audrey didn't feel she had the energy to deal with Carl. She felt like she was dragging an anvil.

"I will later. Talked to her doctor. No major injuries."

"I know." She didn't want to talk. Once again, sleeping the five years until the turn of the century seemed like a marvelous idea.

"In fact the bomb guys say the detonation caused more destruction than it should have, given the charge. The device itself was more on par with a firecracker, meant to scare, not destroy. They hit the fuel line by accident which ignited the gas tank."

"I'm supposed to be happy they were inept but lucky?"

Carl shrugged.

"Whatever...If it was meant to scare me, it worked." Audrey left an uncomfortable pause before she asked: "Do you know why Street was looking for me?"

"No. You tell me." Carl looked away uncomfortably.

"You don't know?" She forced eye contact with him.

Carl took a deep breath before he answered. "Skitch called. Said she thought Street was looking for you, so I followed you."

"And you don't know why."

"Skitch didn't say."

"But you could speculate."

"I really can't."

"Can't or won't?" she challenged him.

"Can't. I would if I could. Look, I didn't kill Street. I presume you didn't, so that sorta leaves Nate or Dr. Kevorkian."

"Why would Skitch call you?" Audrey asked suspiciously. Now Carl seemed at a loss for words. He shook his head during the long pause, before he finally spoke.

"I called her, pressed her about Nate and Street. I figured she probably knew everything that was going on."

"And?"

"And she didn't tell me anything, but I gave her my number and she just called out of the blue. Said you'd talked to her today. Wouldn't reveal anything about Nate's involvement, but she did tell me about Street. I had the police put out an APB on him and one on Nate."

They entered the elevator, and Audrey pressed the ground floor button. As the door closed, Carl put both hands on her shoulders and turned her toward him. His eyes had a klieg-light intensity.

"I know you haven't been keeping me up on what's going on, and it doesn't matter. But if you've got something somebody wants... just give it to them."

Alarm bells sounded in her head. Audrey tried to pull away from him, but he held her more firmly. "Why would you think they'd want something from me?"

"Somebody wants whatever was on Street's computer. Fred copied it. You were the last person to see Fred alive." He said it as though it weren't even a revelation and maybe it wasn't; maybe it was just a simple deduction. Or maybe he knew because he knew about the kidnapping.

"I don't have it. And the last person to see Fred alive was his murderer." As the elevator neared the ground floor, Carl reached back and flipped the power switch. The machine shuddered to an abrupt halt. Audrey looked at Carl as if for the first time. She hadn't wanted to confide in him before because she knew he would want to "handle it", want her to go to the police. Now, she couldn't tell him, because she suspected his involvement on some level. He might even know a lot more than she did.

"But you have other information you're not sharing. Why?" Carl's face was open, imploring.

"Because I don't know who to trust." The pain on Carl's face hurt Audrey in the way that a wound incurred by a loved one can elicit a sympathetic ache in the same spot. She looked away, flipped the switch and felt some relief as the elevator started again. Suddenly, he grabbed her and kissed her deeply. It so surprised her that she didn't resist, in fact, kissed him back, realizing that it was something that she had wanted to do for a long time, something she hadn't let herself even think about since that one time. The opening door jolted her back to reality. She jerked away from him and ran down the hall toward the exit. When she glanced back over her shoulder, she saw Carl smash his fist into the wall next to the elevator.

Audrey fled from her elevator encounter with Carl and hurried toward the courtyard fountain. She had a passing urge to dive into it, swim to China. But even if she could swim down the drain, through the sewer, out across the ocean, she didn't speak Chinese, and she had nothing to wear. She reasoned that there was never a final solution to anything. That life, for her, was an infinite Chinese box whose answer lay at the center but always beyond her ability to open the infinitesimal box at the core.

She felt a kinship with those who described near death experiences as floating above one's body. She sensed she was viewing her psyche from another plane. Viewing her dying psyche but unable to do anything to save it, much like Woody Allen parading his neuroses on film, displaying an intellectual grasp of his problems, yet unable to mitigate the damage they do in real life. She felt that her essential self was being swept away because she had no anchor.

Fred appeared beside her as she stared into the fountain.

"What was that all about?"

Audrey walked toward the curb. "What?"

"You and Carl in the elevator."

Couldn't he see that she had no time for petty reality? "I don't know," she answered, hoping to end the conversation.

"You weren't exactly resisting."

Anger suffused and energized her body. "I don't have to justify myself to...myself...or whatever you are."

Fred looked stung, but defiant. "Fine. Are we still interested in solving this little problem of a missing teenager or shall we go back and have another go at it in the elevator?"

She finally understood what the term "seeing red" meant. Images seemed filtered through a blood colored film. Anger exploded from a depth she hadn't fathomed until that moment.

"If you're going to help me, help me. Otherwise, get the hell out of my life."

Fred's body relaxed, slumped slightly, a physical disarmament. Her anger had pierced something in him. He swallowed with difficulty before he spoke. "Okay. I'll help. This is what you need to think about. Your suspect's probably up in that hospital with an outside shot that it's your ex-husband or Nate. I don't know why Miles would want me dead unless he thought you and I were an item, and I sure can't figure out what he'd want with the disc so he gets lowest priority. Now Nate looks like he's in the thick of things, but he's got family, business and all that. Too much to lose to be screwing around unless that disc holds something lethal for him. My top suspect's Coburn— and Katherine by extension—because of the drug link to Street. Carl could be in on it with them; he's connected to Coburn in the doctor patient relationship and to Katherine through that foundation he set up, but then again it could be something about his cover-up when he shot the kid. Maybe somebody found out about it and is blackmailing him to get him to help them."

"Forget Katherine," she ordered.

"You can't count her out."

"Yes I can!" she screamed.

The tension returned to Fred's physique, his words were clipped, bitten off. "I'm here to help you with your judgment. If you aren't going to listen to me—"

Audrey placed both hands firmly over her ears and walked away. As before, she spoke rapidly and in monotone. "Once upon a midnight dreary/ While I pondered weak and weary/ Over a many quaint..."

"Use your head!" he shouted after her.

"and curious volume of forgotten lore/ While I nodded..."

He caught up with her and roughly jerked her hands from her ears. "You don't want to know?"

Tears streamed down Audrey's face. "If my best friend tried to kill me? I'd rather die not knowing." She jerked free of him and ran to the curb where she hopped into a taxi, roused its napping driver, and fled.

Audrey had always used Mrs. Greenland's poems as a sanctuary. When her mind stormed, "The Raven" gave her shelter. She knew it was odd, but the macabre story of the possibly all-knowing bird had been a warm nest she could sink into. Its cadence had lulled her, its alliteration had soothed her, and even its hopelessness had been despair shared. It had been her mental refuge when her mind became overloaded, when a particular tape played and replayed until she visualized ripping it out and trailing the offending celluloid from the top of her head as she ran screaming down the street.

But now, even the poems couldn't force aside the tumult that had touched down like a tornado in her brain. Had she overstated her case? Would she rather be dead than learn something she couldn't live with? She had neither children nor a husband who, according to Dickinson, would suffer the hell of her parting. She no longer had a father, and her mother hadn't recognized her in years. She really would rather die than believe in a world where someone she had known, had trusted, had loved for most of her life could suddenly become—or have been all along—evil.

She wanted to bundle Coburn in with Katherine. Not that she thought he was blameless, but she wanted him to share her friend's immunity from suspicion so that she wouldn't have to dwell on the possibility that Katherine was living with a murderer; that a murderer was the father of her godchild. Why weren't people built with lie detectors on their foreheads? Litmus-like papers which would change color at the first sign of deception. She would settle for a slight lengthening of the nose. Anything, so she wouldn't have to guess.

She wanted to add Carl to the blanket immunity, but something stopped her. When he had kissed her, she had felt an odd fear. Odd in that it was not entirely unpleasant as was her general association with fear. She tried to isolate rational thought from the clutter in her brain. He may have been unstable at some point, but he was too decent a human being to be involved. She didn't need a chemically sensitive paper to tell her that. He lived his decency. She wanted to exclude Carl as a suspect, but something stopped her. Something connected to Fred? Or maybe it was just Carl.

It had been just that once. And it began so innocuously. She was in the salad dressing aisle because she had run out of mayonnaise and was just reaching for the full fat Best Foods when she was bowled over by a charging dog. Not just any dog, Annabel. She was so thrilled to see her ex-dog that it took a moment before her spirits sank in preparation for seeing her ex-husband. But rather than Miles, Carl rounded the corner in pursuit of the stampeding canine.

"I wondered why she took off like a rocket," he said. Annabel continued to bath Audrey in kisses, and Audrey hugged and stroked her like the long lost friend she was. She had blocked her feelings for the dog much in the way she had blocked her feelings for Miles after their encounter at the Hotel Del Coronado. Now she reveled in the doggie love.

"Let me give you a hand." Carl helped her to her feet, but Annabel continued to jump on her.

"I've missed her so much. Oh, and you, too. How've you been?"

"Great, Miles's surfing in Baja, so I'm dog sitting."

Audrey looked wistfully at her former pet. "I wish I could."

"Look, it's fine with me if you want to take her. I don't mind telling Miles he should work out some custody deal with you."

"I live in a 'no pets' building now."

"Oh, sorry. But, hey, it's a good excuse to have you over for some albacore a buddy of mine caught yesterday. It'll be a supervised visitation."

"I, uh, I don't think...Well, if it wouldn't put you out. I wouldn't mind spending a little more time with her."

"And what am I, chopped liver?" he said as if born in the borsch belt.

"Well, you, too."

Carl's house was one of the only non-mansionized homes on the side of the hill overlooking Santa Monica canyon. From his small, tiled deck one could survey the canyon, Santa Monica Bay, and the highway all the way up to Point Dume. Audrey thought this was where she would like to live when she grew up.

They had the excellent albacore and a crisp Sauvignon Blanc and before either knew it, Audrey was crying about how much she hated Miles.

"Don't you see? If you hate him that means that you still have strong feelings for him. And if you still have strong feelings for him, that means you're not over him," said the recently doctrinated shrink. They were seated on a cushioned glider with Annabel between them overlooking the sparse lights along the coast while finishing those last few drops of Sauvignon.

"I am over him."

"If you say so."

"I am, and I'll prove it."

"Oh, yeah? How?"

Audrey unceremoniously shoved Annabel off the glider and planted a decidedly un-platonic kiss on Carl's lips. Only Annabel's insistent nosing between them ended the protracted lip-lock.

Audrey straightened her clothes. "Sorry, guess that wasn't really appropriate."

"No. I mean, yes, or it was, or, God! I feel like I'm in Jr. High again and I'm tongue-tied because I'm just so...bowled over." He looked at her with, what, desire? No. Love.

"Look, I shouldn't have...I've just always felt an immediate kinship with you. I don't ever want to jeopardize that...that friendship."

Carl tried to cover his disappointment as he rose from the glider. "Right. Friends. How about some ice cream?"

"Thanks any way," Audrey said as she made her way through the compact living room toward the front door. "I need to get home."

"Sure." Carl followed her. "I'd better keep a firm grip on Annabel." He grabbed the dog's collar.

"Thanks for dinner. And the supervised visitation," said Audrey as she reached the door.

"No problem. Any time." Carl held the dog as he opened the door for her. She gave him a quick peck goodnight and turned to leave. Carl grabbed her with his free hand and pulled her into a tender, lingering kiss. He kicked the door closed and let go of Annabel.

Their lovemaking was characterized by an emotional urgency that played out in an intricate ballet which both of their bodies intuited. Audrey felt a physical and emotional "fit" that she never before had experienced. The heights she climbed were vertiginous, frightening.

Annabel was whining excitedly in the early morning light and awoke both of them even before the pounding started.

"Hey! Wake up! Surf's gnarly in Ventura, bro." It was Miles.

Audrey darted out of bed and threw on her clothes. "I'm so sorry. It's my fault. I never should have let it happen."

Carl tried to grab at her hand. "Wait."

"We're friends, Carl, friends." And with that, she climbed out the side window and disappeared through the neighbor's hedge.

They never ran into each other again until Miles and she started seeing each other the second time. Nothing was ever said about the incident. Audrey and Carl picked up their easy friendship without missing a beat.

※

The pleasant looking officer touched his hat as he exited her house after a cursory canvas for murderers.

"I checked the closets and under the bed, so you don't have to worry. We'll be patrolling all night, just hit nine-one-one if you need us."

"Thank you, officer. Good night." Should she tip him? She figured police officers should be tipped if anyone should. Please take this five for risking a bullet for me. Really, officer, keep the twenty. Put it in your child's college fund. You never know when you might not be around to add to it.

She thought people would be judged by how they treated those who served them. Served in the broadest possible sense. Or even how they treated anyone who couldn't help them in some way. There would be a special line for the boss who denigrated his underlings, the child who didn't honor worthy parents, the person who didn't pass a panhandler without thinking "There but for fortune." And on judgment day, the egregious over tipper would be seen, not as the spoiler of good help, but rather, as sitting at the right hand of God.

All this raced through her mind as she entered her brightly-lit house. She let her things drop to the floor in fatigue. Fred appeared with a chilled bottle of champagne in one hand and her terry cloth bathrobe in the other. She smiled unconvincingly.

"Thanks, but all I really need is a hot bath and a nap. Opal and I brainstormed on any place the damn disc could be." Audrey shook her head dejectedly. "She thinks I can bluff the kidnappers until we can figure something out in the morning." She tried to move past Fred, but he stood in her way. "I haven't slept more than three hours in two days."

He put an arm around her. "A nap's not all you need." He bent down and kissed her passionately. She disengaged herself as kindly as she could.

"Just a bath and a nap."

He threw the robe at her. "What happens? A guy kisses you and that's it, you're crazy about him?"

She turned back around, furious at his jealousy. "Didn't happen when you were alive, did it?"

Fred clenched his jaw, but tried to be casual, though his eyes conveyed injury. "So...what, you in love with this guy?"

"No!" But the response was too emphatic. "I mean...I don't know what I mean," her voice thin, scratchy, forced through reluctant vocal chords. After a deep breath: "He's like family. Someone I could always count on."

"And I'm not?"

She looked at him and imagined looking through him, then had to look away because of a tightness in her chest. Enervation overtook her. Was she having a heart attack? Is this what it felt like to die? This weakness that permeates every cell? She spoke quietly, resignedly. "You're a mental illness, a figment. No, I can't count on you."

Now he had to turn away from her, but she caught the glint of light reflected off the watery film on his eye. It cut her like a laser. "You can if you need me," he said.

Audrey shook her head, unable to deal with the pain she had inflicted. On whom? Herself? Her psychosis? Her guardian angel?

The tiny canister of mace was on the floor next to her bathrobe. Audrey had listened to Carl even if she hadn't completely trusted him. As she soaked in a tub of bubbles, she leafed through the file on Street that Katherine gave her in the parking lot before the explosion. There was a notation, "questioned and released", next to the name Street McClean on the same date that Katherine had allowed her friend to exclude Coburn from the bust. Is that what Katherine was going to tell her about before the explosion? It didn't matter. The rest of the file was much as Carl had described; numerous minor arrests followed by the murder charge that was dropped when the only material witness vanished. Street was now truly a dead end. She let the file drop next to the tub and sank down into the steaming bubbles.

Now, nearly falling asleep, her mind tried to think about the other Fred, the one who had been alive, the one who was slow of speech, not by any stretch articulate, who had dressed like an impoverished biker with long hair and bad teeth, but who yearned to atone. With him, there had never been the familiarity she felt with the, well, post-dead-Fred. It was as if the dead man were related to her, someone she had known for years. She thought how absurd it was, especially since he wasn't anything, really, didn't exist, except when she set foot in the waters of madness.

The living Fred desired only one thing at the end: to help his sister. He had asked her to help and she had failed him. How would the tapes ever devise a fantasy that would fix that reality? Would she be forever stuck with myriad possible rescue fantasies? Would there be a matched set now? Failing her parents, failing Frances?

She forced her mind to review her memories of the living Fred, the fight with Street, his help with the sheetrock, his bringing Frances to her house, their last meeting the night before he went up North. With sudden clarity, she knew where it was. She sat bolt upright in the tub, causing a tsunami to wash over the side, then reached for her towel, but it wasn't where she had left it near her robe. She tried to wipe the soap out of her eyes but before she could, the towel was suddenly wrapped around her mouth and neck and twisted. She fought and writhed until she could see that the towel was being wrenched by Nate.

"Quiet! Quiet!" Nate's voice cracked with tension. Audrey fought to loose the towel with one hand while the other groped for the mace on the floor beside the tub. Nate saw what she was after and lunged for the tiny canister. Audrey pulled the towel from her face and screamed.

"Fred!" He appeared and it looked as if Fred tripped Nate as he tried to reach the mace. Or did Nate just slip on the papers from Street's file? Audrey dove for the mace, grabbed it and pointed it at Nate who clutched his knee in obvious pain.

"Stay down!" Audrey's voice sounded foreign to her ears, low, raspy, full of command. Her nakedness occurred to her as an after-thought. She grabbed her robe and put it on awkwardly not wanting to take her finger off the mace for more than a second. Nate clutched his knee with both hands.

"Listen, I'm on your side. I was only trying to keep you from screaming when I came in."

"Sorry, Nate, but my crisis of judgment is surpassed only by my paranoia. Don't take it personally, but I don't believe a word you say."

"It's okay, I wouldn't either." He looked down at his knee, which was already starting to swell.

"The cop said he searched this place."

"I got into the ceiling panel in the hall when I saw him pull up. You gotta get this place rewired. You got some scary splices up there." He indicated his knee. "Could I get some ice for this?"

Fred looked at her incredulously. "You're going to trust him aren't you?" Fred, now in the role of disappointed teacher.

"No," she said directly to Fred. "Just shut up."

"Please?" Nate begged for the ice.

Flustered, concentrating on the mace in her hand, she turned back to Nate. "Fine, fine. I'm just burnt out. Can you make it into the kitchen?"

"Sure." He used the towel rack to hoist himself up, then hobbled into the living room. Audrey followed at a safe distance, the mace held carefully in front of her.

Nate sat at the dining room table and put his leg up on another chair. Audrey moved warily into the kitchen, which was open to the dining room, and removed a plastic ice tray from the freezer. With one hand, she ran it under the water then, pulling a plastic bag from a drawer, handed both ice and bag to Nate.

"What are you doing here?" she demanded.

"I'm on my way to Mexico. I wanted to warn you that Street's going to try to give you some information he has. Something he wants your help on, but he didn't tell me what it was."

"Didn't he trust you?"

"It's not that. We like, go way back. When my construction firm was in the toilet, he bailed me out. It was only later I realized he owned it...and me. He had enough character to feel bad about it, but that didn't stop him. We did have this unspoken thing. I didn't want to know about where the money was coming from. Or, in the case of graft payments, where it was going. He lost his shirt when the art market crashed. That's where he was doing his major laundering. Then he started doing more and more through my company. He was on a short leash to his suppliers and he wasn't getting the quantities he used to, so my company suited his purposes. He always thought he'd get out of the hole with his suppliers one day. Always workin' an angle to get back on top, you know?"

"Oh, yeah, that sounds like Street," said Fred.

She glanced at the dead man. Ignored him. "Why did Fred go to you. He must've known you and Street were still tight."

"Yeah, but Street was always more of a fuck up than we were. Fred and me were closer. That probably bothers Street some. But you know, in the end, even when Street was pissed at Fred for crashing his computer, he was friend enough to tell him he had dangerous information on the disc. Not just danger from him, but from the person he was blackmailing. See he figures this person offed Fred to get the disc and he's next 'cause he knows what's on it.

"He was next. Street was killed this afternoon at the courthouse."

"Shit! I gotta get out of here."

"Think with me. Who was he blackmailing?"

"He never told me, but whoever it is might think I know and come after me next. That's why I can't be anywhere near my family. That's why I wanted to tell you so you could protect yourself in case they think you know."

"So go to the police."

"You gotta've figured out by now, it's somebody connected. Street as much as said there's ties to the cops or the DA's office—somebody in the justice system. That's how you got hooked up in all this."

"What? No, I got involved because I happened to be walking across the street with a piece of sheetrock and Fred happened to be a taper who needed to atone."

"Yeah, well, he was sincere about atoning and all that, but he searched you out 'cause he heard your real estate guy tell Terry you were with the DA"

Audrey was taken aback. She never considered that their meeting was anything but serendipity. She recalled that he knew she was a lawyer, but didn't realize he had sought her out.

"But he never followed through." Audrey suddenly remembered the visit to the DA's office with the bubble pack. He had left without saying anything about it. Audrey's mind raced. Street was blackmailing someone with ties to the DA or police. Maybe about a cover up in a police shooting? Maybe about getting your husband out of a bust? No. Not Katherine. She had drawn that line and wouldn't cross it. Still, she couldn't exclude Coburn. Street could have been blackmailing him. Coburn could have been in on one of the corporate covers. Or Opal. Something that could reflect badly on her valued reputation? Miles wasn't in the DA's office, but Audrey was. Did they have something on him? And then there was Carl with ties to both police and the DAs office and a cover-up. She looked at Nate's knee, now nearing the size of a volleyball. "You need to find a doctor."

"I'll see one when I get to Mexico. I gotta lay low 'til this blows over."

"Carl put an APB out on you."

"Carl, huh? That's interesting."

"What?"

"A shrink putting out an APB."

"He used to be a cop."

"Still..." Nate centered the bag of ice on his knee. "Got anything I can tie this on with?"

"Sure." Audrey went back into the bathroom, followed by Fred, to retrieve the first aid kit.

He sat on the edge of the tub. "Jesus. You're trusting him not to grab a butcher knife and chop you into tuna tartare."

She looked over at him with a slight smile. "I've still got my mace. Besides, it's time to start trusting. It's like holding my breath when I don't." First Katherine, next, maybe Nate. Slowly she would weigh and decide whom to trust.

"What if you're wrong?"

She shrugged. "People will disappoint you. It's as certain as not winning the lottery."

She returned to the dining room and wrapped the ace bandage around the ice bag on Nate's leg, then pinned it to his shorts.

"You have a car?" Audrey asked.

"Swapped with a buddy of mine. It's parked on the next street over."

"I'll give you a hand."

"I can manage." Nate hoisted himself out of the chair and limped stiff legged toward the door. Before he opened it he turned back toward her.

"You'd've been good for Fred."

Audrey smiled at him. "Thanks, Nate. Be careful."

"I'll be okay. You take your own advice."

She nodded and waved as he closed the door. The minute he was gone, Audrey strode to the door off the kitchen leading to the garage. Inside, she flipped on the overhead light and crossed to her tool cabinet and work bench where she removed the sledge hammer, the cat's paw and a large flashlight.

Fred watched her, arms folded in front of him. "Same with me. I get the urge to remodel whenever my life's threatened."

Audrey rolled her eyes at him as she headed toward the living room. She recalled how Fred had told her not to fire up the gas log unit until he could have someone check it out.

"Remember how we said we'd literally torn the place apart?"

"Vaguely," said the dead man.

"We were speaking figuratively. Now it's time to be literal." She moved to the wall above the fireplace and swung the sledgehammer with all the power she could summon. It chewed a hole the size of its head through the drywall. A few more swings and a few more holes allowed her room to pry, with the cat's paw, large chunks of the gypsum from the studs which supported the board. When she opened a large enough hole, she stopped, put her hand inside and felt around. Nothing. Now she ripped away the wall with a fury, almost a rage at possibly having been wrong. When most of the lower part of the sheetrock was torn away, she could stick her head inside the wall. She shined the flashlight from corner to corner. Nothing. As she was about to give up, she spotted something nailed to one of the wall studs: the bubble pack envelope. Ripping it off the stud, she tore it open and found a nondescript disc.

"The dingus," she said.

Fred beamed like a proud parent. "Congratulations, Ms. Spade."

Audrey smiled back triumphantly. "And we still have five hours."

Audrey, fully clothed, dozed on the futon, clutching the phone to her chest. Fred stood by the window peering out the slit between the blind and the window frame.

When the phone rang, Audrey immediately sat up as though she had been awake all along. "This is Audrey."

The voice echoed through the receiver. "You have it?"

"Yes."

"Bring it to the carousel. Meet us inside. Now."

"I will, but I—" A loud click ended the conversation. She looked up at Fred. "Let's go."

chapter 20

AUDREY CONSIDERED THAT at some point she had probably looked more ridiculous than she did now, furiously pedaling down the Ocean Avenue bike lane on her florescent green mountain bike, dressed like a cat burglar, but probably not since she had joined her mother as Sheena Queen of the Jungle. It was four in the morning and Fred was perched on the rack behind her, which would have added to the ludicrous picture, had anyone been able to see him.

he bike had been a gift from Miles. She discounted it when he presented it to her because he had won it in a pro-celebrity skiing tournament, that and because of its ghastly green color. But now she was beginning to see many of Miles' actions in a new light. He had tried, to the extent of his abilities, to be married. He had loved her. She had loved him. They'd make good siblings.

The tapes were oddly silent. Clarity of purpose had descended; a confidence that even if she made the wrong decision as seen from some future armchair, she would be making the right one for her. For now. She still wasn't certain whom to trust, but she trusted that she would know when she needed to.

She coasted down the ramp leading to the pier, happy for the respite from pedaling. The ocean beyond threw back a hazy glow from the Ferris wheel before it faded into a seamless whole with the foggy night sky. The pier itself looked like a giant-child's bedroom, a jumble of enormous toys awaiting the next day's play. She turned sharply toward the carousel and pulled up in front of a flight of stairs that led to a footpath below. Fred climbed off the back rack.

"That was the least comfortable ride I've ever had. Carl's convertible included."

"It was no picnic for me. Next time I'm going to conjure up somebody lighter." She had said it casually but instantly hoped she would never conjure anyone again. Hoped Fred was an aberration rather than a member of some ghost filled metropolis in her brain.

She reached up and touched the nearly healed cut on his forehead. "It's almost gone."

"I know," he said. She noted his wistful tone, then turned to lock her bike to the stair rail. Fred sniffed derisively. "Think that'll guarantee it'll be here when you get back?" He was baiting her and she wasn't going to rise to it.

She shook her head. "But I'll be glad if it is." Audrey dropped the key in the small shoulder bag she carried. They both scanned the area around the circular building that housed the carousel. No sign of life, no cars in the parking lot below, no movement but the wispy fog fingers, which played the coast like a harp.

"We should've gotten a gun somewhere," said Fred.

"Where? 'Guns R Us'? This isn't Texas, besides, I have my mace."

"And a car. We couldn't have stolen a car? What if it's a simple, 'Here's the disc. Here's the girl.' You going to pedal her to the valley?"

"We'll call Carl to pick us up."

"Oh, yeah...the arsonist-firefighter will put out the flames," Fred mumbled almost inaudibly. But Audrey wasn't buying into it.

The building was enclosed by a series of glass doors which Audrey and Fred tried discretely. When none opened, an edginess surfaced in Audrey.

"We're supposed to meet inside. Am I supposed to break in?"

"They're testing your resolve," responded the apparition, testing her patience.

The pair crept around to the back of the building where it abutted a nightclub which seemed to change owners with the tides. They found a flight of stairs angling up the outside of the carousel building and Audrey mounted them as quietly as she could. At the top she tried a wooden door and found that the knob turned but the door itself wouldn't budge. She jammed her shoulder against it a couple of times with nothing for the effort but a bruise. Fred stood behind her, leaning against the landing rail. She looked back at him with an expression that made a verbal barb redundant.

"All right, all right," he said. "Together on three. One, two..." He made as if to assault the door with her, but when he said, "three", she put all her effort into it and the door finally gave way—without his help.

She shook her head. "Thanks for nothing."

"And I delivered," deadpanned the dead man.

They walked through a short hallway that merged with a longer corridor circling the interior of the building. It had windows along the inside, which opened on to the carousel below, and walls with doors on the opposite side. Audrey looked out one window and saw the top of the merry-go-round, its inner workings exposed from above. Her eyes darted around the perimeter, searching the area for whomever she was supposed to meet. Security lights forced ghostly shadows from the wooden figures below.

She thought of contexts and expectations. The same prancing horses, which delighted her by day, now conjured specters by night. Audrey tried to contain her apprehension, tried to feign confidence. Fred followed her as she boldly walked around the upper level, through small offices, storage areas, and a lounge.

One door proclaimed, in large ornate letters, "Knowledge Is At Hand" and beneath that: "Madam Cassandra—The Truth Through Palmistry". It was the last room before a flight of interior stairs. Audrey pushed the door open and saw an inviting, if gaudy, sitting room. She involuntarily glanced at her hand, wishing Madam Cassandra were around to divine the truth for her. She backed out and closed the door, then shoved past Fred, who seemed content in her wake.

They moved stealthily down the stairs and onto the main floor, which was dominated by the carousel, though there were little shops and display enclaves at various points along the windowed exterior walls. Audrey stepped up onto the carousel's platform and walked along the outer edge. She decided it was unlikely that she would sneak up on anyone, so she might as well take the direct approach.

"Hello…I'm here. I have the disc." She began to feel foolish which was a more comfortable feeling than fear. Certainly a more familiar one. "It's like being on stage here. Not my top choice for a furtive rendezvous."

"And your top choice is?" Fred inquired.

"I don't know, a Paris sewer?" A cat leapt from the chariot in front of her. "Whoa!" Audrey jumped off the platform, then looked back to see the harmless animal. "Think he lives here?"

"Sure. He's probably a ratter." It was Carl's voice. She wheeled around to see him sauntering toward her, hand casually in one pocket. The other, the left that he hooked into the wall by the elevator, was bandaged.

Fred vanished. Audrey tried to cover her apprehension.

"And you're here because…?"

"Because you have to come with me without asking any questions."

"What do you think the chance of that is?"

"Right off the bat…"

She started to move toward him, but he held up his hand. Audrey stopped, leaving a ten-yard gap between them. "How's this one. Where's Frances?"

"Listen, we can talk about that, but not here. We don't have time, and…the truth is, I'm in over my head, too."

"Yeah? Who got you in?" Her voice was strong, no nonsense. Carl made his living by manipulating people and she was determined that he wouldn't talk her into or out of anything.

"I can't tell you any more. It's a patient privilege thing."

"Coburn?"

"I can't say."

"And I can't come with you."

He pulled a small handgun from inside his jacket. "You don't have a lot of choice, Audrey. Toss me the mace."

She was incredulous. "Why'd you give it to me in the first place? So I'd trust you?"

"So you'd use it on somebody if you needed to."

"Well, I did. I used it on Nate."

Carl looked disconcerted. "Nothing about it on the police scanner."

"I sent him on his way when I realized he was telling the truth. Street was blackmailing somebody with ties to the police or D.A's office."

"I know."

"You?"

Carl shook his head dejectedly. "Believe that if it'll get you moving. I don't want to have to prove how serious I am, Audrey." He attempted to wave the gun threateningly, but his expression negated the gesture.

"This is a big waste of time, Carl. You'd never shoot me." She stood with her arms open, her purse dangling from her elbow. A shot rang out and Audrey looked down to see that the bullet had pierced her handbag. Appalled, she opened the bag and withdrew her organizer with a bullet lodged near the center. "You shot my Day Runner. You might as well kill me. Now come on, Carl…"

"Are you ready to take me seriously?" Audrey didn't respond. When another shot landed to the right of her feet, Audrey felt an internal chill, the dull cold pain of a slush drink chugged. The coldness immobilized her momentarily, but she finally found her voice. "Carl…"

"I'll do whatever it takes to get you out of here now." Carl's voice held a similar chill, that of detachment.

"Oh, you'd actually shoot me? The way you shot that child?" It was her only weapon. She hadn't thought about it before she used it, and as soon as it was out of her mouth, wished it hadn't been in her arsenal, wondered what she would have come up with if it hadn't been at hand. But then again, why was she worrying about Carl's feelings when he was shooting at her? Her arrow did hit its mark. A sequence of rapid-fire emotions ignited Carl's features: pain, anguish, resolve. He struggled to resume his composure.

"No, not the same way. Then I was given false information by a man who knew his son was in the building, but was willing to sacrifice him for a few extra hours of freedom. He said his connection was inside, armed and holding. Turned out to be his eleven year old son with an air rifle."

"And the cover-up?"

"My partner planted some crack in the john. Said it would keep IA off our backs. I never told anyone but Miles."

"That's when you left the force."

"And spent a year in a 'recovery program'."

"Who are you working with now?"

"No more questions, Audrey. Just move." He indicated the door with a flick of the gun. Audrey paused, considered her options, and finally complied.

Their footsteps punctuated the silence, but not enough to mask the ominous click that caused them both to stop and attend to their surroundings. Darkness enveloped them as the security lights went out, leaving the carousel lit only by dim streetlights, rendering the shadows amorphous gray puddles.

Two shots sliced through the stillness. Two flashes of light. An image of Carl seeming to jump up before slumping to the ground. Audrey felt the same time-fracture she had experienced during previous traumas, as if time itself wanted to assist her observation so as to reinforce the ordinariness of disaster. A scream became strangled in her throat and gurgled out in what she had intended to be his name.

"Carl!" She rushed to him, placed one hand over the spot where blood gushed from his mid-section, the other on a head wound above his eye. Blood oozed through the fingers of both of her hands, but bleeding seemed most pronounced from the head wound. Ripping the bandage from around his previously injured hand, she closed the wound as much as possible before wrapping the gauze tightly around his head.

Opal emerged from the murky shadows, a gun in hand. "Oh, my God. Not Carl." She knelt beside them. "I couldn't see who it was... Only that he was shooting at you."

"Call an ambulance!" Audrey barked the order as she tossed her Katherine's cell phone. She pulled her sweatshirt over her head and wrapped it around Carl's chest.

Opal picked up Carl's wrist and felt for a pulse. She shook her head. "Looks like it's too late."

"We'll start CPR. Just call!"

Opal punched nine-one-one. "Yes, this is Senior Deputy district attorney Opal Nichols. I need an ambulance at the Santa Monica Carousel—gun shot wounds. Immediately." Audrey touched Carl's carotid artery and felt a faint pulse. At first, relief flooded her but then she looked at Opal, perplexed.

"I'm getting a pulse."

Opal put the phone down and pulled Audrey away from the injured man. "That happens sometimes, a spontaneous recovery. I was a nurse before I went to law school. I'll take care of him." Opal began checking the bandages Audrey had fashioned.

Audrey, dazed, almost incoherent, sat back on her haunches. Her mind didn't clamor with the usual clutter. Instead, it seemed to be clear, no static, no tapes but the machinery was clogged, molasses in the gears.

Opal spoke in a soft, soothing, almost hypnotic voice. "Remember, there's someone else to consider here. No matter how we feel about Carl, what he may have done, or been forced to do, we have to think of Frances. If I were you, I'd check the disc to be sure it's the right one." Slowly, the gummy mechanism began to function again. How did Opal know she had the disc? Why was Carl willing to shoot her? Because she knew or guessed too much? Or was it to get her to leave before Coburn came? She looked at Opal.

"How do you know I have it?"

"I tapped your phone. In the hospital I realized how serious it was getting and I moved fast. I was afraid to involve the police for fear the kidnappers had direct access. You said you thought there was someone inside. The only thing I could do was come here and watch your back."

Audrey thought Opal expected thanks, but somehow couldn't bring herself to give it. She picked up Carl's hand and began to stroke it. "If we haven't already scared him off, the ambulance will."

"He'll contact us again...or he may be nearby right now. If that's not the right disc though, who knows what he'll do? I brought my notebook. Over on that bench." Opal nodded toward the laptop, as her hands reworked the makeshift bandages.

"Can't I do something to help with Carl?"

Opal shook her head with a look she probably used when she was disappointed by a naughty child, one who wouldn't take directions. It conveyed a cool sadness that people could be so flawed. Audrey picked up the laptop, removed it from the case and turned it on, using Opal's `XJUDGEMENTX' password. She tried to open the disc, but received the message saying it was password protected.

"Damn." Audrey muttered.

"What? What is it?" Opal snapped. Was the pressure finally getting to her?

"Nothing, just a password protecting the disc. I'll see what I can do."

Opal took off her jacket and placed it under Carl's head, then she tucked his gun inside her belt at the small of her back.

Audrey racked her brain trying to recall anything that Fred may have used as a password. She tapped out "Frances", nothing; "Harley", again nothing. She continued typing becoming more and more frustrated: "Clapton", "Eric", "Demons", "Demons will get you". Then she knew with certainty that she had it. She typed "Layla". Nothing. As she continued through every song she could think of from Cream, Derek and the Dominos, Blind Faith, Yardbirds, Delaney & Bonnie, and Clapton's solo work, she looked around for Fred. Always around when she didn't need him, where was he when she did? She tried to consciously conjure him, closing her eyes and concentrating on a mental picture of him as she thought the words: "Fred, I need you. Fred, I need you." She listened to the silence around her, tried to listen to the silence within her but when her powers of concentration proved ineffective, she spoke into the ether.

"I could use some help here."

Opal looked up immediately. "What can I do?"

"Sorry, I was talking to myself." Something was gnawing at her. Something to do with congruity. Pieces weren't fitting, but she couldn't isolate the nebulous, ill-fitting images. When Audrey had mused aloud about what made Opal so driven, Carl had told her that

Opal's childhood had been a tough one, lots of siblings, little money. Opal had made it to the top through hard work and playing by the rules. Playing by the rules. There was the inconsistency.

Audrey studied Opal as she asked, "You sure got that wire tap quickly. Who'd you have to wake up to sign for it?"

"I was forced to circumvent the law a little."

At that moment, a phrase popped into her head and Audrey typed, "Love my hog". The directory opened. Instead of alerting Opal to this victory, she began browsing through the files. "That's not like you, Opal." A perfectly organized Excel file clearly denoted weekly amounts of an unnamed product next to a column that was probably the money owed each week by the "client".

"We do what we have to," Opal said.

All the names were in code, but one in particular caught her eye: "JudgeNotLeast". The amounts in both the putative "substance" and "money owed" columns were large. Audrey returned to the directory and found a jpg file with the initials, JNL. She clicked on it. It seemed to take an eternity to load. As she waited, she found herself not thinking, not calculating. Some odd mental mechanism was at work akin, she thought, to the feeling she called overdrive, which she occasionally experienced while running. The run would begin with her body protesting the first mile, then the next two or three miles would have no characteristic ease or difficulty, but suddenly, somewhere in the fourth or fifth mile, she would notice that she was gliding effortlessly and with the glide, came a sense that she could continue as easily to the moon. All things were possible. Now this parallel mental state had left her mind open, gliding. It was as though the possibility of Carl's death had knocked out all the circuit breakers and had left the power on full, some intense direct link unfettered by fail-safes. In a flash, she knew what she would see when the image emerged: Frances with Judge Nichols. And there she was in a lacy teddy, smoking a joint with a bored expression on her face while draped across a naked judge Nichols' lap. He was spanking her.

She exited the disc. "I've got it," said Audrey.

Opal jumped up leaving Carl like so much dirty laundry on the ground. She hid her own gun in the folds of her skirt as she moved toward Audrey.

"Here it is." Audrey strode toward her and handed Opal the open computer with both hands. When Opal reached for it with her free hand, Audrey pulled it to one side, forcing her boss off balance. In that moment, Audrey grabbed Opal's other hand and wrenched the gun from it as she shouldered her boss to the ground. Bruised but essentially uninjured, Opal rose with some difficulty and looked into the barrel of the gun that Audrey had trained on her. Audrey moved to Carl, picked up Katherine's cell phone and dialed nine-one-one.

"Send an ambulance and police to the Santa Monica carousel. Someone's been shot. Hurry!" She looked at Opal who had retrieved the computer. "I don't think you had my phone tapped. That'd mean you'd have to get rid of the phone tappers as well as Street and your shrink."

Opal backed toward the carousel and sat on the edge of the platform. She didn't look up as she responded. "Audrey, you've been under a lot of strain. I think you're delusional."

"Normally, I'd tend to agree with you, but I'm pretty clear on this. You had access to my keys at the office and you knew my every move."

"So did Carl."

"That's true. Let's see. Which one of you is overly concerned with the contents of that disc and which one's bleeding to death?"

"Audrey..." Opal began.

"Also, his husband wasn't caught on camera in flagrante with a minor."

Opal sat and rocked the computer like a baby. After a few moments, tears welled in her eyes and her voice held the quality of someone much younger, more vulnerable than the woman Audrey had looked up to.

"Oh, Audrey, if that photo gets out, it'll ruin us. Not just me, my children, their futures."

The tough exterior Audrey had been affecting melted as she looked at Opal with eyes that begged the older woman for more of a rationale. "Why did you have to kill Fred?"

Opal's face bore a hint of an ironic smile. "I didn't kill him. That really was an accident. And I didn't have Frances that night: I just told him that to get him to meet me with the disc. I cut the phone lines to his cousin's house so he couldn't call to see if she was there."

"He didn't even try to call," said Audrey.

Opal shrugged. "When he didn't show, I drove toward the motel and saw where he'd gone over. Who do you think called the rescue team? Then I went back to the cabin while you were out and searched it."

"But why kidnap Frances? Jealousy? Revenge?"

"Hardly. I didn't give a damn what my husband did until it began to affect our family. The rest I had to orchestrate to get you to find the disc. You were throwing in the towel. I had to keep you piecing together Fred's final movements since I could hardly hire a private detective or do it myself. I had faith in you. Knew you would do it, if anyone could."

"Why didn't you just ask me for it? I'd have given it to you."

"You'd have wondered why I didn't turn it over to the D.A. Besides, that do-gooder in you is a much more powerful motivator."

The icy clarity began to fade. Guilt descended, weighing on her like chain mail. "You kidnapped Frances because of me." Audrey shook her head. "How?"

"I told her Street wanted to meet with her at my place in Big Bear. She's still there. She's my guest. Look, the world's a better place without Street." Opal's voice had a frantic edge to it. "Fred was an accident and Frances's not going to want this in the open any more than I do. We'll just destroy the disc and all go back to our lives."

"What about Carl?"

"I swear, I thought it was somebody trying to kill you. I had no idea it was Carl."

Audrey stared at this woman whom she had admired, looked deeply at her strained, tear-streaked face and wondered how she hadn't seen it before.

"My mother's been institutionalized for years, but she's the picture of mental health compared to you."

Opal wiped the tears from her eyes and stared at Audrey. In the next few seconds Audrey felt an odd confusion because there was nothing to read in Opal's expression. It was as though she had been lobotomized. Without the slightest alteration of her blank expression, Opal sprang up and hurled the laptop at Audrey while pulling Carl's gun from the back of her waistband. Audrey fired while raising her hands to protect her head, but the shot missed its target. As the computer smashed into her, Audrey fell to the floor, dropping the gun. Opal now stood over her with Carl's gun trained on her.

"They're on the way," Audrey said in a cajoling voice. "There'll be a swarm of people here in minutes. Give me the gun. I'll testify about the strain you've been under. You can't kill me. I'm the one who called. It's on tape. How would you explain that?"

Opal, suddenly composed, dry-eyed and all business picked up the gun Audrey dropped with her thumb and index finger.

"Your prints will be on my gun of course, since it was the one you shot Carl with. You must have stolen it from my desk. I gave you access to all my keys. You see, you became convinced of your wild theories and drew Carl into them. When he tried to tell you that you were crazy, you killed him."

"Sounds like one of your therapy sessions, Opal."

But Opal didn't appear to be listening. "Then later, full of remorse, you killed yourself. It's not as though I'll have to convince anybody of your mental instability."

"I don't think Katherine will buy it." Audrey watched as Opal sat on the edge of the carousel platform and laid her own gun next to her, keeping Carl's gun trained on Audrey.

Opal stared off in supreme concentration. Her veneer of certainty began to crack. Her speech became hurried, shaky. "Okay, so we'll both be shot by an assailant—you unfortunately mortally; I'll incur a flesh wound while struggling with him. Probably get some kind of a citation...Any way, he'll run off when he hears sirens." And thus invoked, the sirens began to wail in the distance.

As Opal spun her scenarios, Audrey recalled her mother that long ago morning when she had found her earnestly speaking to no one in the front yard.

Opal spoke to the air. "'He was wearing a ski mask, officer, maybe six-feet, two-hundred pounds.'" Real remorse flooded Opal's face, the gun wavered in her hand, but then she steeled herself. "I don't know how things got this complicated. I did try to reason with you. I liked you."

A number of scenarios, most of which involved flight flashed through Audrey's brain as Opal's arm stiffened in preparation to fire. But before she could pull the trigger, the carousel lurched forward, throwing Opal off balance. It moved slowly at first, then more quickly. Opal scrambled to get off the moving platform, while Audrey took the opportunity to put her randomly selected plan into action. She sprinted for all she was worth.

Fred had said he would be there when she needed him. He had to have been the one who started the carousel. Suffused with hope, which translated to power, Audrey dashed toward the ornate band organ at the corner of the building.

The report of the gunshot was deafening and Audrey dove into a roll as the bullet creased the side of her forehead, opening a gash next to her eye. She quietly thanked her volleyball coach in high school as she sprang up and continued toward the band organ, reached it, then vaulted the waist high wooden barrier to reach temporary safety behind the massive instrument. She marveled at the power of adrenaline even as blood gushed into her eye momentarily blinding her. She swiped at it with the back of her sleeve until she could see again. Above her she found the switch to the organ which she threw, causing it to burst forth its fractured version of "Let It Be".

She shouted over the din of the organ which now blended with the wail of sirens. "Please Opal, it's over. Please."

Squad cars, rending the night's stillness, pulled up on the deck outside the carousel, their lights assaulting the interior with white, red and blue strobes.

When Audrey poked her head around the side of the band organ, she saw Opal running toward the computer. Audrey moved stealthily from her hiding place and jumped on the still moving carousel. She alighted from the platform a few yards away from Opal and ducked behind the ticket booth. Opal was intent on tearing the disc from the computer.

"Opal, we can work something out…" Opal looked at her, then at the team of police surrounding the glass-enclosed building. She raised her gun toward Audrey and fired twice. Audrey darted back behind the ticket booth.

A bull horn blared from outside. "Drop your weapons. Put your hands up and keep them where we can see them."

When Audrey peered around the side of the ticket booth, she saw Opal throw the disc to the ground and fire at it repeatedly. Then she experienced the time stretch phenomenon again. Audrey watched in horror as Opal put her gun into her mouth. Without thinking, Audrey jumped up and jetted toward her, screaming. "No!"

A final shot rang out. Opal sprang backward as if hurled by some unseen specter then landed in a heap of lifeless flesh. The back of her head fanned out in horrid little fragments in her wake. Almost simultaneously, four bulletproof vested police kicked in one of the glass doors.

"Freeze!" they said in a disjointed chorus. They didn't have to tell her to. Audrey did. In fact she felt the moment freeze, her whole body freeze, her life lock in ice.

"Keep your hands in sight at all times." Her icy prison made this request simple. It was one of the officers who had searched her house. He moved toward Audrey, patted her down. "Hey, this is Carl Rogers' friend."

Audrey found her voice. "He needs help. Around the other side. Hurry." She found some measure of strength in the thought that there was still Frances. In the hope that there was still Carl. She pointed toward Opal's inert body. "And that's Opal Nichols."

"You okay?" he asked as he went about his business. Audrey nodded listlessly, wiped some blood out of her eye. "Anybody else here?" Another officer stepped toward her with his hand outstretched to lead her away, but she held up her own to stop him.

"Can I just have a moment alone?" The officer nodded and Audrey moved toward the now motionless carousel. She stepped onto the platform, searching the air for Fred. She spoke quietly. "Well, you waited 'til the last minute—guess that's part of letting me make my own decisions. I thought I didn't need you any more...anyway, thanks. Show yourself to me, please." She heard a faint sound from the interior where the carousel machinery and controls were located. She moved through the horses toward a small door in the interior paneling.

"Fred?" She heard another sound, a slight moan, then saw blood in front of the door. She opened it hesitantly. Carl fell into her arms and she saw herself as the skeleton in a danse macabre, leading a poor soul to his grave. Their bodies wrapped around each other as they twisted slowly to the ground, choreography derived not from entropy but from some cosmic harmony. As their blood mingled, Audrey found her voice. "Help! Over here!" Finally, she cried.

chapter 21

AUDREY PERSUADED THE reluctant police captain that Frances could be irreparably psychologically harmed if someone she trusted wasn't immediately available to her when she was rescued. She never said "lawsuit", but her mastery of implication and her job at the D.A.'s office had weighed in her favor, which was why she had been allowed to accompany the law enforcement team to Opal's cabin in Big Bear.

It had been tough to avoid being taken to the hospital for her head wound, that crease above her right eye just where Fred's had been. The paramedic made her sign a release form before applying the four butterfly bandages in lieu of sutures.

Now she sat in the back of a squad car, behind a mesh grate which separated her from the officers in the front seat. It reminded her of the first mental hospital her mother had been confined to. Wire mesh over every window. Double locks on every door. Each symbol of constricted freedom represented her own failure to keep her mother from the frustration of captivity. This sense of failure returned to her even as she clung to the hope that Frances would be found unharmed.

They parked down the street from the pink cottage nestled into the hillside. After she strapped on her bulletproof vest, she slipped on a windbreaker with "SMPD" stenciled on the back. San Bernardino county sheriffs also accompanied the team. Protocol. It made her wonder: a young girl could be hurt, dying; yet there are people who have rules governing such things. To whom such things are routine. To whom everyday madness is a job.

The team approached the building silently. Audrey was kept well to the back of the group and, when they were properly positioned, a bullhorn blared a warning to anyone inside.

"This is the police. Come out with your hands on your heads." No response from the darkened cabin. Three officers raced toward the back door, then stood against the wall on either side of it. One officer smashed a pane of glass and slipped a gloved hand through to unlock the deadbolt. They all crouched before entering with their weapons poised. Checking every corner and possible hiding place in the kitchen, they signaled a "clear" and the young officer assigned to protect her led Audrey into the house.

The group moved down the hall, securing each room in succession. Audrey followed without the least apprehension for her own safety. All her apprehension was focused on Frances. What if she were dead? Would finding a young girl's body finally push her over the edge, just when she was beginning to feel strong again? Who could live with that kind of culpability?

When they opened a door to a stairwell, two officers proceeded down, but waved Audrey back. She peered from the top of the stairs but couldn't see beyond a few feet from the bottom.

One of the officers shouted up. "Down here!"

Audrey scrambled down the stairs to the basement that appeared to be a large workroom where she saw a ten-foot cubicle built into the corner. It had no windows and only one door. The officers battered it down.

Audrey's heart nearly burst when she saw the teenager handcuffed, cowering between a sink and toilet, the only furnishings besides a cot in the cell. A pizza box and some fast food bags lay near the young girl on the floor.

"Frances!" Audrey screamed in relief as she rushed to the girl.

"You came!" The teenager started to whimper the minute her cuffs were removed and she could return Audrey's embrace. "I can't believe you're here. Thank you. Thank you."

"Of course I'm here."

Frances now sobbed uncontrollably into Audrey's shoulder. Audrey stroked her hair. No, thank you, she thought. Frances had allowed her to help rescue her. She had been more accommodating than her mother had been. Audrey could finally retire some of the tapes.

*　※　*

Then finally, she slept. In her own bed. Alone. When Fred crossed her mind, she utilized the Poe defense to erase him. So far it had been effective. She no longer felt in imminent danger of going crazy...imminent being the operative word. She had hoped for an epiphany, some defining moment, which would assure her absolutely that she wouldn't follow in her mother's footsteps. It hadn't happened.

*　※　*

Gingerly, Audrey opened the door to Katherine's hospital room. Katherine was feeding Brent Austin, who seemed to have fallen asleep. The mother gently pulled her breast away and raised the groggy infant toward Audrey.

"You're the godmother. Why can't you help with some of the breast feedings? My nipples are killing me."

Audrey took the dazed child and rested him on her shoulder where she patted his back to burp him. "I would if I could," Audrey said, and meant it. "How are you feeling, excluding your nipples?"

"I feel good. Don't tell Coburn, but the whole thing was pretty much a piece of cake after the initial drama."

"Good. Hope you're getting some rest."

"Oh, yeah. Lots of sleep—whenever Brent says I can. Lot's of thinking." Katherine grabbed Audrey's arm. "I'm so sorry for screaming at you, you know, before."

"Forget it. Everything you said was true," said Audrey.

"No. I should've told you about Street right away. I knew Judge Nichols let him slide. I just didn't know why. But it was like I was paralyzed. I started to relive the nightmare of Coburn's drug involvement...started wondering if I was going to lose my baby's father."

"Of course you were worried."

"I was going to tell you in the parking lot, then when you said Street was dead, I figured it was over. The truth is I still didn't know for sure whether Coburn had, you know, slipped back. I wanted to confront him before I said anything to you. In the corridor I was pissed off about you doubting him because I was doubting him myself."

"I'm sorry you got dragged into it."

"Don't be. It made us talk about his problem, something we haven't done in a long time. He'd fallen off the wagon a couple of times, which I ignored because I didn't want to see. But now he's going to meetings and in therapy again, with Carl, and he says he's confident he can stay clean. We'll see."

"I'm glad something good came out of it. I've been feeling sort of like an albatross," Audrey said.

Katherine shook her head. "Make that a phoenix. You're alive to tell about it."

"Yeah, not like Opal."

"Sorry, but it's hard to work up much sympathy for her. I mean, she could've blown us both up—all three of us if you count Brent."

"It was supposed to be a small explosion, just enough to make me trust her and exclude her from the possible candidates for Street's murder."

"What a nutball. Murder and suicide just to keep her old fart husband's name clean. I thought the disc just had drug information on it."

"I think Fred did, too...at least I hope he never saw the photo. He was just getting back at Street for dealing to his sister. As Audrey gently patted Brent's back, the infant contributed a yeoman's belch.

"Damn, I wish Coburn had heard that. If he ever doubted his paternity, that would've settled it." Katherine repositioned the pillows behind her. "How'd you end up smack in the middle of everything?"

"Because I happened to move next door to Street's sister, Terry."

Katherine shook her head, amazed. Audrey handed back the now sleeping child. Katherine positioned him next to her in the crook of her arm and tried to sound casual. "How's Carl doing?"

Audrey felt an involuntary contraction in her abdomen; the mixture of pain and longing which physically presented itself when she thought of Carl. "He's out of intensive care, but they still won't let me in."

"You'll see him soon—"

"Sure, I'll be the first person on his phone list." She walked to the window, tried to sound casual. "So, can you tell me anything about SandCastle? In my paranoia I imagined Carl set it up to pay blackmail."

"Well, I can't technically talk about it because I'm counsel for the foundation."

"I wouldn't want to tread on your ethics," Audrey said, smiling.

"Okay, but only because I know he wouldn't care. It's not non-profit, but the cash generated by its investments goes into a college fund for the kid he shot. The principal can be accessed by his own parents when they need money. He just replaces it out of his pocket. He told them that the investments generate the income they take. You didn't hear it from me."

Audrey smiled and shook her head. Of course he would take care of the child he shot. His own parents had borrowed money from him during the lean times since he was a kid himself. So that was SandCastle.

Brent stirred, started to whimper, then broke into a full-blown scream. Katherine peeked inside the back of his diaper. She picked him up and handed him to Audrey.

"Your half needs attention."

Audrey laughed and took Brent Austin Dale to the changing table.

⌖

Everything at the carousel that night had been taken in as evidence, including Carl's clothes, but the police were most concerned about the disc and whether the information it contained was worth the cost of having it salvaged by a specialized software firm. Was it important for anyone to learn that a respected judge was sexually twisted? Did anyone need to see a young girl degrade herself for dope? Audrey hoped Opal had done an efficient job of destroying the disc.

The road vaulted over the highway before it dipped down to the Santa Monica pier. Audrey sauntered along it, drawing a parallel between this stroll and Katherine's admonition to get back on a horse after having been thrown. Until the night she was forced to ride Fred's motorcycle, she hadn't been on one since her accident. It didn't faze her that night. She knew she could ride if she needed to. Her accident had happened at a time when she was young, when death hadn't occurred to her until that very day. But she was older now, and thoughts of mortality encroach with age, piling caution upon fear until one's world could shrink to the size of a room. She needed to take the onus off the pier, off the carousel, needed to revisit the place where her life had altered. Where she had witnessed an attempted murder. Witnessed a suicide.

Audrey climbed on one of the carousel's outside horses just before it began to move. Crime and violence. It was hard not to let them rule your life, color how you looked at strangers on the street. Hard, but not impossible. She could understand why someone would buy a handgun. Understand he felt secure with the knowledge of its presence. But Audrey couldn't conceive of owning one herself, of having the responsibility for an accident. Of having its presence constantly announce the fear of having to use it. Suspicion as a lifestyle. Audrey was realistic, but hopeful.

As she rode her wooden stallion, she glanced outside and saw her bicycle still chained to the stair rail. Realistic but hopeful. Sometimes things worked out.

Pedaling up the bike path toward home, Audrey thought of Miles. She knew it was over, knew they would never be "us" again, beat herself up for the next thought, but, she missed him. Odd images flashed through her mind—not tapes, memories—and not of fabulous parties or treasured moments of good sex, but of the two of them reading the paper on the couch in the morning, eating a thrown-together meal on the deck overlooking the ocean, arguing politics from their respective opposite and intransigent stances. She loved him because there were many things about him to love. She left him because his particular behavior was something she couldn't live with. He could only see the "lock" in wedlock.

She remembered overhearing a friend say to Katherine, "We're all damaged property. We're all double parked for life." At the time she had chuckled, thought it was cute, but now she thought it an excellent criterion for any relationship. Are our flaws compatible? Somehow the things that fit turn out to be less important than those that don't.

An essential self-loathing had lifted. She had married him both times for the same good reason. She had loved him. She still loved him in some nether corner of her heart where recent ex-loves are sent to molder in exile, but those loves eventually acquire a patina of fondness which honors the love once shared. She realized she could now send Miles to join Jimmy Taylor and Eddy Christy, junior high and high school respectively. He would be comfortable with them. They surfed.

Audrey drove Katherine's Mercedes down a tree-lined highway in the hills behind Malibu. The drive up to the rural "home" was made without the dread that usually accompanied these visits. John le Carre had written in THE PILGRIM: "In desperation we find a natural kinship with the mad." Audrey had known desperation and was now more forgiving of her mother's frailties; had a greater understanding of her state, having been a visitor herself. And so Audrey drove without the burning longing for recognition that usually accompanied these visits; with nothing but the desire to see her mother happy in whatever world she happened to be in, and to smile at her.

She pulled up to a walled Mediterranean compound and parked under an old oak. A massive wooden door with a smaller door cut into it was the main entrance. She rang the bell. A casually dressed security guard admitted her with a smile of recognition. Audrey found her favorite nurse.

"Hi, Gladdy. Any good news about Mom?"

Gladdy shrugged. "She's still with us. That's always good news."

"Good point." She was shown to a small garden off the main back yard. Her mother sat in a high-backed wicker chair, wearing a somewhat threadbare, yet beautiful flowing silk caftan. The result was an otherworldly vision. The queen of an ancient lost civilization awaiting the return of her subjects so that life at court might resume.

Audrey approached her gingerly, pulled up a stool next to her, noticed the absence of the cribbage board and felt a rising bubble of hope. Her mother regarded her imperiously.

"You're very pretty."

"Thank you. I'm your daughter, Audrey. I come by my looks honestly."

Her mother eyed her suspiciously. "I have my own daughter."

No matter how much she prepared herself, Audrey was still crushed by the feeling of being a stranger to this person to whom she owed her very existence. The bubble burst, but still, she smiled at her mother.

"And I'm sure she loves you very much," said Audrey.

"Oh, yes, she lives with me." Now her mother's tone was confiding.

Audrey wondered if she had adopted one of the nurses or even another patient as a surrogate daughter. "In this home?"

"Closer than that."

"In your room?"

Her mother looked around to see if anyone was spying on her. Surreptitiously, she cupped her hand over her heart. "In here. She comes out to play sometimes."

Audrey hugged her. "I'll bet she's a perfect daughter."

"I knew you'd understand." The older woman held her daughter's face in her palms and kissed her on the forehead.

As she drove away from the hospital, Audrey thought about her parents. About how lucky they were to have had each other for the time that they did. She admired her father for having lived his credo: Eat dessert first. They may not have made it to the exotic places the three of them had dreamed of, but he found and lived with the woman he loved, a Valhalla certainly. Her mother had been his dessert. With the peace this notion brought, Audrey was able to discard the idea of getting another Jeep and to look forward to fixing up the

Mustang knowing she could withstand the fallout of any memories it might radiate.

On the drive back down the coast, she also reflected on her propensity to decide what people were like and then to be disappointed by them when they didn't live up to her fantasies. It wasn't wrong to believe the best of others, or even to want to help them, it was only wrong to want them to conform to her expectations. Just accept. Accept and make amends where need be. Accept and forgive when appropriate. She remembered her mother's mantra about why one should treat everyone with kindness: "You will be rewarded". The reward is in the smile exchanged. The reward is in recognizing what a reward is. And her mother's mother of all maxims: It's not what you have, but what you appreciate.

⁂

Audrey's living room communicated warmth, nearly spoke to visitors, inviting them to come in and sit down. Katherine had given Audrey a beautiful cashmere and silk rug which broke up the expanse of gleaming hardwood floors. Audrey had been on leave for two weeks and had tackled the arduous task of laying the wooden planks herself. It was the kind of job she needed to keep herself busy, to keep from thinking about Carl who still couldn't or wouldn't have visitors.

The disquieting tapes had ceased that night at the carousel. In their place were memories. Real memories, not distorted by the need to have them turn out right. Most of the early ones did all by themselves.

Now her disquieting moments centered on the lingering sense that her tilting at windmills had been responsible for Frances' ordeal. She hoped that someday that sense wouldn't be as immediate as it was now, wouldn't be the last thing she thought about before falling asleep, wouldn't be her initial thought in the morning.

As she looked at her beautiful floors, she thought about Fred who hadn't been around since he disappeared that night at the carousel. She wished the real Fred could see what a good job she had done on her floors, even though he had thought her efforts analogous to his making a pair of ill-fitting pants. She would have been able to gloat because she had taken her time, measured twice, cut once.

All things he had taught her. He had given her the confidence to do things she hadn't thought herself capable of.

She left the fireplace wall until the very end, and now she sanded the final seam of her newly taped sheetrock. As she ran her fingers along the seam, searching for any raised areas, any surfaces not perfectly smooth; she suddenly felt Fred's presence. Her hand stopped, but she didn't turn around.

"Nice place ya got here." He looked around the room approvingly. A slight fear, of herself, of her own mind, floated to the surface. Audrey's voice needed extra breath to animate her vocal chords.

"I worked at it."

He nodded, then moved to the fireplace wall to inspect her work. "Mine was a little smoother."

"Yeah, well, you did it for a living." She finally turned to look at him. They held each other's eyes a moment and she noticed that any trace of the cut above his eye had vanished. She looked away, intent on some imagined rough spot, which she sanded with the finest grain paper. "Where were you when I needed you? I told you I couldn't count on you."

Fred wandered around the room inspecting the rest of the work she had done. "That's the point, remember? If you'd needed me I'd have been there. Anyway, it's a good lesson. Nobody's going to save you."

She thought of Carl. "I had a little help."

"Yeah." He nodded thoughtfully.

She turned back around abruptly. "So how do I get rid of you?"

Fred smiled at her, a smile tinged with regret. "You already have. I just dropped by so you'd know it was official."

Suddenly there was so much she wanted to say, so many things to clear up. "You weren't exactly infallible. You weren't even murdered, something you could have told me and saved us all a lot of time and trouble."

"What were you really trying to do?" asked the vaporous presence.

"Solve your non-murder."

Again he assumed the role of teacher trying to prompt the right answer, and failing. "Get Frances into rehab. You got her into a good program that she seems committed to. She wouldn't have checked herself in if she hadn't been scared shitless."

"I don't know." Audrey smiled at him for the first time. "You're saying I got where I was supposed to go, I just went by way of Cleveland."

"Not a bad city. Now if you just remember to enjoy the ride, you'll have life knocked."

She moved close to him, put a hand on his arm, and teased him but with a poignancy. "You're really leaving? I'm not going to wake up in your persona knocking back a beer and picking up chicks in a biker bar?"

"Kinda kinky, but, no, don't worry."

"Your cut healed." She reached up and touched the spot above his eye where it had been.

"And you've got one." He touched hers lightly.

"When you said it meant we were soul-mates, you said I had had one."

"Had, have, will have...it's all the same." He moved a step closer to her and planted a friendly kiss on her forehead. As he started to pull away, she grabbed him closely to her for a last hug. After a moment he pulled back and turned to leave.

"You're taking the door?" she asked.

"There's some finality about closing a door that's appropriate here."

She watched as he walked away, then she smiled. "I just find it interesting that my mission and yours happened to coincide. I'm sure some angel up there is happy things turned out the way they did."

He turned back and flashed her a radiant smile, beyond anything she had seen from him before. "I'm sure there is. And I'm sure he'll be watching out for you for a long time." With that, he stepped out and closed the door.

Audrey fought the urge momentarily, then succumbed to it. She flew to the door, opened it and looked out upon the empty walkway that led to the curb where her Mustang was parked.

Most of us spend so much time and energy defining the world around us in logical terms that we necessarily exclude the magical, the spiritual. Are all the Napoleons and Marie Antoinettes now confined to institutions, arms in force-wrap around their bodies, more in touch with the cosmos than those who only navigate the normal range? Must it be either/or? Or is there a possibility that one can remain in some sense grounded and yet open to the otherness of the universe? Audrey hoped there was.

She planted herself outside Carl's hospital room for the fourth day running. The doctor said that Carl had refused all visitors, but she thought she might wear him down. She read THE INFORMATION by Martin Amos and thought how bleak the world could be for some on their slide toward the extremes of the mental health continuum. How cold the world could be. The only real warmth in the universe was generated not by thermonuclear reactions—for one could die from emotional hypothermia on the equator—but by love. "And in the end the love you take is equal to the love you make." She had always thought Lennon was full of shit on that score; some people gave and others took. But then maybe it was like the nouveau riche matron, babbling ever louder at her foreign housekeeper, convinced that volume could somehow surmount the language barrier. You can't understand it unless you speak it. Can't really even take love if you don't know how to give it.

Which led her to the non-epiphany. Nothing dramatic. Nothing earth shattering, just a fairly sound belief that she wouldn't go off the deep end. Not now, not for a while anyway. She believed that anyone could take that plunge. The death of a child could put the most stalwart near the edge, no matter how long she had remained in the middle. No matter what kinds of coping skills she might have developed. Never say never. But for now, she realized that she was one of the lucky ones who had been given the gift of early love. And though she would continue to ply the dangerous shoals of the unbalanced, from time to time, she was unlikely to ever wreck upon them. She had grown up in a safe harbor and it would always exist within her.

Audrey opened Carl's door a crack and saw him lying face down on a slender bed encased in a wheel-like metal contraption. His arms were free to hold the book he was reading. A mirror afforded him a limited view of the room. As Audrey opened the door fully, he adjusted the mirror to watch her.

"I heard you weren't admitting visitors."

"Yet that doesn't seem to be stopping you." His answer came clearly, in a full-bodied voice.

"It did for a while. So, was that anybody? Or me in particular."

"Anybody and you in particular."

Undaunted, she sat in a chair at some distance from the bed. "So, how are you feeling?"

"Exactly as if I'd been shot in the head and the gut."

"Heard it clipped a vertebra on the way out."

"Yup."

Audrey got the impression that he was enjoying her discomfort. She pulled a box from her satchel. "I brought some chocolates."

"Your favorite."

"Yes, but they're for the nurses. My mom always told me to bring chocolates to people in the hospital so that the nurses would check on them more."

Carl was looking her over. She could tell by the way his eyes moved in the mirror. "I get enough attention." His scrutiny made her more uncomfortable.

"I'm sure you do...I've been waiting for you to be able to have visitors so that..." She took a deep breath, but he jumped in before she could continue.

"So that you could say how very sorry you are."

"Well, yes...that and—"

"How grateful you are."

"Of course, but also—"

"How stupid you were not to see that I was your friend and always had your best interests at heart?"

"You're not making this any easier."

He signaled with his right hand. "Come down here. Your image doesn't show up in the mirror." She relaxed. If he could tease her about being a vampire, he couldn't be completely closed to her. She moved the paraphernalia out of the way and crouched down on the floor so that their heads were at the same level. "Guess I was pretty bad."

"Worse."

"Well, I've come to make a clean breast of it...so to speak."

"I'd like to see that."

Audrey smiled at him. He'd forgiven her. "I'm not sure you would at this point...but I have to—"

"I had a long talk with Miles...he wasn't happy about it—" Carl looked a little guilty.

"Do we have to discuss Miles?"

"Do you love him?"

"Miles? Yes, but I'm not in love with him any more."

"How 'bout your dead friend?"

She smiled and shook her head at the thought. "No."

He ran his finger along the wound above her eye where the bullet had grazed her; his touch was as gentle as a butterfly kiss. "So I was talking to Miles, and I told him I was in love with his wife and would he please sign the divorce papers so I could have a shot at her."

Audrey was blown away. So that was why Miles had warned her to watch her back around Carl. He had felt betrayed, and on an emotional level, had been. She swallowed, her voice not quite her own. "And what did he say?"

"That I was as nuts as you are."

"And you said?"

"That mental health is such a relative thing, that if I had to be nuts to be in love with you, it was a small price to pay."

"You'd risk your sanity on me?"

"In a heart beat."

The wound above his eye that matched hers was fairly accessible, so she kissed it first. Then, with no little difficulty, she positioned her head under his and kissed him and knew that she was home.

CPSIA information can be obtained at www.ICGtesting.com
Printed in the USA
BVOW08s1621031113

335366BV00001B/64/P